# THE
# WAITING

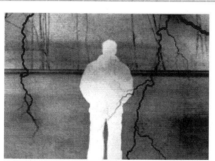

## JOE HART

The Waiting

Text copyright © 2013 by Joe Hart
All rights reserved.

This is a work of fiction. The names, characters, places, and incidents are the products of the author's imagination or are used fictitiously. Any resemblance to actual events or persons, living or dead, is purely coincidental.

*To the ghosts inside us all. You are our treasures and curses. Never go away.*

# Special Thanks

As always, there are a number of people to thank for their help and input during the course of creating a novel. First off, thank you to Nicole Lampi, who gave me great feedback about speech and occupational therapy—your help is much appreciated. To my wife: you provide not only time for me to write but also inspiration and insight that are invaluable. To my mother, who let me read pretty much whatever I wanted growing up—Mom, you helped shape me as a writer with your love of books. And thank you to all the readers, especially the ones who loved my first novel, *Lineage*. Thank you for the continual kind words; you keep me rolling onward every day.

# Contents

# Prologue

*It's coming.*

The words chanted inside his head as he ran, his arthritic joints exploding with each painful step. Blood dripped from his fingertips, smeared on the screen door as he pushed through it into the warm night air. Stars hung above the lake, their cascade of pinpricks joined to one another like a dot-to-dot in the sky, their portrait reflected in the calm face of water beyond the shore. A soft breeze spoke in the pines and nudged Maggie's chime into life. The jangle of the hollow steel spurred him on as his lungs began to burn.

He felt a twinge in his shoulder, and it lanced down the inside of his biceps and stabbed a shot of fire into the left side of his chest. Heart attack, finally. He knew it would take him one day, just like it took his grandfather, father, and son. He welcomed it, hoped it would drop him on the dewy grass. But the pain relented and vanished, a phantom of the nerves that came and went with his age.

He ran.

His socks were already soaked when he hit the water, but the chill that set into the lake each night still made him grimace. What did he care now, with Maggie gone? His insides shrunk with the renewed epiphany: he would never see his wife again. Unless ...

He stopped in the waist-deep water, the liquid darkness rippling with his movements. Tears rolled down his face, catching in the lines of his years. His family flitted through his mind's eye—births, graduations, anniversaries.

His reverie was broken by a splash behind him, like something diving into the lake. His eyes widened as he craned his neck around, looking for movement but knowing it didn't matter. He was done.

*Curiosity killed the cat, and nothing in the world can bring him back.*

He cried, tears dropping from his face like the blood from his fingers. Knowing it was his fault would be the last thought he would take with him.

He doubled over, his face inches from the water, and saw his blackened reflection. He was only shadow, an outline. Nothing more. He took a last breath, savoring the sweet taste of it on his tongue before exhaling as much as he could; he would need a lungful to do it right.

He made to push his face into the water, but two hands shot up from the depths, their fingers fish-belly white, and found the back of his neck.

A garbled scream of pure terror fell from his mouth and was cut off the moment his head slammed into the lake. His feet surfaced, two pale, thrashing things as he kicked, and then they were gone as well.

Concentric waves rolled away in ever-increasing circles, and soon they flattened, leaving the water unbroken and smooth like the silence of the night.

# 1

"Evan, we're going to have to let you go."

Evan Tormer raised his face from his hand and let the words reverberate inside him. He stared across the corner office, the office that should have been his, at Christy Weathers sitting behind the desk. Her hair perched in a gravity-defying jumble of curls on top of her head, her mascaraed eyes watching him, cold, unblinking.

"Christy, look, we can talk about this, please."

The man leaning against a desk near the panoramic window made a sound like a cough that could've been a laugh. Evan glared at him. Calling him a man was pushing it. Colt was a kid, at least seven years his junior. Evan took in his trendily hipster clothes—the too tight slacks, the vibrant clashing dress shirt, the oversized black-framed glasses—along with the sneering mouth beneath a poor attempt at a mustache.

"I'm sorry, Evan, there's no wiggle room here, and you know it. Mr. Tillins is already aware of this, and the best I've been able to do is convince him not to press charges," Christy said.

Evan swallowed. His throat was as dry as a streambed in a drought. Tears stung his eyes, and he forced them back down. He would not cry in front of these people.

"I paid everything back, every cent." He searched Christy's face for a semblance of compassion, a smile, something of the person he had worked with for four years before her *promotion*.

When she didn't move a muscle, he continued: "Look, I was desperate, Elle was so sick and the treatments were more than we could handle."

"Nontraditional treatments, is what I heard," Colt said, taking his glasses off to polish them while gazing out at the afternoon sweep of Minneapolis.

Evan stared at the younger man until Colt returned his gaze. "What does that have to do with anything?" A cold flame lit in the bottom of his stomach.

Christy waved the question away like a buzzing fly. "Listen, Evan, I don't want this any more than you do, you're a vital part of the company. You do good work, you're a team player, and your recent setbacks—"

"My wife died, that's not really what I'd call a setback," Evan said.

The tears were back, and they weren't heeding his efforts. One slipped over the rim of his eyelid and traced down his cheek to his chin. Christy stiffened, her jaw tightening.

"Evan, we're all very sorry about Elle, but the fact is, you took fifty thousand dollars from the company, and that can't be overlooked."

Christy paused and tipped her head to one side, a bundle of curls catching light from the setting sun. Evan wanted to tell her that her hair looked nice. In fact, he wanted to say he remembered the first time he saw her wear it like that, at the company Christmas party a year ago. He could still see that mop of blond curls bobbing at Tillins's crotch while the man reclined in his office chair, oblivious to Evan retreating, the page of marketing reports still in his hand, and closing the CEO's door without a sound.

Instead, he prepared to beg. "Christy, please, I won't be able to afford Shaun's medical bills without the health care."

"My thoughts are, you should have contemplated that before stealing from the company, Evan," Colt said, moving to the side of Christy's desk.

Evan ignored him, focused on Christy. "Please, let me speak to Mr. Tillins, I'm sure he'll understand."

The curls shook. "No, Evan, this is final. Please pack your desk up. We'll have your last check delivered to your house. Your health care will continue for the next two months, until the quarter ends."

Evan's jaw worked as though more pleas wanted to come out, but there was nothing left. The aching worry that had begun early in the morning with Christy's email asking him for a meeting became a sour explosion of reality. They'd found out. He'd lost his job.

Colt come closer, and he stood, staring down at the kid's snarky face. What kind of name was Colt anyway?

"If you have any further questions, direct them at the HR department," Christy said, now looking at a stack of papers that her fingers shuffled through.

Evan turned toward the thick double doors and began to walk, hearing Colt's footsteps a few inches behind his own.

"Well, on the bright side, now you have some extra time to spend with your retard," Colt said, just above a whisper.

Evan moved without thought, oblivious to the static charge in his limbs as he spun. His elbow came up in a short arc and connected with Colt's face. A sound like an aluminum can being crushed filled the office, and then there was blood—a lot of it.

The kid's hands cupped his shattered nose as his broken glasses slid, now in two pieces, off his head. Colt stumbled back, clutching at his face with delicate piano-player fingers.

Christy sat stock-still in her chair, her eyes saucer plates dabbed with blue at their centers.

"Uhhh! Uhhh! He fucking hit me!" Colt yelled.

He tripped over a chair and fell to his ass, the impact jolting a fresh gout of blood through his shaking fingers.

Evan stared, his jaw loosened. So much blood. The sound of the phone on Christy's desk being picked up pulled his eyes from the bleeding office worker.

"Don't!" Evan said, pointing at Christy, her finger hovering over the button that would bring the two security guards from the lobby rushing toward the office. "Or I'll call Tillins's wife."

Christy's mouth formed words that died in her throat. She set the phone back into the cradle.

"Get out."

Evan looked one last time at Colt and wondered if the hipster would bleed to death right there on the floor, then turned and hurried through the double doors.

Evan walked as calmly as he could down the hallway, saying hello to several people who passed him by. His legs moved on their own accord, propelling him forward as his slamming heart threatened to burst from his chest. He rounded a corner and saw the sign for the bathroom. In a few seconds he was inside the farthest stall, with barely a pause to see if anyone else was present. He fell to his knees and vomited into the toilet, the light salad he'd had for lunch an unrecognizable mess before him. Evan clutched the handicap bar to his left and heaved again, and again.

He was unemployed. He'd broken Colt's nose, threatened Christy with blackmail. What the hell was he doing? And more importantly, what the hell was he going to do? The stall spun, and he closed his eyes, spitting acid into the water.

When he managed to make it to the sink—the bathroom still blessedly empty—his reflection met him, but he avoided it entirely. He didn't care to see what waited there for him. Instead, he bent and splashed cold water over his face until his skin stung.

He left the bathroom and walked to a set of doors at the far end of the corridor, opting to take the stairs rather than risk bumping into someone in the elevator who might ask a question he didn't want to answer. After six flights of steps, he swung a door open, stepped out on the ground floor, and made his way to his office at the rear of the building.

Office. It wasn't more than a glorified broom closet, just wide enough for a small desk, no window, and two file cabinets. He'd attempted to make it nicer several years before everything fell apart, by hanging photos of Elle and Shaun on the walls. He removed them, pausing to take in his wife's and son's features.

They both had a fair complexion and light, wispy hair. Elle's smile radiated from the picture and struck a bell in the center of Evan, as it had when she was alive. Shaun's arms were wrapped around his mother's neck, his face partially buried in her hair. The white scar on the side of his small head was all but invisible in the picture unless you knew what you were looking for, and Evan couldn't help seeing it each time he gazed at the photo.

He swallowed and turned in a slow circle to survey his office, searching for anything else to take, but other than a warm can of Coke inside his desk drawer, his favorite pen, and his jacket, there was nothing.

He stood in the doorway to the office in which he'd toiled for eight years writing promotions, ads, and marketing strategies. He remembered all the time spent in the little room, away from his family. And what did it mean now? All his effort culminated at this point—alone, with nothing but his pictures beneath his arm to show for it. He snapped the light off and shut the door behind him, listening to the hollow *thunk* as it closed. The end of his career.

Before he could take a step, his cell phone sprang to life in his pocket, trilling and vibrating against his thigh. When he saw the name and number on the display, he almost hit the ignore button, but the thought of having to call his best friend later and tell him what had happened wasn't appealing either. He answered the phone as he walked toward the lobby, slinging his jacket around his shoulders as he went.

"Hey, man."

"Wow, you sound like complete shit. Do me a favor next time I call and don't answer if you're having a bad day," Jason said.

Evan sighed. "I almost didn't."

"Well fuck you too."

Evan heard the tap of a keyboard in the background. "Yeah."

A long pause from Jason's end. "Ev, what's wrong?"

Evan nodded to a security guard near the front desk in the lobby, marveling that it was the last time he would do so, and pushed into the crisp spring air of the city.

"I don't want to get into it on the phone."

"Shit. Okay. Meet me at Aran's after work."

A light mist fell as he strode across the parking lot, the mid-afternoon sounds of traffic and smells of wet concrete invading his senses.

"I'm leaving work now."

Another pause. "I'll be there in ten minutes."

"Jason, no, I'm going home—"

"Aran's, ten."

The call ended, and Evan stared at the screen as he stood beside his minivan. "Shit," he said to the deserted parking lot, and climbed inside the vehicle.

# 2

"You're kidding me."

The bar was quiet for this time of day, the regulars that adorned the barstools like drunken hood ornaments each night still at their day jobs, or wherever they spent their time when they weren't here. No clack of pool balls rang out, and no calls for another beer echoed off the stained oak walls. Even the sun seemed less inclined to shine through the wide glass windows near the door, opting instead to hide behind a cluster of tumorous-looking clouds above the buildings across the street.

Evan took a sip of his beer, quenching the dryness in his throat, which hadn't left since his meeting with Christy and Colt. He shook his head and met Jason's stare from across the table.

"No, I'm afraid I'm not."

Jason's mouth, almost always curled in a half smile, hung partially open. His wavy blond hair, still wet from the mist outside, fell limp on his forehead.

"I can't believe you did that."

Evan nodded. "I know."

"You never stole as much as a dime in your life, you always left that to me."

"And you ended up as an investment banker, how's that for fate."

Jason looked poised to offer a contradiction and then merely shrugged. "I wish you would've come to me, buddy."

Evan shook his head. "This was when everyone was hurting, remember? You didn't have fifty grand to loan me, and I wasn't going to ask."

"So you took it from your company?"

"Yes," Evan said, with more force than he meant to. The bartender looked over a set of bifocals at their table before returning his gaze to a report on CNN. "Yes," Evan repeated, in a lower voice. "There was sixty-three thousand dollars in their wonderful little account for the annual party every year. I took out fifty and paid it back from Elle's—" He glanced across the bar. "Elle's life insurance."

"Christ," Jason said.

Evan brought his gaze back to his friend. Jason stared off into space, his fingers stroking the blond stubble of his goatee. How many times had he watched him do that? Evan wondered. Ever since he was old enough to grow it, he supposed. He recalled the first time they'd met in third grade, their desks pushed together by the firm hands of Mrs. Carmichael. *Evan Tormer, meet Jason Price. You two are going to be friends,* she'd said. And they had been. Two kids couldn't have been more different: Jason tall and lanky, with *GQ*-model good looks; Evan shorter and dark. Years later he'd read *Something Wicked This Way Comes* and thought, *That's us, except I look like Jim Nightshade and Jason is more like Will Halloway.* Jason always took the risks, his calculations paying off every time, while Evan stood by his side no matter what, along for the ride, for better or worse.

"I still would've helped you guys, you know that. I would've found a way."

Jason's words brought Evan back to the present, and he blinked. "You mean you would've ripped off Kimball and Owens to help pay our bills? No, I'm good with how things went down, the Zine didn't lose anything when I took that money. No one knew it was gone until a week ago, and if I had any inkling that a few more thousand would've made a difference for Elle, I would've taken that too."

Evan took a long pull from his beer, the last dregs washing against his upper lip. He set the mug down and looked at Jason, his friend's face full of concern.

"Will you be okay?"

"Yeah," Evan answered, too fast, he realized a moment too late. "Yes, we'll be fine."

"What's your plan?"

"I'm going to finish one more beer, go down to the corner of Broadway and Central, and take my pants off. Everything will work itself out."

Jason burst out laughing and shook his head. Evan offered a small smile and spun his empty mug in a circle.

"Seriously, though, what's your plan?" Jason asked.

"I don't fucking have one," Evan said. Tears sprung to his eyes without warning, and suddenly the bar became a blurry mess. "I'm two months behind on our mortgage, Shaun needs more oxygen therapy that I don't have the money for because I have to pay for his personal-care attendant every day I'm at work."

"What about," Jason said, in a soft voice, "what about the rest of Elle's—"

"Her life insurance?" His words cracked with emotion. "Her policy was for a hundred grand. I mean, who would've thought we should've had it for more? Elle was thirty when she got diagnosed. Fifty of the hundred went back to the Zine. The other fifty went to the hospital, and guess what. I still owe them over forty thousand dollars." He gritted his teeth. "For my dead wife."

Evan placed a hand against his forehead and braced himself. More anguish, like a rotten soup, wanted to spill out from inside him. Years of turmoil and pain, festering, a sore that wouldn't heal like everyone else claimed it would with time. It only got worse with each passing day, with the addition of bills, the weight of Shaun's treatments, *her* absence.

Jason placed his hand on Evan's arm. "Ev, it's going to be okay."

Evan jerked away from Jason's touch and pointed a finger into his face. "No, it's not. No, it's not. It'll be all right for you, and for the fuckers that fired me today, it'll be okay for them, but not for me, not for us. Not ever again."

He wiped away tears and watched Jason's face fold.

A young waitress strode toward them, and Evan turned his head away. Jason ordered two more beers, and Evan thought about getting up to walk out. He wanted to but didn't feel he had the strength. His muscles were atrophied with such crushing depression, he felt he might never move again. A few moments later, he heard the waitress set their beers down and turned to stare at his.

"I have an idea," Jason said, breaking the uncomfortable silence.

"I'm not taking a loan from you. I won't do that to you and Lisa."

"That wasn't what I was thinking. How long does Shaun have left in the school year? Can't be more than a month now, right?"

Evan's brow furrowed. "He's done on May twenty-fifth— why?"

"Now hear me out," Jason said, holding his hands before him as though talking to a hostage taker. "I don't know if you remember, but my grandfather has this cabin up north—actually, I shouldn't say that since it's technically mine, but anyways. It's this really nice cabin on an island in the middle of Long Lake near Mill River. You know where I mean?"

Evan squinted. "Maybe. You visited them sometimes when we were younger, right? It's west from Kelliston, isn't it?"

Jason nodded. "Yep, we went there every so often when Dad was still alive. The island is smack-dab in the middle of the lake, and it's not really big, but definitely a few acres or more. The house is in good shape, Gramps always kept it up, he was fanatic about it since he was a carpenter most of his life. After he and Grandma passed away, it was willed to me since Dad was already gone and Mom was in Florida. Lisa and I took Lily up there quite a few times, but we slowly quit going. It's a long drive, and Lily wasn't actually too keen on staying in such an isolated place, no Wi-Fi or anything." Jason took a sip of his beer.

"It sounds really nice, but I'm not following you," Evan said.

"Here's the thing." Jason held up his hand. "Since we haven't gone there in years, I've had to hire a caretaker to stay there—you know, do maintenance around the place, make sure no one's breaking in or shit like that. My most recent guy just quit, and I was thinking—"

"No, I'm not doing that," Evan said, shaking his head. "Thanks, but no. How would I get Shaun his treatments? He has physical and occupational therapy twice a week."

"There's a great clinic in Mill, we had to take Lily there once when she stepped on a fishhook on the dock. The place comes with a fishing boat and a little cruising pontoon. You could bring him back and forth across the lake, no problem, he'd love it."

Evan began another protest, but Jason continued: "Plus, he won't be in school that much longer. You could take him out a couple of weeks early to get settled up there."

"No, Jason, no, okay? I can't run away from my problems here, it won't fix anything."

"Listen, I pay the caretakers that I hire well. They get to live there in the middle of paradise with a nice wage. I would pay you the same just to house-sit, and it would be more than enough to catch you up on your mortgage, I guarantee it. You could spend the summer there and write the articles you've wanted to finish for years. Justin over at *Dachlund* said the other day he'd love to print something of yours again. Now you have the time since you won't be writing ads for that fucking e-rag anymore."

Evan laughed and sipped at his beer. Jason, always with the plan, always looking out for him. He recalled the day of Elle's funeral. The sunshine beating against his black suit in mock joy as the long, honey-colored box dropped away into the darkness of the earth. He would've fallen to his knees right then if Jason hadn't had his arm tight around his shoulders.

"What do you say?" Jason asked, finishing his beer.

"I say, your intentions are good and I love you, but no. Our home is here, Shaun's treatments are here, even our problems are here, and that's something I have to deal with. I'll have to readjust, that's all. I'll find work again, I'm a little shell-shocked right now. I mean, I hit a guy today, broke his nose."

"Little bastard deserved more than that."

"Yeah, he did, but that's not like me. I need to decompress and things will seem better in the morning."

Jason sighed and nodded. "Okay, okay. Just know the offer is out there. I won't start looking for a new guy for another two weeks."

"Thank you."

"No, thank you for getting these beers."

"Yeah, leave the unemployed guy with the check, nice."

Jason grinned and dropped a fifty on the table before standing. His eyes sobered. "Are you going to be okay?"

"We'll be fine."

Evan stood and gave Jason a rough hug. As he watched his friend move out the door and into the afternoon drizzle, he wondered if Jason believed his last words any more than he did.

## 3

Evan shut the minivan off and watched the falling rain bead on the windshield and run in silver rivulets.

His house glowed. Each window looked like a rectangle cut from the sun. Shaun's PCA, Farah, always turned on every light she could find. During the first months of her employment, her habit drove him nuts. He would come home from work and spend ten minutes pacing through the house, flipping switches and turning knobs. But after a time, the sight of the lights burning in the windows wasn't irritating anymore; it became a welcoming that he looked forward to each time he pulled into the driveway.

Thoughts of what he would say to Farah when he went inside barraged him, making him feel like he'd consumed more beer than he had.

Lightning threaded across the sky, flickering in pulses that lit up the neighbors' yards. Rain hammered against the roof of the car, and he decided to make a run for it before the storm intensified further. The icy drops were like cold needles as he jogged to the front door and slid inside, the warmth and dryness of the house embracing him. Evan peeled his soaking jacket off and threw it in the dryer, listening to the sounds of dishes being stacked in cabinets. When he entered the kitchen, he saw Farah straining to put away the heavy crockpot on a high shelf, her round body shaking with effort.

"Jeez, Farah, let me help you," Evan said, hurrying across the kitchen and taking the crockpot from her hands.

"Oh, I would've got it, I'm just short, that's all. Put it up there every other time, you know."

Evan closed the cabinet door and turned to his son's PCA. The retired nurse looked like the embodiment of Mrs. Claus, with her curled white hair and miniature features. The red color in her cheeks from the effort of lifting the crockpot only furthered the likeness.

"I know, and I've told you, you don't have to put away the dishes."

Farah waved a hand at him and grasped a gallon of milk from the counter. She stowed it in the refrigerator. "Shauny's resting, so I thought I'd do something useful until you got home. Nice that it's Friday, huh? Glad to be done with work?"

Evan opened his mouth, an insane giggle wanting to burst out. "Yes, definitely," he said, sitting at the kitchen table. He pulled off his damp socks.

Farah paused. "Everything okay?"

"Yeah, perfect," he said, without raising his head. "How was he today?"

"Very good. He did magnificent at physical therapy, took a dozen steps using only the rolling walker."

"That's great. Did we get anything in the mail from the doctor?"

Farah walked to the counter and sifted through a short stack of envelopes. Evan eyed the pile with distaste; no doubt, it contained mostly bills and past-due letters.

"Ah, yep, here you go," Farah said, handing him a thick envelope.

He took the letter and set it on the table. "I asked for more information on the seizures he had two weeks ago. I wanted to know if that's something we can look forward to from now on."

Sickness soured his stomach as the memory of Shaun shaking and jittering on the floor washed over him. The overwhelming helplessness of that morning hadn't diminished in the least.

"I asked Lindsey today if seizures were common with TBI, and she said that they were."

"I knew they were, but he'd never had one before, so ..."

Farah nodded. "We also did some flash cards this afternoon, he remembered 'hammer' and 'window' this time, so that was good. He had a bath, and he ate great at supper. He wanted to watch one of his little shows, so I put one in, and the poor thing didn't even make it through the credits before he fell asleep on the couch." Farah's face crinkled with a smile, her eyes glimmering warmth.

It wasn't the first time, or the hundredth, Evan felt a swelling of appreciation at having such a wonderful caretaker for Shaun. But the stabbing knowledge that he might have to let her go became too much, and he stood, moving through the archway to the living room.

Shaun sat propped against two overstuffed pillows on the couch. The dancing light from the TV illuminated his son's delicate face with myriad colors. Evan knelt beside the couch and took one of Shaun's soft hands in his own. Shaun's light hair fell in a sweep across his forehead, and Evan brushed it away. It was longer than normal, another reminder of Elle's absence. She used to always cut Shaun's hair, in his medical chair under the bright lights of the kitchen. Evan remembered the sound of Shaun's laughter as his hair fell beneath the clips of Elle's scissors, his small legs kicking with glee.

Shaun's eyes opened into slits, and Evan blinked back a layer of tears, determined not to cry in front of his son again.

"Hi, buddy."

Shaun smiled, gripping his hand tighter. "Da."

"How was your day?"

Shaun's mouth worked, and he licked his lips. After a few moments of struggling, his forehead wrinkled. "Yesh," he said, and frowned.

"Farah said you did great today. She said you walked a mile."

Shaun giggled and wiped at his eyes, tried to sit up but only managed to slide down farther into the pillows.

"Here, buddy," Evan said, hoisting him into a better sitting position. "You can go back to sleep again if you want."

Shaun shook his head and pointed at the TV. "Tains."

Evan glanced at the television, where Thomas the Train raced along beside another tank engine.

"Okay, you watch your trains," Evan said, and tousled his son's hair, feeling the rough scar tissue on the left side of his scalp.

When he turned, he saw Farah watching them from the kitchen. She moved aside to let him pass, but her eyes remained on the little boy.

"He's doing so good," Farah said, finally turning away.

"Yes, he is. I think we'll try tracing again tonight, if he's up to it."

"Sounds like a plan. Well, I should get home to Steve, he'll be worried, what with the storm. But I whipped up some hot dish, it's in the fridge."

"Thank you," Evan said.

He followed her to the foyer, where she donned a plain set of slip-on boots as well as a light jacket.

"I'll see you both Monday morning then, bright and early," Farah said, gripping the door handle. She glanced at Evan and must have seen something flit across his face, because she stopped, her eyes penetrating. "Are you okay?"

He swallowed. "Yeah, long day."

Farah smiled sadly and grasped his arm in her short fingers. "You're doing splendid, you know?"

"Am I?"

"Yes. When I met you, you were in a terrible place, with challenges most people never even think of, but you and Shaun are strong. You've both got stout spirits, as my father used to say." She squeezed his arm. "You're doing great."

He smiled and put his hand over hers. "We wouldn't have made it without you."

Farah released her hold and made a batting motion with her hand. "Pah, I just make sure you both don't starve." She turned, and pulled the door open to the storm. "I'll see you Monday," she said, and was gone in a whirl of wind that spit rain onto the floor before she shut the door.

"Monday," Evan said, not liking the dead sound of his voice in the empty hall, as thunder rolled in a renewed wave outside.

~

They spent the rest of the evening playing. Evan helped Shaun to the table, holding his son's hands in his own while Shaun walked in an awkward limp to his chair. After strapping him in, Evan dealt out a game of brightly colored, numbered cards designed to stimulate eye focus and cognitive function. They played for an hour, Shaun's laughter echoing through the warmth of the house while the rain poured down outside and thunder shook the roof from time to time.

When Evan finally glanced at the clock, he saw that it was eight thirty, a half hour past Shaun's bedtime. They proceeded through their evening ritual. He helped Shaun go to the bathroom, steadying him on the toilet so he wouldn't fall off. He brushed his son's teeth and combed his hair, then carried him into his room, Shaun's eyes already beginning to close.

"Moon?" Shaun asked, as Evan tucked him beneath his blankets.

"Moon?" Evan smiled. *"Goodnight Moon?"*

"Moon," Shaun said. His small face brightened as Evan pulled the ever-present book from the bedside table and began to read.

Before the third page, Shaun's breathing became deep, his eyelids closed, and an occasional snore drifted out of his open mouth.

"Night, buddy," Evan said, folding the book closed before returning it to its place. He leaned down and kissed Shaun's forehead, the boy's skin soft and cool, always smelling of soap. "We're going to be okay, son, Daddy's going to make sure."

Evan hesitated, his eyes becoming watery again. Without needing to look, he reached to the table and snapped the baby monitor on and stood. The storm had quieted, and now only a light drizzle fell in slithering streams against the windows. He watched Shaun for a moment longer, then moved to the door, swinging it partially shut but not closed.

~

*He walks down the hallway, the doors to either side of him bustling and beeping with life and activity, his eyes searching for her room number. He feels flattened inside, ironed by the foreknowledge that something is terribly wrong. There it is—436. He angles inside and sees the doctor with white hair sitting on a stool, one hand on the desk, the other perched on Elle's knee. Tears on her face, not good ones, the sad kind. She looks up and he knows.*

*He knows.*

~

He came awake, opening his eyes to the darkness of the room, his breath still calm in his chest, his heart not beating too fast. He licked his lips and rolled to the side, Elle's side—*so empty*—and checked Shaun's monitor. The low hiss of white noise and soft breathing came from its speaker. Evan lay back, closing his eyes again, but couldn't help himself and glanced at the clock: *5:33*.

He walked to the kitchen, gazed out of the windows, and watched the horizon change from shadow upon shadow to tinged gray to a mushroom of golden light growing with each minute in the east. His eyes never left the glow, and when the first edge of sun cut the new day into dawn, he picked up his cell phone, hitting a single button to dial the number.

"My God, it's called sleep, you should try it sometime," Jason said, his voice thick.

Evan smiled a little. "When can I start?"

# 4

Long Lake appeared on the right when Evan least expected it.

The white birch, oaks, and towering pines lining either side of the road fell away and gave them their first view of the lake. Its name became apparent within a glance. The body of water was wide and curving, resembling a crescent moon. Whitecap waves rolled toward the highway and broke on the rock-studded shore. The wind, slight when they'd left the last gas station twenty miles back, became prominent, pushing and pulling the minivan as they drove.

"Shaun, do you see the lake?" Evan asked, pointing toward the water while he navigated a curve.

Shaun shifted in his seat. "Ahhh," he said, as the lake vanished behind a veil of trees. "Wha?"

Evan glanced in the rearview mirror, taking in his son's disappointed features. "It'll come back, buddy, wait a second."

The road twisted to the right, and a sign appeared, hewn in rustic letters and hanging from a post made to look like a pine tree. "Mill River welcomes you, population six hundred ninety-three," Evan read aloud. "Six hundred ninety-five now, huh, buddy?"

Shaun smiled in the mirror.

*Does he even understand you?*

Evan clenched his jaw and shoved the niggling voice away. He understands me, he thought. I can look into his eyes and see that he does.

The thorn of doubt that accompanied him everywhere tried to raise its voice again, but he shut it down, humming a tuneless melody instead. Ahead, Mill River came into view.

It was a postcard come to life. The highway became Main Street, with a fifteen-mile-per-hour speed limit. Storefronts lined the left side of the road, while the lake made a panoramic sweep opposite the buildings. A few cafés and coffee shops studded the beginning of the first block, followed by a general store, then a small grocery, and finally a Holiday station. The street rose, and at its top sat a white, steepled church, its bell tower at least fifty feet from the ground.

"Let's take a little drive and see if we can find the hospital," Evan said.

When he checked on Shaun in the mirror again, he saw that the boy's attention hadn't left the lake since it came back into view. Evan turned left at the first stoplight and followed the side street for two blocks before a brick building marked as "Mill River Elementary" appeared. They drove past the school, traveling deeper into what looked like several connected neighborhoods. Just when he was about to turn around, Evan spotted a small sign bearing a blue *H* with an arrow straight ahead. The road dipped and made a hard left turn before running past a low, glass building set on the right.

Evan coasted into the parking lot but didn't stop, letting the minivan roll past the automatic front doors of the hospital. Its size and architecture were impressive for a town as small as Mill River. When he'd called the pediatric-therapy department two weeks before, the scheduler he spoke with sounded polite and businesslike. She assured him that they could definitely handle all of Shaun's therapy needs and told him to stop in for a tour of the facility when they got settled.

"This is it, buddy, this is where you're going to do some work and play. What do you think?"

Shaun laughed, and Evan guided the van back out of the parking lot and returned to the main street. He hadn't seen the small marina that Jason had described, so Evan turned left and drove toward the looming church at the top of the hill. A battered sign came into view, a badly drawn bass leaping from an equally childish-looking pond gracing its center, with "Collins Outfitters" arched over the top. Evan turned into the parking lot, which provided an excellent view of Long Lake.

Shaun laughed again, and Evan's spirits buoyed. Perhaps this had been a good idea. Shaun seemed to love the lake, and the town was picturesque. He sent a silent thanks to Jason, promising himself he would deliver it verbally next time they spoke.

Collins Outfitters consisted of three buildings pieced together by rudely constructed hallways topped with a mixture of shingles and faded tin. The front of the structure had a long overhang, with several benches and chairs stacked beneath it. Two of the chairs were occupied by a pair of men dressed almost identically in faded jeans, red suspenders, and blue chambray work shirts. Even their bald heads glistened the same way, and Evan had to make himself quit staring at the twins, who had to be approaching their eighties. Instead he looked to the right and saw a long, concrete ramp leading down to a makeshift pier and boat landing. Four aluminum fishing boats and a wide pontoon bobbed in the waves beside the long dock. A man and a boy, each clutching fishing rods, stood at its end, casting into the rolling water.

Evan shut the van off and turned to face Shaun. "Ready to go on a boat ride?"

A look of delight lit up Shaun's face, and he began to fiddle with his seat harness. But his small fingers couldn't manipulate the two buttons to release the fastener.

"Let me help you," Evan said, climbing out. He strode around the side of the van and opened Shaun's door, uncoupling the belts before lifting him from his seat.

Immediately Shaun pointed toward the lake. "Dere?"

"Yep, we're going out there," Evan said, walking toward the screen door of the building.

A gust of wind came off the lake and ruffled their hair with the cool touch of spring. Spring breezes always smelled and felt different than autumn winds. There was hope in the air during spring, and only a promise of frost with fall.

"Mornin' ta ya!"

The voice brought Evan out of his musing, and he stopped a few yards before the door as a man pushed through it. His clean-shaven face beamed, and a pair of coal-black eyebrows stood out beneath a shock of white hair. He held out his hand as he approached.

"Jacob Collins," he said, shaking Evan's hand with a callused grip. "You must be Evan." Jacob's voice had a Celtic lilt that sounded a little like song when he spoke. "And this must be Shaun."

He flattened his hand so that Shaun could slap it with his own. After two tries that missed their mark, Evan guided Shaun's hand onto Jacob's.

"What a nice smile you've got, boyo!" Jacob said, as Shaun grinned. "Jason told me ta look fer ya this mornin'," he said to Evan.

"Yes, sorry if we're early," Evan said. He shifted Shaun into a more comfortable spot against his hip.

"Been up since the crack a dawn, you won't see me sleepin' late, specially this time a year. The opener was last weekend, ya know."

"Oh yeah, I forgot. My dad and I used to go out every year. Funny how you forget if you don't keep the tradition."

"Aye. Jason's father, God rest his soul, and I used ta go out each spring together. I've known Jason since he was wee-high. He tells me ya grew up side by side?"

Evan smiled. "Yes we did, and that's a good way to put it, we didn't spend too much time apart."

"Jason's a good lad, and we're glad ta have ya both up in the north again."

"Thanks, we're excited to get settled in, and thank you for agreeing to bring us to the island."

Jacob waved his words away. "Ain't nothin'. Now, I'm guessin' ya got some gear. I'll have ya back down ta the dock."

Evan returned to the van and, after placing Shaun in his car seat, reversed the vehicle down to the pier, backing up until Jacob gave him the signal to stop. The rear end of the van was packed full of their belongings, and Evan felt a sense of pride at having managed to fit everything that they needed.

As he and Jacob hauled various suitcases and bags onto the pontoon, Evan surveyed the lake. It was wider than he'd first estimated, at least half a mile across in some places, and when he looked to the left, he couldn't see its opposite end. Several fishing boats swayed in the swells, their occupants only dots that shifted from time to time, betraying the illusion that they were parts of the crafts.

"Somethin', ain't it?" Jacob asked.

Evan glanced at him before setting his laptop bag onto the heaping pile within the pontoon. "It sure is. I forgot how beautiful it is up here."

"It's a sight, that's fer sure." Jacob pointed northeast, across the water, his finger guiding Evan's eyes to a dark mass he'd mistaken for a large boat. "That's yer island there. The Fin, it's called round here."

"The Fin?"

"Looks like a shark's dorsal when you get closer."

Evan stared at the black speck, trying to discern any features. "How far out is it?"

"Eh, maybe a kilometer from the dock. Takes ten minutes on a calm day, take us fifteen today." Jacob moved to the back of the minivan and took Shaun's walker out, then shut the hatch.

Evan watched a boat pass by before returning his attention to the island. It was so far from shore. He hadn't anticipated it being that far away. What if Shaun had another seizure? What if he got hurt and couldn't call for help?

He caught himself before the questions pushed him into a full-blown anxiety attack.

"You can park yer van in me lot. I live right here, so I'll be able ta keep an eye on it," Jacob said, setting the walker in the pontoon.

"Thank you," Evan said, but his voice sounded distant, as if the wind had blown it away.

~

The pontoon bounced up and down as they crossed the lake, and several sprays of water speckled them with cold drops, eliciting cries of glee from Shaun each time. Jacob piloted the pontoon without effort, animatedly talking with them about the history of the lake and his own story of how he came to live there.

"Me mum and dad moved here when I was twelve. Bought the land that the shop sits on and started a guidin' service. Dad would take people out, help 'em catch some fish, and Mum would knit sweaters, sell 'em in the shop."

"Pretty industrious," Evan said, readjusting Shaun on his lap.

"Aye, they were workers, and once we got here, I never wanted ta leave. Took over the family business thirty years back when Dad passed."

The growing mass of trees and rock jutted from the water ahead of the pontoon. Like the lake, the island had appeared smaller at first. The closer they got, the more the land lengthened and took on character. Its shape mimicked the lake around it, but its crescent curved the opposite way, creating the impression of a massive boomerang. Tall pines along the rocky shoreline swayed, while reed grass, not yet above a person's knee, curled and bent along the banks.

"Did you know Jason's grandparents very well?" Evan asked.

Jacob shook his head. "Not very. I'd stop out here from time ta time with Ray, but I never knew his parents more than the passing hello."

Evan nodded, and looked at the island again. The pontoon moved closer to the landmass and Jacob idled the engine down. The outline of a house became clearer above an old dock sticking out into the water like a rude tongue. The house was large, with an attached three-season porch at one end and wide windows cut into its sides. A musical tinkle played on the breeze, and he saw swaying wind chimes attached to the porch's closest end. Several tall oaks towered over the structure on either side, their branches newly budded with leaves. A gently sloping hill covered in fine grass rolled down to the edge of the property, where it met the lapping waves on a manicured beach. A small, canopied boatlift held a miniature version of the pontoon they rode in, and an aluminum boat lay belly-up near the sand, like some kind of silver fish out of water.

"It's beautiful," Evan said.

Shaun jerked excitedly on his lap. "Dere?"

"Yep, buddy, that's where we're headed."

Jacob steered the pontoon to the left side of the dock. Evan spun in his seat and reached out, catching one of the dock's steel supports, and held on until Jacob climbed out and secured the craft with a few ropes. The gentle rush of waves washing onto the beach was so calming, Evan imagined sitting in the pontoon with Shaun on his lap all day. He was sure they could watch the water run onto the sand and slide away again without ever getting bored.

"What would you like brought out first?" Jacob called from the dock.

"Shaun's chair, then he can sit in the shade while we unload."

Jacob nodded and hauled the medical seat, which was equipped with several straps to help keep Shaun upright along with wheels. Evan carried his son to the front of the pontoon and opened the side door, then stepped onto the dock. After positioning Shaun in his chair beneath the shade of a large pine, he helped Jacob unload the pontoon. As he carried a large suitcase up the hill toward the house, Jacob called to him, making him turn back.

"I hope you'll forgive me, I've got ta get back ta the shop, but I'll unload everythin' onta the dock fer ya."

Evan hesitated, a frown attempting to darken his face, then nodded. "That's fine, Jacob, we really appreciate it."

Jacob continued stacking their belongings upon the dock in an ever-growing pile. Within a few minutes the pontoon was empty, and Evan helped untie the craft from the dock's moorings.

He held out a twenty-dollar bill to Jacob, who immediately waved it away. "You have to take it," Evan said, pushing the money at the older man again.

"No, I don't," Jacob said, smiling. "That's the nice thing about bein' yer own boss. I'll settle fer a handshake and maybe a beer next time yer in town. How's that?"

Evan finally relented and shoved the money into his pocket, then shook Jacob's outstretched hand. "Sounds like a deal, and thank you again."

"No problem, boyo. Keep yer daddy in line, eh, Shaun?" Jacob waved at the boy.

Shaun raised a hand, kicked his feet, and smiled.

"Take care, now," Jacob said, as Evan pushed the pontoon away from the dock.

Soon the motor purred to life, and the boat as well as its captain grew smaller and smaller across the waves.

Evan turned back to the island, surveying the lush forest on the acreage, listening to the wind cutting through the trees, and breathing in the scent of fresh water and pine needles. Shaun waved at him, and he waved back before picking up one of their bags. When he glanced over his shoulder, Jacob had disappeared from sight.

They were alone.

## 5

A musty blast of air swept past Evan's face when he opened the door to the house.

*Like a crypt opening.*

He shook his head, forcing the odd thought away. Hefting Shaun into a better position, he nudged the door open and stepped inside.

They were in a small entryway, with a closet directly opposite them. To the left, a living room opened into a wide space interspersed with comfortable-looking leather furniture. An entertainment center stood against the far wall, with a large flat-screen TV above it. The bank of windows in the room overlooking the lake were dusty but gave a great view of the yard and water.

Evan walked farther into the house, pausing every so often to take in a painting on the wall or a knickknack standing on a shelf. Past the living room was the kitchen, modest and clean, with a long, wooden table in its center. A fridge stood beside a small dishwasher, and another series of windows looked over the backyard, which was more overgrown than the front, hemmed in by trees that obscured the lake from view save a shimmer here and there between their trunks. To the right of the kitchen were two doors.

"Let's see what's in here, buddy," Evan said, and grasped the handle of the door on the left.

It was the master bedroom, a neatly made bed in its center and a walk-in closet off to one side. The windows faced the woods to the south, their growth even thicker than those in the backyard.

A wave of self-consciousness rolled over him as he looked at Jason's grandparents' bedroom, as if they would come through the front door any moment and catch him and Shaun intruding in their private space. He shut the door, stanching the invasive feeling.

"How about door number two?" he said, tousling Shaun's hair. The boy giggled.

Evan grasped the doorknob and pulled. The door swung open—

—to darkness. A set of stairs led straight down and disappeared from sight.

"Basement," Evan said.

Reaching out, he felt along the wall for a light switch he knew must be there. His fingers found it, a disproportionate amount of relief flowing through him, and snapped it on.

Nothing happened.

Everything below them remained shrouded in black. Evan stepped back and shut the door, pulling his palm away from the knob as though it were hot.

"Let's go find your room," Evan said.

They moved through the living room to the opposite end of the house. The three-season porch branched off to the left, its hexagonal shape holding a gas grill, four lawn chairs, and a small table. The only bathroom in the house sat before two other doors, and when Evan opened them, he found that they were almost identical guest bedrooms. Picking the larger of the two, he went inside and set Shaun down on the edge of a twin bed.

"What do you think, buddy? Is this your room?"

Shaun's eyes roamed the ceiling and flitted across the closet and chest of drawers. He pointed above Evan's head, his upper teeth biting into his lower lip.

"Fa, fff ..."

Shaun paused, his jaw working to dislodge the word he wanted. Evan mimicked his expression and coaxed him with the same sound.

"Fffff."

"F-f-f-fan," Shaun said, and smiled at the ceiling fan hanging in the middle of the room.

"Good boy," Evan said, and hugged his son close. "That's right, that's a fan. Can you say it again?"

"F-fan!"

"High-five!"

Shaun raised his small hand and placed it against his father's much larger one. "Five."

Evan grinned, and in that moment Shaun looked so much like Elle it hurt his heart. How she would have loved to see his progress. Biting back a line of tears that threatened to spill out, he stood and gazed out of the window at the swaying trees.

"Come on, son. Let's get the rest of our gear inside."

~

They worked for the next two hours, Evan hauling their belongings up the short hill and into the house while Shaun watched from his chair in the shade near the front door. Every so often Evan would stop to take in their surroundings. Spring birdsong filtered into the yard from the dense copses of trees to either side of the house. The fresh air tasted good on his tongue, and his muscles burned in an almost pleasant way.

He took the other guest room, mostly because he wanted to be within feet of Shaun in case he had a seizure or needed him in the middle of the night, and only partially because he didn't think he'd be able to sleep in the master bedroom. As he set his suitcase on the bed, a silver wristwatch on the bedside table, atop the cover of a paperback thriller, caught his eye. Evan picked it up and saw that it was a self-winder, the kind that used energy from the movement of its wearer. Its hands were stopped at 12:17. Frowning, he set it down and made a mental note to tell Jason his prior caretaker had left it behind.

After Evan deemed them adequately moved in, he made them sandwiches from the meager supplies he'd brought to get them through the first day or two. They ate on the screened-in porch, enjoying the view and listening to the wind and occasional whine of an outboard motor on the lake.

"This is beautiful, huh, buddy? We're going to stay here for the summer. Is that okay?"

Shaun gazed around at the trees, his eyes returning to the lake over and over.

"A lot of people would pay a bunch of money to stay in place like this, but Uncle Jason is paying us."

Evan glanced over his shoulder at the house that wasn't anything near a cabin. It didn't need a full-time caretaker, not really. Someone could've handled the chores one day a week, if that.

"Uncle Jason's too good to us, you know that?"

Shaun looked his way and smiled, his head tipping forward so that he looked at Evan from beneath his eyebrows.

Evan chuckled. "You're a ham."

When they were done eating, he left Shaun on the porch, reclining his chair enough so the boy could comfortably fall asleep if he wanted to. In the kitchen he gathered the bread, turkey, cheese, and mayonnaise and opened the fridge to put them away.

The stench hit him like a baseball bat.

Rotten, molded food soaked in its own juices. Containers and bags filled with unrecognizable contents sat on each shelf. A single milk carton looked normal, but the crisper held nothing but a brown soup.

"Fuck me," Evan said, and stepped back, covering his mouth and nose.

He stared at the inside of the fridge, almost tasting the rot on his tongue. The sandwich in his stomach made a leap for the back of his throat, but he swallowed, forcing it down. He glanced at the temperature setting, noting it was a little warm, but not enough to cause the decay before him.

Evan shoved the door shut to cut off the smell. He moved back until his ass hit the counter beside the sink, watching the fridge as though it were some feral animal crouched in the corner. Without thinking about it, he dug his cell phone from his pocket and made his way to the porch. Shaun dozed in the chair, the breeze ruffling his light hair.

When he glanced at the phone only one bar was visible for service. "Shit."

He walked through the living room. As he neared the windows overlooking the lake, the signal gained another bar, and he hit Jason's number. It rang only once before there was a click on the other end.

"Make it okay?" Jason said.

Evan heard the murmur of other people in the background. "Yeah. Hey, can you talk right now, or is it not a good time?"

"Sure, I'm good. Just left a board meeting. What's up?"

Evan paced to the front door and then back again, shooting a look at the kitchen. "Something's off here."

"What do you mean, 'off'?"

"Who was this last guy you had in the house?"

A pause. "Why?"

"Well, for one, he left his watch and a paperback in the guest room, which isn't a big deal. But the fucking fridge is full of rotten food, man. When I opened it up the smell about knocked me over."

"Really? Was it unplugged?"

"No."

"What the hell? Yeah, I mean, his name was Bob something ... Garrison? Something like that, anyway. He was a normal guy. Single, lived in Colorado before he moved here, did some handyman stuff to get by. Never had a problem with him until this spring."

"You said he quit—what happened?"

Another pause. "Well, to be honest, he stopped answering my calls—not that I called him all the time. I gave him a ring in late March, and then again in mid-April. When he didn't get back to me the second time, I had Jacob go out there and check it out. He said that the place was empty and everything was fine, but no sign of Bob. He cashed the last check I sent him in March, so I thought he got sick of being there and jetted."

Evan chewed at the inside of his cheek. The house looked slightly different now. Not quite as open and bright as before.

"It looks like he up and left everything sitting here, like he just took off. If he left in March, that would explain why the fridge is so nasty. But how the hell did he leave? Both boats are still here."

"I'm guessing he hoofed it across the lake since it was still frozen in early April."

Evan shook his head. "Weird."

A ding of an elevator came from Jason's end.

"I don't know what to tell you, my friend, people are loopy. I'm sorry you guys have to deal with the shitbag's mess. How's everything else, though? Jacob get you there okay?"

"Yeah, yeah, he was great, didn't even charge us for the ride."

"That's how he is. He was Dad's best friend, good guy, except he's Irish."

"I'm Irish, you asshole."

"I know."

Evan laughed. "I'm sorry, man, I'm not complaining. The house is great and the island is beautiful. Shaun loves it here so far."

"Good deal. Hey, I gotta run, there's a client waiting in my office. I'll give you a ring later."

"Okay, talk to you then."

Jason began speaking to someone else a second before the line disconnected, and Evan felt the warm glow he always did when he reflected on their friendship. There wasn't another person in the world who knew him better. Now that Elle was gone.

He swallowed and sighed before going to check on Shaun again. When he saw that the boy hadn't moved a muscle, he turned and headed for the kitchen, mentally preparing himself for the cleaning session he was about to endure.

~

It took him an hour to clean the fridge. Somehow, amongst three gagging episodes and two breaks to check on Shaun, he managed to evict all signs of the decaying food from the GE. After tossing two bags of refuse into a large garbage can outside, Evan finished putting away their food and separated Shaun's clothes into the chest of drawers in his room. It was nearing five in the evening when Shaun awoke, and they sat down to a simple meal of canned soup.

"Wanna go for a walk, buddy?" Evan asked, as he placed their dirty dishes onto the counter.

Shaun nodded, and he smiled at how rested his little face looked. Sleep was his ally, and Evan tried not to wake him if at all possible, no matter the time of day.

They left the house and made their way around the right side of the building, toward the heavy cover of trees, Evan walking backward and holding Shaun's hands while Shaun tottered along, concentration etched across his features. Evan had him walk until they reached the boundary of the yard, and then picked him up, swinging him high in the air before depositing him on his shoulders. They threaded their way between the massive trunks and a few brambles that were beginning to sprout, into green foliage. A worn path no more than a foot wide appeared and he angled them toward it. The trail looked beaten, whether by animals or humans, he didn't know. They followed the track as it snaked ever downward, over exposed rocks and roots. Eventually the wavering surface of the lake became visible. A small ring of rocks sat in a clearing above the waterline, the earth permanently black in its center.

"Wow, nice party spot, buddy," Evan said, holding Shaun's hands. "Fire ring," he annunciated, hoping that Shaun would mimic his words.

"Help!"

The cry was loud and came out of nowhere, turning Evan's guts with icy surprise. He stopped, trying to determine where the call came from.

"Help! I dropped my paddle in the water."

He hurried down to the clearing and caught sight of a woman in a canoe some fifteen yards offshore. Her hands gripped the sides of the little boat, and her dark brown hair was buffeted by the wind that pushed across the lake.

"My paddle," she yelled, pointing toward a clump of reeds growing from the foremost tip of the island. A faded wooden canoe paddle floated there, its handle hooked on a bent reed.

Evan glanced back at the canoe and saw the woman's dilemma. The wind was gradually pushing her farther and farther away, turning her in a gentle circle. He moved to the nearest tree and took Shaun off his shoulders, setting him at the pine's base with his back resting against its trunk.

"You sit right here, don't move."

Evan jogged to the water's edge and looked for a way to grab the paddle without getting soaked, but soon saw the canoe and the woman would be out of sight before he devised a plan. With a grimace, he waded into the water, the cold spring lake rushing in to fill his shoes and socks. Leaning forward, he reached out and snagged the paddle's handle and drew it toward him.

"I'm going to toss it to you, okay?"

"Okay."

He took aim and launched the paddle over the water with an underhand push. It sailed up and flipped once, and came down within feet of the canoe, bumping its side with a hollow thud. The woman pulled the paddle into the canoe, then stroked at the lake with long, practiced movements. Evan sidestepped through the muddy bottom until his feet were on solid ground again. To his relief, Shaun still sat where he'd left him. When he turned back to the lake, he saw that the canoe was closer and the woman aboard smiled at him as she neared.

"Where's Elle?"

Evan's heart jittered in his chest, and his mouth dropped open. "Wha ... what did you say?"

The front of the canoe scraped onto the bank and stopped, and its rear end drifted sideways. The woman placed a hand against her brow, blocking the setting sun, and looked at him.

"I said, it fell." When Evan didn't move, she lifted the paddle up and set it back down. "I was floating by your island and thought I saw a cardinal. When I set the paddle down and picked up my binoculars, it slipped into the water and drifted out of reach."

Evan shut his mouth and blinked. "Sorry," he said, stepping forward to pull the bow of the canoe farther onto land.

It was an old craft, with chunks of paint peeling off here and there, the inside speckled with bits of twigs and mud. He steadied the front as the woman stood and made her way out of the canoe and onto the island.

She was thin, in a way that spoke of athleticism and lean muscle rather than frailty, and not much over five feet tall. She wore a long-sleeved T-shirt and brown cargo pants that nearly matched the shade of her hair. Evan straightened up and broke from his inspection when the woman held her hand out.

"Selena Belgaurd."

Evan grasped her small hand. "Evan Tormer, and this is my son, Shaun," he said, motioning to Shaun, who tried to wave.

"Very nice to meet you both, and thank you," Selena said, letting go of his hand. She smiled. Her lips curved up in a way that accentuated her blue eyes.

"You're welcome," Evan said. He glanced away.

"Do you guys live here?"

"Yeah, kind of. We moved in today. We're house-sitting for my friend who owns it."

"Well, it's a beautiful place. Do you like it here, Shaun?"

Shaun smiled and his small mouth worked to form a word.

"He doesn't speak well," Evan said.

Selena's face fell, and it looked as if she wanted to ask more. But Evan turned away.

"We really have to be getting back to the house."

Selena nodded. "Sure, okay. Well, thank you again. If you wouldn't have come along, I don't know where I would've ended up."

"You're welcome," Evan said, and picked up Shaun.

Selena raised a hand and then turned, shoving the canoe back into the water and jumping inside in one motion. Evan hitched Shaun a little higher onto his hip and didn't wait until the canoe was out of sight before climbing up the hill, toward the house.

# 6

They sat on the porch and watched the sun bleed its last rays onto the water. The trees ceased their movement, and birds washed the evening with song that seemed to fill up not only the island but the whole world.

After some rummaging through their belongings, Evan found two tracing books and a dry-erase marker. He stood behind Shaun, guiding his son's hand beneath his own over letters and numbers alike, pronouncing their names as the marker traced the dotted lines.

"Okay, now you're gonna do it on your own," Evan said, letting go of Shaun's hand.

The boy's head bent closer to the book, and his fingers began to slip off the marker before he could trace a row of figure eights. Shaun grunted in frustration and tried to re-grip the marker, but it fell from his hand and rolled off the table.

"It's okay, buddy, it's okay," Evan said, kneeling to retrieve the fallen writing utensil. He placed it back between his son's fingers. "Try again."

Shaun started the eight and made it only inches before the marker spun away, this time to the opposite side of the porch.

"No," Shaun yelled, and banged both his hands against the table.

"Hey, hey, it's all right, you did good. We just need more practice," Evan said, and wrapped his arms around Shaun.

The boy strained against him, anger fueling his motions. A hot burning filled the back of Evan's eyes. What terrible karmic atrocity had he committed that made the universe glance his family's way and shake its head? In response, he heard the same answer he received each time he asked the question, spoken by the voice he hated inside his own mind.

*Because this is your life, this is what it is.*

"It's okay, it's okay, we can be done for tonight. You did really good." Slowly Shaun calmed, and Evan released him, repeating the words in his mind, *it's okay, it's okay.* "Do you want to watch trains?"

Shaun whimpered one more time and then stilled, his breathing slowing, skin sweaty from his exertions. "Tains?"

"Okay, buddy, we'll watch some trains."

He centered Shaun in the couch and sought out the DVD from the duffel in his room. After a few moments of fussing with the unfamiliar player, Thomas the Train began to race across the screen. Evan adjusted the volume and returned to the couch, putting an arm around Shaun's slight shoulders. The sun fell completely out of sight as they watched, replaced by an inky darkness that crept closer until the lake sat in gloom, the open windows no longer admitting birdsong.

Evan glanced to the left, his eyes straying from the episode playing out on the screen, and found himself staring at the basement door. Shaun giggled at one of the train's antics, and Evan focused again on the TV. Minutes later, his eyes rested once more on the door. He watched it. He studied the knob like prey looking for a predator, waiting, not willing to glance away, afraid that if he did, it would ... turn.

Shaun's sharp snore tore him out of his trance, and he jerked with the sound. Evan shifted, sliding his arm from beneath the boy's back. He breathed even and deep, his eyes shut, mouth open.

"Tired guy," Evan whispered. "Long day."

With gentle movements, he laid Shaun on his side, nestling him into the couch. Evan unfurled a folded comforter that hung from the arm of an easy chair, and spread it over his sleeping son. He listened to Shaun's soft inhalations for a long time in the faint glow of the only lamp burning in the room. Gradually his attention returned to the basement door.

In a few strides he crossed the room, and flipped on two of the kitchen lights, chasing the shadows from beneath the long table and behind the breakfast bar. He paused, listening for what? Sounds from below? Evan huffed and walked to the door, throwing it wide.

Darkness greeted him, deeper than earlier that afternoon, thicker. It swallowed the treads and gave nothing in return, rebuffing the cheerful light of the kitchen. His earlier desire for exploring the basement wilted, and he nearly slammed the door shut, the muscles in his arm already tensing to do so.

However, he reached out and found the switch once again, knowing the outcome but having to flip it on and off several times without effect before he was satisfied. The overwhelming urge to step back and close the door came again. Revolting against the warnings sounding within him, he took the first step. The wooden stair emitted a short shriek beneath his weight. He swallowed, looked over his shoulder at the rounded shape of Shaun on the couch, then continued down.

The light at his back died within the dark. In all his years, the only other experience he could compare it to was at a lock-in party at his high school. Several other boys in his grade had snuck out of the locker room in which they'd been changing, knowing full well Evan was sitting on the toilet. He'd been lost in thought about how to ask Kimberly Shell to the dance later that evening when the fluorescents winked out, the silence broken only by the retreating laughter of the other boys. He'd sat there, petrified on the toilet, frozen in the cold darkness of a place that held no malice in the light, but without it, became something else.

Memories of staggering out of the windowless locker room and into the hall full of giggling teenagers left him as he stepped down again, the shadows rising ever upward as though he were dropping deeper and deeper into a subterranean sea.

His left hand brushed against the smooth wall, the only sound above his hushed breathing. Five steps, six, seven. The eighth tread wasn't where it should have been, and he almost fell headlong, the surface under his foot remaining level instead of dropping away—a landing.

Evan slid his hand forward and found that the wall turned, and he pivoted with it, his opposite arm now out before him, stretched into the black maw. The next step edge met his foot, and he went down. One, two, three. At the fourth stair his arm brushed something, and he nearly cried out before realizing it was a pillar near the foot of the stairway.

He searched blindly until his fingers met a switch box. Knowing full well if this switch produced no light he would retreat up the stairs, he flipped it up. Three dim bulbs blinked on in a line across the basement, casting everything in a sick glow. He was about to step onto the basement floor when he looked down—

—and saw a small child standing less than a foot away.

His feet tried to backpedal, and a strangled moan fell from his mouth as he tripped and landed hard on the stairs behind him. The treads bit into his ass and lower back, but he barely noticed, his gaping eyes locked on the child facing away from him. As he was about to spin and flee up the stairs, already forming a plan to grab Shaun from the couch and haul him to the pontoon, Evan realized that the child hadn't moved. He waited, his breath too large for his lungs. His eyes traveled down the back of a little girl with dark hair wearing a purple dress, except something was wrong. Several slits were cut into the back of her knees.

Evan sighed and placed his sweating face into one palm.

A doll.

"Shit."

His voice sounded hollow, but speaking gave him the strength to stand and wince at the throbbing ache settling into his back. He moved down the last two treads, his heart returning into the realm of normality as the doll's face came into view.

Its eyes stared across the basement, its mouth covered in duct tape.

The bubbling dread within his stomach that had receded only moments ago built again, the hairs rising on the back of his neck. Evan didn't move any farther into the basement, his eyes fixed on the doll's face. Visions of its head slowly turning toward him corkscrewed through his mind. If that happened, he wouldn't simply cry out, he would become a scream embodied.

Trying to shove aside the blaring fear within, he bent and grasped the doll's miniature arm. Its plastic flesh was cold to the touch, as if it had been soaking in ice water. He shuddered, waiting for the frigid limb to writhe in his palm. Even as the rational part of his mind tried to quell the stampeding fear, his hands continued to shake. He turned the doll over once, studying it. It didn't look very old or used. In fact, it appeared almost new. When he flipped it over again, he flinched as its bright blue eyes blinked shut, but realized it was designed to do that when lying flat. The gray tape covering the doll's mouth was smooth, its chubby cheeks visible above its gag. Evan set the doll on the floor beside a stack of cardboard boxes, giving it another sidelong glance before stepping fully into the room.

The basement ran the full length and width of the house, and even with its low ceiling, it felt like a cavernous space. To his right he saw what must have been Jason's grandmother's sewing area; a dust-covered sewing machine sat amidst a field of threaded bobbins atop a desk. Beside it, several baskets of yarn lay in bundles, their wrapping sealed and new.

He moved forward, running his hand along a workbench that stretched along the wall. A pegboard of hanging tools glinted in the soft light, and numerous drawers lined the front of the bench. A few support beams studded the floor in random places, furthering the feeling of being in a cave.

As he approached the opposite end of the room, he saw a wide worktable covered with a white sheet and littered with several stacks of papers held down by oblong brass paperweights. Toothy sprockets and thin chains were coiled within trails of oil. Beyond the table stood a massive shape partially concealed by another sheet, this one dark and splotched.

Evan moved closer to the hidden shape, noting the electrical panel in one corner as well as a hulking furnace and water heater. Several cobwebs danced in the rafters above, and gradually the silhouette beneath the makeshift tarp became apparent.

A grandfather clock.

But it was the biggest he had ever seen. Rounding the table, he tugged once at the sheet covering its bulk. It fell to the floor, and he stepped back.

The clock didn't have a single pendulum encasement, but three. The two towers to either side of the center lacked actual pendulums and sat lower, like the shoulders of a crouching giant. The wood frame was dark, stained a deep obsidian, with elaborate molding that swirled and curved on the outside of the frame. Three glass doors covered the pendulum encasements, their handles and hinges cast iron, with the center door being the widest, almost big enough for a man to walk through comfortably. The clock's shining face was the size of a large dinner plate and had four separate sets of timing hands. Instead of numbers around the outer edges, bunches of delicate, curving lines were etched into the silver plating. The slicing brink of a moon dial peeked over the top of the clock's face; the crescent moon carved into the steel bore an uncanny malevolent smile, with two empty sockets for eyes. Above the face, the molding came together in two pointed horns that nearly met in the middle.

*That's the scariest fucking clock I've ever seen.*

He frowned. How could a timepiece be scary? He chided himself but couldn't deny the aura the clock gave off. It hadn't been engineered to be beautiful. As far as he could see, it was quite the opposite.

His hip bumped the worktable, and one of the paperweights rolled off the pile it held down. He reached out and stopped it before it plummeted to the floor, marveling at its weight. Only after lifting it close to his face did he realize that's exactly what it was—a weight for the clock. Its brass casing shone beneath the light, and a small pulley grew from its top.

Evan spun the little wheel a few times before placing the weight back on the table. A diagram on one of the pieces of paper drew his attention. He picked the paper up and spent several seconds squinting before realizing it was an inner illustration of the clock's face, "the bonnet," as it was apparently called.

"On it like a bonnet," Evan said to the empty room, as he placed the paper back on the pile. He turned toward the clock, wondering whether or not he should replace the sheet. The soulless eyes of the moon at the clock's peak gazed at him, almost imploring him to come closer.

"No thanks," Evan said, and crossed the basement to the stairway, shooting only a cursory glance at the doll as he passed.

He paused at the light switch, running through different options before sighing and flipping off the power to the lights. The basement plunged into darkness, and with all the restraint he held in his body, he managed not to pelt up the stairs into the welcoming light of the kitchen.

After closing the door behind him, he moved to the sofa, letting out an unconscious sigh of relief at seeing Shaun still sleeping soundly on the cushions. He brushed at the boy's hair once before retrieving a pull-up from the bathroom. Shaun barely moved as Evan put on the small diaper and then carried him to his room. A few moonbeams shone through the window, dappling the floor in an aquatic way, and Shaun shrugged in his sleep as he laid him down.

"Mama."

Evan froze in the process of pulling the covers up over his son. His lower lip trembled, and he hoped that Shaun would and wouldn't repeat the word. The boy licked the corner of his mouth and then resumed snoring in barely audible breaths. He swallowed and placed a kiss on Shaun's forehead.

"Night, buddy, sleep good."

Evan flicked the baby monitor on beside the bed and crossed the hall to his own room, not bothering to shut either door. With a groan, he tugged his shirt over his head, massaging the spot on his lower back where he'd fallen. His eyes swept the room and landed on the crack in the folding doors of the closet. Knowing that sleep wouldn't come if he ignored it, he stepped to the closet and drew open the doors.

Several men's T-shirts and sweaters hung inside.

He knelt and saw a pair of dress shoes on the floor in the corner and a short stack of jeans on the wire shelf off to one side of the space. He stood and snapped the doors shut, leaving the questions to reside within the closet, at least for the night.

After brushing his teeth and checking on Shaun one last time, he lay down within the cool sheets of the bed, too tired to care that he'd changed only Shaun's bedding earlier that day. Swirling thoughts attempted and failed to amount an attack on his fatigued mind. He turned on Shaun's receiver and closed his eyes, falling into sleep's embrace almost at once.

~

Hours later he awoke, the moon having shifted its light enough for him to see the room in which he rested. Evan sat up, his heart thumping from the terror of the fading nightmare, its shape and fear an amalgam of shifting unease hanging above him yet failing to reveal itself fully. His mouth was dry, cracked and parched beyond desert soil.

He swung his feet to the floor and shuffled out of the room, crossed the hallway to the bathroom door, which was closed. Had he left it that way? He nearly paused to consider it, but his thirst pushed him onward, nudging away the concern. His hand gripped the handle, and he opened the door—

—and stepped out of the clock, into the basement.

Shaun screamed somewhere above him.

Evan sat up straight in bed. The cry, longing to break free of his throat, dying on his tongue. His eyes widened and sweat rolled down the center of his back as he scanned the room. His room. He was in his room. A nightmare, that's all it had been. A doozy, but only a dream within a dream.

The monitor beside the bed remained steady while he listened to Shaun rustle beneath his covers. His heaving breath gradually slowed, but the sweat kept rolling off him in waves.

He stood and moved to Shaun's room, hovering in the doorway for more than a minute before returning to bed. Using his T-shirt from the day before, he toweled off as best he could before lying back down to stare at the ceiling of the unfamiliar room.

After a long time, he closed his eyes, sleep waiting even longer before claiming him for its own. As he drifted, he told himself that the quiet ticking coming from somewhere below was only a dream.

# 7

The morning dawned bright, with long rays of sun that spread throughout the house and colored the lake gold.

Evan and Shaun rose early and ate a meager breakfast of peanut-butter toast, the whole while Evan vowing to go grocery shopping that afternoon to replenish their supplies. After breakfast, they made their way to the edge of the lake, where Evan lowered the small pontoon into the water from its cradled lift. When he'd successfully started the motor and swept the leaves and other refuse of winter from the decking, he brought Shaun aboard. He buckled him into the seat beside the pilot's chair, and folded his walker and placed it in the front of the boat.

As they cruised into open water, the morning sunshine, and even Shaun's delighted laughter, couldn't fully engross Evan's thoughts. His head kept turning back to the island growing smaller and smaller behind them, the house no longer visible amongst the trees. The nightmare from the night before replayed in his mind on a sickening loop, and it became more unsettling each time he watched it spool out.

"Dere?" Shaun asked, his finger pointing toward the approaching docks of Collins Outfitters.

"There," Evan corrected him. "Yes, that's where we're going."

Evan lowered the pontoon's speed as they neared the dock, and was pleased with himself at parking the craft in an empty spot on the first try without bashing into anything.

"Your old man's a pirate at heart," he said, and then cackled in a mock evil voice as he tickled Shaun.

The parking lot was empty, save their minivan, and though Evan looked for Jacob through the windows as they passed, he failed to see the old man within the store.

"We'll stop in on the way back," he told Shaun as he buckled him into the backseat.

They drove through the quiet of Mill River, their vehicle seemingly the only one on the road but for a trundling school bus, its yellow paint a shining reflection of the sun. When they arrived at the hospital, Evan unloaded Shaun's walker, and they made their way inside the glass building. They found the pediatric therapy department without any trouble. A woman with wispy gray hair pulled back tight into a bun met them in the waiting room after Evan checked in with the desk.

"I'm Dr. Doris Netler, pleased to meet you both," she said, first shaking Evan's hand and then Shaun's.

Dr. Netler led them down a short hallway. "I don't have a lot of time to spare this morning, but I definitely can give you a short tour," she said over her shoulder.

"Thank you," Evan said, taking in the colorful posters and paintings that adorned the walls. Even with the cheery atmosphere the hospital staff had tried to create, it still felt as if he were being pressed beneath a giant thumb. The last time he'd been happy in a hospital was the day Shaun was born.

Dr. Netler introduced them to the head of the pediatric-therapy department as well as the speech pathologist who would be Shaun's therapist for the summer. When Dr. Netler opened the last door on their tour, Shaun let out a yell of happiness.

"And this is our therapy gym," she said, stepping inside a room with a padded floor, a zip line running along one wall, and a giant ball pit filled with every color of the rainbow.

"You remember this, buddy?" Evan asked.

Shaun bounced with excitement in his arms.

"Would you like to play for a few minutes?" Dr. Netler asked Shaun. He nodded and she laughed. "You can put him in the ball pit if you like. Before you leave, stop by the admission desk and set up his appointments as well as your insurance program."

"Thank you, doctor," Evan said. "Just one more quick question. You wouldn't be able to recommend any good personal-care assistants, would you?"

"Absolutely. Becky Tram works part-time in OT and is a PCA on the side. I'll let the desk know, and they'll give you her information."

"We're a little out of the way," Evan said.

"I'm sure she won't mind. Where are you staying?"

"The island ..." Evan searched for the nickname Jacob had said the day before. "The Fin."

Something flashed across Netler's eyes. It was there and then gone like a bird's shadow on the ground. She smiled. "I'm guessing she'd still be able to help, but you'll have to ask her. Take care, guys."

Without another look, Netler left the room. He watched her go, and stood still for a moment after the door closed behind her.

"Dere?" Shaun pointed toward the ball pit.

"There," Evan said, still looking at the door, then lowered Shaun into the large playpen.

~

They spent the rest of the morning grocery shopping and exploring the shops along Main Street. They stopped at a quaint coffee shop with a great view of the lake. Evan got a large dark roast, and Shaun, a small hot chocolate that he drank through a straw once it was cool enough. A little boy, no older than five, wandered over to their table on the patio, a green balloon clutched in a chubby fist. He stared at Shaun, who sat in a chair pulled up next to Evan's. Shaun smiled and reached toward the floating balloon.

"Hi there," Evan said, and glanced over the boy's head at a woman who must've been his mother ordering a drink at the counter.

The boy examined Shaun and tilted his head when Shaun made an excited sound.

"What's wrong with him?" the boy asked.

Evan was figuring out a response when the boy's mother grasped her son by the shoulder, guiding him away.

"I'm sorry," she said, shoving the boy toward their car parked along the sidewalk.

Evan smiled halfheartedly. "It's okay." He didn't think she heard him. The mother admonished the boy in hushed tones as she stowed him away inside the car.

"It's okay," he repeated, and stroked the side of Shaun's face.

When they finished their drinks, they stopped at a liquor store near the landing, and Evan picked up a few bottles of cabernet sauvignon. They were unloading the van when Jacob came out of his store and made his way to them down the ramp, his face one big smile.

"There ya are. Missed ya this mornin'."

Evan shook hands with the older man.

"And how's Shaun t'day?" Jacob said, stooping beside the minivan. Jacob held out a hand that Shaun managed to slap lightly. "Aye, you got it! Lemme help ya with yer things," Jacob said to Evan.

The two men loaded the groceries and wine into the pontoon while Shaun watched. The lake was a mirror, flat blue stretching out beyond sight. A pair of loons paddled by the docks, their pointed black heads dark against the contrast of the water.

"Beautiful day," Evan said, slamming the hatch of the van.

"Yessir," Jacob said, leaning against the vehicle.

"Fishing been good?"

Jacob tipped his head back and forth. "So-so. Been better years before, might improve in a weeks' time."

Evan waited a few beats, trying to find the right way to ask the questions that had needled him since he opened the refrigerator at the house.

"Can I ask you something, Jacob?"

"Aye, boyo."

"What do you know about the last caretaker Jason had at the house?"

Jacob sucked on his lower lip for a few moments before replying. "Name was Bob, I believe. Di'n't come ta town too often, stayed mostly on the Fin. Quiet fella."

"And you didn't see him leave this spring?"

Jacob shook his head. "Di'n't know nothin' was askew till Jason called an I went out there ta check. Shamed ta say I di'n't inspect too much, just poked around the house a bit, saw he wasn't there, an told Jason."

"What do you think happened to him?"

"Jest wandered off, I s'pose. People do that sometimes durin' a long winter. Get a bit restless, cabin fever an whatnot. Mighta got lost 'n' froze in the woods, never know."

"Wasn't there a search for him?"

"Sure, local sheriff went ta the Fin, had a look around. Seemed that Bob di'n't have much, if any, family, none that came callin' anyway."

Evan frowned and sought out the dark spot on the lake's surface. "It's pretty weird."

"Yeh, life's tha' way, weird shit till we die, I s'pose."

"You can say that again." Evan reached out and shook Jacob's hand. "Now I owe you two beers."

"I've got a tally up in the shop."

Both men laughed, and Jacob headed up the ramp, toward the store. After parking the van and carrying Shaun back to the pontoon, Evan untied them and set off across the lake. His mind wandered as they cruised along, his eyes scanning the woods bordering the lake. Was Bob's body somewhere out there, a rotting carcass now bloated beyond recognition?

*Or is he still in the house?*

Evan shivered despite the warmth of the sun, and shook his head to clear it, as the pontoon's motor labored to bring them closer and closer to the growing mass of land.

# 8

The afternoon drifted away from them in a humid curl of time.

They spent an hour outside practicing balancing techniques for Shaun, Evan holding his hand firm at first and then less and less, until he stood for a few seconds on his own. The triumph on his small face sent a warm hum deep in Evan's chest, and he hugged Shaun close before letting him try again.

Later, Evan laid out a blanket on the grass below the house and they practiced flash cards on the iPad, the interspersed shafts of sunlight rippling around them with the movement of the trees above. The program's odd mechanical voice sounded out of place in the peaceful yard as Shaun touched each object on the screen. When they finished, they lay side by side, listening to the waves on the shore, Evan telling Shaun a story he made up as he went along. They watched for birds in the branches overhead, Evan drawing a laugh from his son each time he exclaimed loudly and caused the birds to take flight, or at least to ruffle their feathers indignantly.

When Shaun fell asleep, Evan picked him up and carried him inside to his bed, tucking him beneath a single sheet. He watched the slow rise and fall of his chest, the twitch of his fingers as he dreamed. Evan wondered what his dreams were like. Were they full of color and peaceful? Could he walk like other children and speak the words that refused to come while awake?

"Someday, buddy, you just wait," he whispered.

A knock at the front door jolted Evan back to himself, and he stepped out of Shaun's room, his heart pounding against his breastbone. He moved to the entry trying to recall if he'd heard a boat motor recently. Should he open it? Who could be calling on them?

*Bob.*

Stop it.

Steadying himself he opened the door to Selena Belgaurd waiting on the stoop, a smile on her pretty face and a pie cradled in her hands.

"Hi, sorry to bother you," she said.

"Oh, no, that's okay," Evan said, trying to find his bearings.

"I wanted to repay you for helping me yesterday. What's the saying? 'Up the creek without a paddle'?"

Evan smiled. "Or across the lake." She laughed. "Sorry, come on in," he said, stepping aside.

"Oh, I don't want to intrude, I just wanted to drop this off for you guys." She held out the pie to him. Evan took it from her hands. "Hope you like blueberry."

"Love it." Evan looked from the pie to Selena's face, a tilting sensation barely balancing within him. The urge to thank her and shut the door was overpowering, but he muscled past it and held out one hand toward the living room.

"Please, come in, you're not intruding."

Selena's eyes pinched a little with her smile, and he noticed again how blue they were, the color of the lake beneath a clear sky.

"Thank you," she said, and stepped inside.

Evan shut the door and walked past her to the kitchen, placing the pie on the counter before returning. Selena stood in the middle of the living room, taking in the surroundings.

"This is a really beautiful house."

"Thanks, we're liking it so far."

Selena nodded and looked out the window at the lake, then returned her gaze to him. A nervous tension tightened around him, and his mind spun its wheels, trying to gain traction.

"I'm sorry, would you like something to drink? We have water, milk, wine."

"Actually, a glass of wine sounds wonderful."

"Perfect."

Evan strode to the kitchen and took a deep, calming breath, then searched for something to pour the wine into. He flipped open cupboards until he found two dusty wineglasses, and rinsed them off before uncorking one of the bottles of cabernet sauvignon. When he returned to the living room, he found Selena sitting in the middle of the couch. He handed her a glass and sat in a nearby chair.

"Thank you."

"No problem."

After taking a sip, Selena glanced around. "Where's your little boy?"

"He's napping," Evan said, and motioned toward Shaun's room.

Selena nodded, opened her mouth, and closed it again, then took another sip of wine.

"He had a traumatic brain injury." Selena looked at him, her eyes soft. "I usually tell people up front so they're not wondering."

"Oh, I wasn't, I didn't mean to press—"

He shook his head, then drained half his glass. "Not at all."

"That's why he has trouble speaking?"

"Yes, along with a range of other developmental disabilities, like walking, fine motor skills, balance, that type of thing."

"I'm sorry."

"Thank you."

"How did it happen, if you don't mind me asking?"

Evan sipped his wine. "We were in a car accident a little over four years ago, when he was three. We got hit by a truck in an intersection, complete accident, it was slippery and the other driver couldn't stop. Shaun's car seat shifted enough with the impact for his head to hit the window. He was in a coma for two weeks, and when he came out, he'd lost most of what he'd learned."

Selena's free hand hovered over her mouth. "That's terrible."

He smiled. "We were lucky, and he's making progress every day. Not much more I can ask for."

"It must be so hard for you and your wife."

Evan's hand holding his glass halted midway to his mouth, and then continued. He finished the rest of his wine. Selena's shoulders slumped and her eyes closed.

"My God, I'm so sorry. I'm having a lot of trouble getting my feet out of my mouth. I'll just—" She stood and set her glass down.

"It's okay, you don't have to leave."

"I'm sorry, I saw your wedding ring and assumed ..."

Evan glanced at his left hand. The tungsten-carbide band shone in the afternoon light. It was hard to miss.

"No, you're fine, don't worry about it."

Selena sat on the couch as though the cushions held shattered glass. "Was it in the same crash?"

"No, two years later. Cancer."

Selena only sighed in response. The house creaked around them with a gust of wind, and Evan looked out the window, the sound of the wind chimes no longer brilliant, but a flat, jangling chorus.

"How have you managed?" Selena asked, a look of incredulity on her face.

"Shaun's the light of my life, I wouldn't have made it without him. Good friends and one day at a time."

"Sorry, I don't mean to pry, just my profession shining through, I guess."

"What do you do?" Evan asked, thankful for the change of subject.

"I'm a psychologist."

"Really? Only one in town?"

Selena laughed, a hearty sound that made Evan smile without realizing it. "Pretty sure, yes. Not too much call for one in Mill River, but I get by."

"You grew up here?"

"No, Minneapolis. I moved about three years ago. I've got a little building over on Outlet Road that I practice out of." Selena held up her ring hand and waggled her fingers. "Divorced once, no kids, and that pretty much sums up my life."

Silence hung between them, and Evan struggled for a moment to keep the conversation flowing. It had been so long.

"What drew you this far up north?" he finally asked.

"I love nature. Loved it since I was a kid. My dad used to bring me up here fishing before he died. I never forgot it. That's actually his canoe that I use now. I've got another, newer one that's way easier to pilot, with paddles that don't slip out." She paused to smile at him. "But the older one has a few memories attached to it. I usually cruise around the lake when it's calm enough, good way to detach yourself."

"I bet. I've never been canoeing before."

"Really? You'll have to try it sometime, it's great."

He nodded. "So, do you live right in town?"

"No, I've got a place on the opposite side of the lake. It's not anything like this," Selena said, motioning to the living room. "But it's home. How about yourself, are you working in town?"

"No, we're basically taking care of the place for my friend, and I do some writing, so I thought I might get a few projects done while we're here."

Selena scooted forward on the couch. "Really? What kind of writing?"

Evan shrugged. "A little of everything. I like nonfiction, editorials, that type of thing. I've dabbled a bit with a screenplay but never pursued it a hundred percent."

"That's great. If there's any place in the world that you could use for inspiration, this is it."

Evan nodded. His eyes came to rest on their empty wineglasses. "Would you like more wine?"

Selena shook her head and stood. "No, actually I should be going. I didn't mean to come in and put you through a bunch of trauma. I swear, I was just dropping off the pie."

Evan laughed and stood as well. "It's fine. It's been hard, but we're doing good, so don't feel bad. It's always awkward to meet new people."

Selena walked to the door, and Evan followed her, a mix of emotions running through him. She paused after stepping outside onto the stoop and turned back to him.

"Thanks for the wine and conversation."

"Thanks for the pie."

"Don't thank me till after you've tried it."

Evan chuckled again, looking down at his feet.

"Have a good evening, Evan."

"You too."

Selena smiled and walked down the steps. He caught his eyes tracing down the slender curve of her back to the formfitting jeans, and looked away. He moved to go inside, but something froze him where he was. And before he knew it, he called out to her.

"Hey, Selena?"

She stopped halfway down the hill and turned.

"Feel free to stop by again."

She smiled, and he saw her eyes shining, even across the distance between them. She nodded once and then continued to her father's canoe.

An unfamiliar springy giddiness vibrated inside his chest as he returned to the living room. The moment he noticed it, another feeling began to coat the excitement with black bile that shriveled his guts with shame. His eyes went to the ring on his hand, and he stared at it, remembering the words the jeweler told him the day he and Elle had picked it out. *Only thing harder than tungsten carbide is diamonds. That's a ring to last an eternity.*

The excitement gone, the familiar hollow filling him up, Evan walked across the room to check on Shaun.

~

Dusk approached, and the water became scorched glass beneath the falling dark. Evan took Shaun down to the lake and showed him the art of skipping rocks. There were quite a few perfect skippers, and he picked out the best, trying to get as many hops out of the rocks as he could. He threw until his shoulder began to ache. Shaun sat in his medical seat, transfixed by the sight of the rocks jumping like living things across the water. Whenever Evan would pause to massage his shoulder, Shaun would cry out "More!"—one of the few words he could say with ease.

"That's all I've got, buddy, we gotta go in," Evan eventually said.

"Na!"

"We have to, it's getting dark."

Shaun responded by kicking his feet against the chair and clawing at the belts that held him in place.

"Shaun, stop, stop," Evan said, hurrying to his side. "It's all done, we have to go up to the house."

"Na!"

Evan sighed and tried to restrain Shaun from banging his head against the back of the chair. "Shaun. Stop," Evan said, raising his voice.

Shaun froze. The anger on his face melted into a sob as he brought his hands up to cover his eyes. Evan lowered his head.

*Good job, you made him cry again.*

"Shaun, Shaun, look at me."

The boy pulled one wet fist away from his eye.

"Do you want to try?"

Shaun gazed at him but didn't move.

"Throwing the rocks?" Evan imitated the motion with his arm and then gestured at Shaun. "You try?"

A grin replaced the frown on the boy's face.

"Okay, let's get you out of that chair."

Evan unbuckled his son and led him down to the water. Keeping him from falling while finding a good rock proved difficult. With one arm wrapped around Shaun's chest, Evan guided his son's hand in the motion, releasing the stone at the correct time. The rock hit the water and skipped once before dropping out of view.

"Yay, Shaun! You did it."

"More?"

"Okay, buddy, one more."

But it was full dark by the time they returned to the house, and they'd thrown so many rocks Shaun could barely keep his head upright. Evan helped him go to the bathroom, brush his teeth, and get into bed.

"That was fun today," he said, smoothing Shaun's hair back from his forehead. "You did good riding in the boat and at the hospital, and I think a couple more times and you'll be skipping rocks by yourself." He spoke in lower and lower tones, each word helping to sink Shaun's drooping eyelids into place. "Mom's proud of you too."

His throat tightened, and he inhaled through his nose, blinked the tears away. After listening to him breathe deeply for over a minute, Evan leaned forward and kissed him on the cheek.

"Night, buddy, sleep good."

He left the room and paced through the quiet house, to the kitchen, putting a mug of water in the microwave for tea. While the unit hummed, he found his laptop case amongst the rest of his luggage and sat with it at the kitchen table. After firing it up, he searched his documents for the last article he'd started, and cringed at the date the document had last been modified: almost two years prior. The disappointment only lasted a minute, and the familiar feeling took its place as he opened it up. It was an article about an Afghanistan veteran who'd run into a burning building to save a little girl, despite the fact that he was a double amputee and had only prosthetics from the knees down. The dates and facts were so old the article was useless now. Evan closed the document and slid its icon into the trash.

The sound of the microwave beeping pulled him from his seat, and he returned a minute later gripping the steaming mug of green tea. As he sat, he sipped the drink, letting his eyes flow over the half-dozen articles remaining in the document folder—an expose on a salmonella outbreak at a grocer near their house in the cities, a few hundred words about a special-education plan that affected Shaun being cut, and a document titled "Young Cancer."

Evan deleted the last on the list, then opened a blank page. He stared at the blinking cursor. He wasn't a fiction writer at heart, and he knew it. Without a subject, facts, something to research, he felt lost. He'd enjoyed many great books throughout his life, and he never understood how the authors did it. How could you venture into the unknown, no guide or map save the one you drew for yourself? He needed a solid groundwork laid out before typing the first word; anything else felt foolish and immaterial. He sighed, and drank more tea and looked out the dark window, as if trying to pluck a subject randomly from thin air.

A sound snapped him from his trance, and he glanced around the empty kitchen, waiting. It came again, a quiet snap, once, there and gone, almost like a coffeepot cooling.

*Or a fingernail tapping on a window.*

Evan stood and walked to the back wall, finding a switch near the sill and flipping it on. The backyard and solid line of trees beyond blazed into life with the glow of the floodlight. He cupped his hands around his face, searching the tree line and ground between. Nothing.

The sound came again, and Evan spun in place, his eyes flitting to the living room. The source was definitely inside the house. After shutting the outside light off, he made his way through the living room, checking behind the sofa and recliners. He threw a glance at the vacant entryway, then walked to the bedrooms.

Shaun still slept peacefully, one arm cocked above his head. Evan stepped fully into the room, and looked behind the door and tugged the curtains over the bed open enough to see nothing was there.

*Tick. Tick.*

His spine stiffened and goose bumps flowed over his exposed forearms, onto his back. The sound had come from the kitchen, he was sure of it. The idea of a weapon came to mind, and he mentally cursed himself for leaving his pistol at their home. He hadn't seen any need to bring it here. Now, it seemed a stupid oversight.

*Tick. Tick. Tick.*

He walked through the living room, in what felt like slow motion. The air in his lungs became hot and uncomfortable with each renewed breath.

*It's Bob, he's come back for his things.*

Evan looked at the front door, recalling the moment he locked it. Yes, he was sure he'd locked it.

*Tick. Tick. Tick. Tick.*

Entering the kitchen, he stopped, his stomach a ball of twisted snakes.

*Tick. Tick. Tick. Tick. Tick.*

The sound was coming from the basement. The broken clock was ticking.

"No," Evan said. He meant the word to be forceful, but it came out barely a whisper.

That wasn't a possibility. He was no clock expert, but the one downstairs couldn't run.

*Tick. Tick. Tick. Tick. Tick. Tick.*

Slowly, methodically, the sound went on, perfectly measured in tempo. Evan found the strength to move to the door, and placed his ear against it.

The ticking stopped.

All at once it was gone. Silence returned.

*It heard you listening.*

Another wave of goose bumps rolled across his skin, and he forced the voice away. With determination, he pulled the door open and started down the stairs. The darkness waited, liquid and pure, just as the night before. Evan backtracked to the kitchen, his resolve unbroken. He found a flashlight in a junk drawer near the bottom of the cabinets. When he flicked his thumb against the switch, a solid beam of yellow light lanced from the lens. Not waiting for his resolve to crumble, he stepped to the basement door and shone the light down.

The doll stood on the landing.

Evan dropped the light, his mouth opening to cry out, but the need to pick up the flashlight was too great. He bent and fumbled with the smooth barrel, his fingers fat and unwieldy. The whole time his eyes were locked on the darkness, ready to run if he saw movement coming toward him. He picked up the light and pointed downward.

The landing was empty.

The bare boards stared back. Silence roared in his ears. He leaned against the doorway, all the strength going out of his legs. He rubbed his eyes.

"You're fucking losing it," he said to himself.

Speaking out loud didn't have the calming effect he hoped for. Evan stepped down onto the first stair, his light illuminating less of the darkness than he liked. Another step. Another. Down. Finally he stood on the landing, and as he turned, he couldn't help but shine the beam in the direction of the doll. It still stood where he'd placed it, its eyes two glinting sapphires, the duct tape over its mouth.

Evan shook his head. He needed a drink. What was he even doing down here? Making sure an ancient clock with missing pieces wasn't ticking? He should turn around and go back upstairs simply to prove he wasn't insane right now. Giving in to your fears only led to more paranoia. He nodded—

—and took another step down. Reaching out, he snapped the switch on, illuminating the basement. Everything looked in place. The table before the clock was the same as he'd left it.

He descended the last few stairs and crossed the room, stopping before the clock. Black. Eerie. Stoic. He stepped closer to it, gathering the nerve to actually touch it, waiting for it to tick again. Reaching out, he ran a hand up its closest pendulum encasement. The wood was cool beneath his palm, the ridges and grooves carved in its trim, almost like braille. An odd thought occurred to him. If he stood there long enough and closed his eyes, the pattern under his fingers would begin to mean something. Perhaps a long-forgotten language waiting for the right person to come along and listen. To hear. To see.

He stepped back, watching the clock's twisted hands for movement. Nothing happened. Why the hell was this thing here? Who built it? Why didn't it have numbers on its face?

His eyes fell to the table beside him, and he scanned the stacks of paper. Upon closer examination, he realized that many of the sheets were handwritten. A hazy scrawl covered the paper with lines of text, written in pencil, pen, and what looked like charcoal. Again he glanced at the clock, its glass doors reflecting three dark images of himself.

"That's enough fun for one night," he said.

With as much composure as he could muster, he walked to the stairway and flipped off the light. He treaded upward until he reached the safety of the kitchen, and let out a held breath like a man rising from beneath water. Evan shut the door and sat at the table, then pulled up his blank document once again. After a moment he tapped at the keyboard.

*Clock's origin, purpose, and history.*

He stared at the dark words against the white background, then shut the computer down. As he left the kitchen, he paused by the light switch near the doorway, listening. After a minute, he shook his head and turned the light off, then headed toward his room.

# 9

*He cries with a vehemence he didn't know he possessed.*

*The agony pours out of him through his eyes as he sits at her bedside, her hand, so warm before, cool now. Everything is cold here, this hospital, the people. But he knows it would be no different going outside, going home; there is no place that would make him feel unlike he does now.*

*"Evan, I love you."*

*He blinks through the tears and swallows his sobs long enough to look at her. "I love you too."*

*"I'll always love you both."*

*He shakes his head, re-grips her hand. "There's still a few tests to run, the doctor said there was this new treatment in Texas, radio waves or something."*

*She smiles, so sad. A longing there for life just out of reach, a chance, a hope. "Yes, we'll have to be patient and strong for Shaun."*

*Shaun.*

*Shaun.*

*Shaun.*

Evan awoke to Shaun's soft crying. The monitor's lights jumped with life. He threw off the covers and crossed the hall before sleep completely left him, the dream receding into what he recognized as relief—relief it wasn't reality, it wasn't actually happening again. When he flipped the light on, he saw that Shaun had kicked his blankets off and rolled close to one edge of the bed. Dark, clumpy stains surrounded his legs and feet.

Blood.

Evan rushed forward and grabbed Shaun's shoulders, ready to run to the pontoon and rush him to the emergency room, but then he smelled it.

Shit. Shaun had soiled the sheets.

"Oh, buddy. You had an accident, that's all," Evan said, his muscles relaxing. "We'll get you in the tub."

"T-t-t-tub," Shaun sobbed.

Evan picked him up and, trying not to get the sticky waste on him in the process, carried him into the bathroom. Stripping off the pull-up, he saw that the diaper hadn't held near the leg holes, overflowing and subsequently waking Shaun. Evan got the water flowing in the tub, and wiped his son's legs and backside as well as he could with a nearby towel, then placed him in the warm water.

"There, we'll get you all cleaned up," Evan said, pouring several dollops of bath soap into the water.

Shaun continued to cry and look up every few seconds, his eyes reddened and ashamed.

"It's okay, honey, it's okay, you had an accident, you're fine." He stroked Shaun's hair and smiled at him, then wiped sleep from the corners of his eyes. "Everyone has accidents. Uncle Jason had an accident once at college, except he wasn't wearing a pull-up, but he probably should have, seeing as how much he drank that night." Evan shook his head at the memory and laughed a little. "He had to clean himself up the next morning, I wouldn't go near him."

As the water crept higher, Shaun's crying diminished, until he sat still while Evan washed him. He tried to remember the last time Shaun had had an accident, and couldn't. It had been at least a year.

Evan drained the water, scrubbing Shaun down one more time before toweling him off and placing him on the couch. He then undertook cleaning the bedroom, balling up the sheets in a garbage bag and scouring the mattress with hot, soapy water. When he was satisfied, he flipped the mattress, but failed to find another set of sheets anywhere in the house. So he covered the bed with an old blanket from the master bedroom's closet. It smelled musty but looked clean, and after unfurling it, he saw it was hand-sewn. Evan finished putting away the cleaning supplies, and finally glanced at the clock: *2:17*.

"You want to watch something?" he asked, as he entered the living room.

"Somfing?" Shaun echoed.

Evan flipped through the TV channels and found a documentary on dinosaurs.

"This okay, buddy?"

Shaun didn't reply. He glanced at his son and saw the entranced look on his face as the ancient creatures trundled across the screen. Evan smiled and yawned. As he watched a brontosaurus roam across a lonely, windswept plain, his mind traveled back to the dream, like a tongue prodding at a sore tooth. He closed his eyes and tried to clear his mind, but Elle's worn face, still beautiful through the pain, kept floating across his vision.

When Shaun fell asleep an hour later, the anxiety hadn't receded, and instead of returning to bed, he opted to sit on the screened-in porch. The night air felt good against his warm skin, and the sound of the lake all around gradually lulled him into calmness.

When the bed called to him, he went and fell into a dreamless slumber without broken clocks or hospital rooms.

~

The next morning dawned bright and hard, a cold wind sweeping in from the north, chopping Long Lake into a rolling bed of saw teeth. After a light breakfast, they stood on the shore, Evan helping balance Shaun with hands on his shoulders. They watched the waves move past the island, toward the southern end of the lake. Cars streamed by on Main Street in Mill River, only gliding dots of different colors to them.

When Shaun began to shiver, they returned to the house. Evan grabbed his phone and walked into the kitchen, while Shaun watched Thomas the Train again. Jason picked up on the second ring.

"How goes life in paradise?" Jason asked, in a breathless voice.

"Pretty good, how about down there?"

"It's god-awful, just got off the treadmill. When the hell did we get so old?"

"I don't know, I didn't get the memo," Evan said, sinking into a kitchen chair. Exhaustion pulled at him, and he promised himself he would nap when Shaun went down later in the day.

"So what's happening up there? No more surprises, I hope."

Evan glanced at the basement door and then looked away. "No, nothing to speak of."

"Good, I was worried about you guys."

"We're fine. I was actually calling to see what you wanted me to do around here for upkeep. The place looks really good."

"Oh, I don't know, do some cleaning, make sure the fucking shingles aren't falling off, that sort of thing," Jason said.

"So I was going to ask you," Evan said, feeling a strange amount of trepidation, "what's with the clock in the basement?"

Jason didn't say anything for moment, and Evan wondered if Jason hadn't meant for them to go into the basement.

"Why do you ask?" he finally said.

"I don't know. I was down there the other day and saw it. Looks like someone was working on it."

"Yeah, I think grandpa tinkered with it for a while."

"Kinda strange looking," Evan said, jokingly. When Jason didn't respond, he continued. "I mean, with it all torn apart, it looks a little weird."

"I think it was the last thing he worked on before he passed away, he never got to finish it. I didn't have the heart to throw it out or sell it, so it got left. Even now, I don't know why I didn't get rid of it."

"Sentimentality."

"Maybe."

"Do you know where it came from?" Evan asked, sitting forward in his chair.

Jason's voice sounded funny. Light and airy, like he was talking in his sleep. "If I remember right, he got it at an auction in town. Carted it home. Grandma hated it."

Evan grabbed a notebook and pen from the table, writing *in town* at the top of the page. "Do you remember where?"

"Not off the top of my head. Ev, what's this about?"

"You won't think I'm crazy?"

"I already think that."

"Good." Evan squinted at the backyard. "Do you think Justin would print a story about the clock if I did a write-up?"

A pause on Jason's end. "What kind of write-up?"

"I don't know yet, but with the way that clock looks, there's got to be a history, you know? I thought I could do a little research while Shaun's at his treatments in town, uncover where it came from, that type of thing."

"Sure, man, I can throw it at him if you want, but I don't know how much you'll find out about it. I think it's older than the hills, and the locals might not appreciate an outsider poking around."

Evan's eyebrows drew down. "I thought you said this was the friendliest town in the state?"

"Yeah, well, you know how small towns can be. Somebody from the outside comes around asking questions ..."

"There's got to be someone around that would be willing to talk, who knows about it, right? You said he got it from a local auction?"

"Yeah, you could definitely check it out anyway."

Jason's voice sounded more normal again, and Evan heard the rasp of wind against the receiver.

"Keep me posted, buddy. I'll shoot an email to Justin this afternoon, see if he'd be willing to run a piece on something like that."

"That would be great, man, really appreciate it."

"No problem. Any other questions about the place while you've got me? Didn't dig up a cannibal graveyard down by the lake, did you?"

Evan huffed laughter. "No, not yet, but if your relatives were cannibals, that's one hell of a story."

Jason laughed without humor, and Evan decided to change the subject. "I met a woman." He regretted the words as soon as he spoke them.

"What? Really? Who?"

Evan smiled in spite of himself. "Her name's Selena Belgaurd, ever heard of her?"

"No, she live in town?"

"No, other side of the lake, but she's a psychologist."

"Oooo, a shrink. Is she hot?"

Evan frowned. "She's kinda pretty."

"She's hot. Where'd you meet her?"

"She lost her canoe paddle."

"Is that a euphemism?"

"No, she dropped it in the lake when she was passing the island. I helped her out."

"I bet you did."

Evan frowned. "I can't tell you anything."

"I'm kidding—that's great! Are you going to see her again?"

"I don't know, maybe."

"Ev, it would be good for you."

Evan stood and went to check on Shaun, a familiar agitation rising inside him. "Listen, I don't even know if I'm ready to go down that road yet. I don't know if I'll ever be."

"Hey, I'm not saying marry her, just get to know her."

Evan watched the TV for a few seconds without seeing it. "Yeah, I gotta get going, Shaun's appointment's in an hour."

"Ev, I'm sorry."

"It's fine. I gotta go."

Evan hung up without saying goodbye. He spun his wedding band around and around his finger, and then began to get them ready for the trip into town.

~

When he left Shaun at the hospital, the occupational therapist they met earlier in the week told Evan that it would be about two hours before they would finish. Shaun's head kept swiveling to inspect all of the colorful drawings attached to the walls of the OT room, and Evan had to lean into his view to tell him he'd be right back.

The day hadn't warmed, but the town held a certain chilly beauty as Evan drove, a scalding coffee clutched in one hand. After buying new sheets, he sat in the store's parking lot, sipping his coffee and thinking about where to go next. This was the part he liked about writing articles: the research. So much could be gleaned from merely asking questions and visiting places. It was almost like he absorbed the feeling of a piece through osmosis. Justin at *Dachlund* magazine had raved over his first article on special education, and had demanded him to write more. But then Elle got sick, and ...

He didn't want to think about that right now. He'd trodden that path too many times, had gotten lost on it. It was unsteady and dangerous. He could cut himself on memories like that. He couldn't control his dreams, but he could make an effort to keep his mind his own while awake.

He put the van in drive and made his way toward the docks. Jacob hadn't been at the shop when they came through earlier; perhaps he would be in now. It would be the simplest place to begin.

When he parked the van in the lot, he saw that the elderly twins were again at their posts outside the front door, beneath the building's awning. Both wore identical jeans and woolen sweaters against the brisk morning air.

"Does their mother dress them like that?" Evan mumbled before getting out of the van.

He smiled at them as he approached, nodding once before beginning to walk past them.

"You the feller out at the Fin?"

Evan stopped before pulling open the door. The twin on the left had his bald head tilted, and he could see just how polished the dome was.

"Yes, Evan Tormer," he said, holding his hand out for the elderly man to shake.

"Arnold Benson, and this is my brother, Wendal."

Evan stepped forward to the other man and shook hands. Wendal smiled, his mouth open slightly, revealing a small stub of grizzled muscle where his tongue should be. Revulsion tried to make him yank his hand away, but he steeled himself and pretended that he hadn't seen it.

"Wendal can't speak, bit his tongue clean off when he was ten falling down a set of stairs to our basement. He does the thinkin', and I do the talkin'," Arnold said.

Evan didn't know what to say, so he nodded and gestured toward the store. "Is Jacob in?"

"No, that old mick brought his wife over to Wilson Springs this morning. They'll be shoppin' and carryin'-on until afternoon, for sure."

Evan nodded again, noting the irony of Arnold calling Jacob "old."

"Okay, maybe you can tell him I stopped in? He can give me a call if he'd like."

"Will do," Arnold said.

Wendal's head bobbed.

Evan took a step toward his van, then stopped and turned back to the twins. "You guys wouldn't know anything about an old grandfather clock that the Prices used to own, would you?"

Wendal's brow furrowed, crinkling his scalp in a multitude of lines, before he glanced at his brother. Arnold sat back in his chair and took a slow sip of coffee.

"What makes you ask such a question?" he said after swallowing.

Jason's prior warning of townsfolk and their distrust of outsiders replayed in Evan's mind. "Just curious, it looks like it could have a history."

Arnold laughed in a harsh bark. "Yeah, you could say that again."

"So you know about it?"

Arnold held out an age-spotted hand and tipped it back and forth. "Before our time. It originally belonged to a man named Abel Kluge. Odd fellow, from what I heard, violent sometimes. Lots of rumors floating around about him." Arnold's eyes twinkled.

"What kind of rumors?" Evan said, taking his cue.

"He was a clockmaker from Chicago back around the turn of the century. There's some that say he was one of the best in the world. And there's others that say there's reasons for that."

"Reasons?"

Arnold lowered his voice and leaned forward. "His success was unnaturally quick in the industry, from what I heard, like people couldn't buy his work fast enough. Almost like he was selling drugs instead of clocks. A friend of my father's once told us that he heard the man came from a bloodline steeped in the occult."

"The occult?" Evan asked. "Like witchcraft?"

Arnold shrugged, leaning back into his chair again. "I don't know about that, but that place he lived in was always dark, in more ways than one. Outsiders tended to stay away from there, people still avoid it like the plague."

"So he lived close by?"

"Oh sure, retired up here and died in his mansion out on Wicker Road, along with his wife."

Evan hunched his shoulders as a gust of cool wind came across the lake and ruffled his hair. "They died together? Were they murdered?"

Wendal glanced at his brother, then shifted his eyes to Evan's. Arnold didn't seem to notice and shrugged.

"That isn't entirely clear. Mostly rumors, long time ago, like I said. Anyway, the clock was from the house, and some say it stood in their bedroom. Old man Price bought it quite a while ago during an estate sale."

"Do you know where I could find out more about this?" The excitement in Evan's chest hadn't relented, and he felt a sense of satisfaction at having followed his hunch about the clock.

Arnold smacked his lips, rolling his eyes toward the sky as he did so. "You could try talkin' to Cecil Fenz. She was tied to the old place somehow or other, I can't remember exactly now."

"Cecil Fenz," Evan said. "Do you think she'd mind me talking to her about it?"

Arnold barked his laugh again. "She minds everyone talkin' to her about everything. She moved out in the sticks years back, orneriest woman I ever met, and I met a few of 'em."

Evan smiled and reached out to shake Arnold's and Wendal's hands again. "Thank you, you've been a big help."

"What you want with all the questions anyway?" Arnold asked.

"I'm doing a little research for an article. I thought the clock would make a good story."

"That it would. Just don't mention me or my brother as a source, we're too old to get all wrapped up in gossip."

Evan laughed and waved goodbye. He got in the van and closed the door, shutting off the bite of the wind. After scribbling down the name in his notebook, he did a quick White Pages search on his phone and found a number listed for Cecil Fenz, along with an address.

Listening to the ringing hum on the other end of the line, Evan readied his most charming voice and tried to think of the best way to bring up the subject. A moment later, the line clicked and a woman's smoky voice answered.

"Hello?"

"Hi, is Cecil Fenz there, please?"

"Who is this?"

Evan grimaced. Right to the point. "My name is Evan Tormer. You don't know me, but my son and I are staying on the island in the middle of Long Lake, and I came across an old grandfather clock in the basement—"

A snap came from Cecil's end, and dead air hissed in his ear.

"Hello?"

He frowned and held the phone out, studied it. Raising his eyes, he noticed Arnold and Wendal looking at him, their expressions smug, as if they knew exactly who he'd called and what kind of reception he'd gotten.

"Yeah, okay," Evan said, starting the van and pulling out of the parking lot.

# 10

After picking up Shaun from his therapy, they stopped for lunch at a small diner.

In honor of how well he did at the hospital, Evan ordered a banana split for dessert, which they shared. The occupational therapist had been extremely pleased with Shaun's capabilities and willingness to work.

"You keep doing this good, you can get ice cream every time," Evan said, helping him with a spoonful of sweets.

Shaun grinned, his teeth stained with chocolate.

They arrived on the island in the early afternoon, the sun making a brief appearance before sliding back into cover behind a wall of gray clouds. Shaun fell asleep on the ride across the lake and didn't wake even when Evan carried him up to the house and laid him on his bed.

With the house quiet, his mind whispered of sleep, the early session of cleaning catching up to him, but the idea of the story behind the clock wouldn't leave his head for more than a few minutes. Cecil's reaction hadn't dulled his interest in the least; quite the opposite, in fact. Hanging up on him spoke of hidden secrets buried within families and time. The prospect of uncovering them became so appealing, he wondered what was wrong with him. You're enthused about something, he told himself, as he sat at the kitchen table. How long had it been since he'd felt like this?

Elle immediately entered his mind, and he stood from his chair, not willing to be dragged down by memories this afternoon. Noticing a little dust and a several specks of dirt on the linoleum, he decided to do some cleaning, to actually earn some of the money that Jason was paying him.

He found a broom in the closet near the entry. Starting at the sink, Evan swept in the direction of the basement door, herding a nest of dust bunnies above a layer of dirt as he went, his mind wandering to the article and its layout. When the dirt formed a small pyramid in the center of the room, he knelt and started to sweep it into a dustpan but stopped. Leaning forward, he reached into the dust pile and plucked a shining white hair from the center. It unwound from the dirt like a snake uncoiling from its lair, and he saw that it stretched at least two feet. Holding it up in the light, he brought it close to his face. It hung in a pale question mark from his fingers, mirroring his thoughts.

"Where the hell did this come from?" he asked out loud.

Had Jason's grandmother worn her hair long? But that couldn't be—his grandparents had passed away a decade ago. And if Bob had supposedly been here up until a couple of months before they arrived, how did the hair get missed?

He dropped it back into the pile, wiping his hand against his jeans. Another glint of white caught his eye, and when he looked closer, he saw that a second strand lay amongst the dust, this one longer than the first.

The phone on the wall rang loud and shrill, and Evan inhaled and almost sucked up a mouthful of dirt. He stood and stared at the phone on the wall as it trilled again. The panic was quelled inside him as he stepped forward and picked the receiver up.

"Hello?"

A slight crackle of static. "Evan?"

"Yes?"

"It's Selena."

He turned toward the backyard, leaning against the wall. "Hi, how are you?"

"Good. I'm calling because I was thinking of going for a paddle later if the lake calms down, and wondered if I could stop in and say hi."

*No.*

The internal answer to her request startled him. "Sure, that'd be fine. What time are you thinking?"

"Oh, late afternoon."

"That would work, we'll be here."

"Sounds great, see you later."

"Bye."

Evan hung the phone up and gazed out at the backyard. "What are you afraid of?" he said.

The tinkling of the wind chimes was the only answer.

~

A knock at the front door pulled Evan away from the cooking beef. He rumpled Shaun's hair as he walked by the kitchen table, where the boy played with several toy cars. Smoothing his own hair forward, he opened the door.

The late-afternoon sunshine outlined Selena in the entryway. Her hair hung past her shoulders in a brown wave that caught the light. She wore a white T-shirt and a pair of khaki shorts that accentuated her legs.

"Hi," she said.

"Hi," he replied, his heart picking up speed. "Come in, dinner will be ready in a bit."

She paused halfway through the entry. "Oh, you don't have to feed me, I just wanted to pop by, maybe meet Shaun properly."

"Come in, it's fine. I have to cook for us anyway."

Evan waved toward the kitchen and Selena smiled, stepping inside.

"Shaun, this is Selena, do you remember her from the other day?" Evan said, turning Shaun in his chair so that he could face her in the doorway.

"Hi, Shaun, how are you?" Selena said, putting her hand out as she knelt before him.

Shaun looked at her for a moment, and then smiled and placed his hand in her own.

"Nice to meet you," she said, pumping his arm up and down.

Selena turned her eyes to Evan's, and he caught himself smiling at her. Hearing the sizzle of the stove, he made his way to the browning hamburger. After adding some salt and pepper, he stirred the meat until he thought of something to say.

"So the lake calmed down, huh?"

Selena gave Shaun one last smile and then stood, framing herself in the doorway. "Yeah, turned out to be great. I was disappointed this morning when I looked outside, I didn't think I'd be able to get out on the lake today."

"Yeah, we went into town when it was rough this morning. Even in the pontoon, it bounced us around. Would you like a glass of wine?" Evan said.

"That would be great." Selena pulled out a chair from the table and sat. "So, are you two getting settled in here?"

He opened a bottle and poured two glasses. "I think so. It's a little more of a commute into town than we're used to, but yeah, it's a good fit for us."

He moved to the table and handed Selena her glass. As he did, their fingers brushed and a flutter of pleasure flitted in his stomach.

"To the evening," she said, tilting her glass toward him.

"To the evening."

He clinked her glass and took a sip, hoping the wine would calm the nervous energy inside him.

They ate spaghetti at the table, their conversation comfortable and easy. Every so often Selena would ask Shaun a question, and he would either respond with a waving of one hand or an excited noise. Evan watched Selena, examining her interactions with his son. She didn't talk baby talk to him, like some other people that knew them, and he was grateful for that. There was nothing more infuriating or frustrating than watching people degrade Shaun's intelligence through pity.

He anticipated that Selena would look uncomfortable with Shaun's movements or lack of proper articulation, but if she was, she didn't show the slightest hint.

After a quick cleaning of the kitchen, the three of them settled into the furniture on the porch. The sun hung above the tree line that marked the boundary of Mill River, its light rippling with gentle waves that rolled in colors of cobalt and amber.

"God, it's pretty out," Selena said, gazing at the lake.

"Yes, it is," Evan said, placing his wineglass on the patio table. "I'm curious, though."

She looked at him, tilting her head.

"How did you find the phone number for the house?"

She blushed and licked her lips, casting her gaze at the floor. "I asked my secretary to find out who owns house, and after she told me, I looked up the name online and found a listing."

Evan laughed. "Wow."

Selena placed a hand over her face. "I know, right? I wasn't even sure if it was correct or not, but since I didn't have your cell phone, I worked with what I had."

"Industrious."

"More like creepy."

"Industrious sounds better."

She laughed, and Shaun giggled too.

"Now everyone's laughing at me," Selena said, shaking her head.

"It's fine, I'm glad you called."

She glanced his way, and their eyes met, holding for less than a second, but something connected and then released as he looked down into his wineglass.

"Me too."

A silence stretched out, broken only by Shaun talking to his cars and the tinkling of the wind chimes.

"Professional question," Evan said after a while.

"Oh no, here it comes," Selena said, smiling.

"Nothing too weird, I'm actually curious about cabin fever."

"Why, are you already feeling isolated out here?"

"No, nothing like that, it's just—"

He hovered over the subject, not knowing whether to get into it or not. The night was going so well.

"The former caretaker here, Bob, he disappeared a couple months ago."

Selena frowned. "Yeah, I think I heard something about that."

Evan nodded. "People seem to think he walked off in the middle of winter. Is that common with someone in isolation?"

Selena pursed her lips. "It can be. The claustrophobia and isolated feeling people get after being alone or confined to a small area for a period of time usually results in them doing something that's out of character."

"Like what?"

"Like someone who is normally an early riser sleeps longer and longer into the day. Peaceful people become irritable, violent sometimes. Reason can be lost if the person doesn't do anything to remedy the situation."

"So wandering off into the woods in the middle of winter could be a possibility?"

"Sure. And mind you, some people are more resistant to isolation than others, they can handle being alone and not be any worse for wear." She studied his expression. "Why do you ask?"

Evan drained the last of his wine, feeling the pleasant buzz weaken with the conversation. "You're going to think I'm crazy."

"If I had a quarter."

He chuckled. "I bet. No, it's—" He glanced at Shaun, who intently watched the lake. "It's disturbing being here when I don't know what happened to the last guy, you know? I have these feelings that ... that he isn't really gone."

"You mean, like he's hiding somewhere on the island?"

Evan frowned. "Maybe? I don't know. It's unsettling, that's all."

"I can see how it could be, you have a ton of responsibility," she said, motioning to Shaun. "The weight of that sometimes does funny things to our minds. Makes us worry when there isn't anything to fear. Not to say you're unstable. A new location coupled with the last caretaker's disappearance might have sent your protectiveness into overdrive."

Evan sat back in his chair, surprised by how much Selena's words made sense. "I never thought about it that way. You're probably right."

"A girl never gets tired of hearing that."

He smiled. "Would you like another glass of wine?"

~

An hour later, he walked Selena to the door. The evening fell around the island in a cool hush that brought stillness to everything. Even the waves along the shoreline seemed calmer.

Selena paused on the stoop. "I had a really nice time tonight with you guys, thank you for dinner."

"No problem, it's great to have company, keeps the cabin fever away."

She laughed and pulled out a business card from her pocket. "My home number's on the back. I transfer it to my cell when I'm out in case I get an emergency call from the office for a patient."

He reached out to take the card from her, a simple act, but one that held so much more weight for him. He hesitated before accepting it. A small flash of uncertainty crossed Selena's face.

"Thank you," he said, as lightly as he could. "And you already have mine."

She blushed again and nodded. "Have a nice night," she said, holding out her hand.

He took it, feeling the softness of her skin again, and instead of shaking it, he just held it for a moment before letting go. "You too."

She turned and moved toward the dock, and he watched her go, wanting to say more, and at the same time, glad the night was over. When she was out of sight, he carried Shaun to the bathroom and helped him brush his teeth.

"So what did you think of Selena, buddy? Was she okay?"

He nodded once and exposed his foamy teeth.

"Does that mean we should have her over for dinner again?"

"Na," he said, smiling.

"No?" Evan laughed and tickled his son's sides. "What do you mean, no? I thought you liked her."

Shaun giggled and tried to bat Evan's hands away.

"Okay, okay, let's finish brushing."

Evan glanced at the clock after they finished in the bathroom. "It's still a little early to go to bed, do you want to find another documentary on the TV?"

Shaun struggled to get down from his arms, in an effort to get to the couch faster.

"All right, let's do it."

He placed Shaun on the couch and walked to the entertainment center to grab the remote, looking out the windows at the evening—

—and saw the outline of a body floating in the water.

His eyes widened, and the remote slipped from his hand, snapping against the floor and spewing its batteries out like a rotten meal.

"Oh God," Evan said.

A moment of indecision gripped him, and then he ran toward the door.

"Shaun, stay right there."

His fingers fumbled at the doorknob for an agonizing second, and then he flew down the steps, onto the grass, the dew of the evening wetting his socks. As he ran, he hoped he was seeing things again, perhaps a trick of the failing light on the water. Maybe a piece of driftwood or something like it. But no, the shape was there, clearer this time, floating past the end of the dock. It looked like a man, facedown ... definitely facedown.

"Hey! Are you okay?"

The figure in the water didn't stir. It bobbed, turning counterclockwise, its feet spinning slowly toward the town.

"Shit," Evan said.

He tore his T-shirt over his head. His feet hit the dock, the planking banging beneath his soles as he ran. Three more strides and he jumped, hung in the air, and dove into the water.

The lake hit him like something alive, its cold unlike anything he'd experienced before. Frozen needles pierced every inch of his skin, and he barely resisted the urge to gasp at the shock. He stroked toward the surface and broke through, heaving a lungful of air in. He tried to shake the water from his eyes, then swam forward, hoping for and dreading the moment his fingers found the body. The moisture filtered from his vision, and he stopped, treading water and spun in a circle.

Nothing was there.

The beating of his heart throbbed in his ears as he searched the calm, flat plane of water all around him. He dove, keeping his eyes open against the blinding cold this time, and swam down, panning the surrounding few feet for the man's body he knew must be there. Straggling weeds grew up from the lake's bottom, but otherwise the water was too dark to see through.

He rose, sucked a breath in, and plunged down again. Over and over he dove, a sickening feeling growing in his stomach the whole time.

*There was nothing there in the first place.*

At last he gave up and swam toward the dock, glancing over his shoulder every other stroke, half expecting the body to be there again. Whenever a weed touched his foot, his heart gave a nasty jump. When his hand found the decking, the relief was almost overwhelming. Pulling himself onto the dock, he stood there shivering, cold water running out of his pants legs in streams, the dripping of the moisture returning to the lake and the chattering of his teeth the only sounds.

Evan hurried back to the house, picking up his dropped T-shirt on the way. When he stepped into the entry and saw Shaun still propped on the couch where he'd left him, his first instinct was to call 911. Picking up his cell phone, he started dialing the numbers, but then turned to face the lake again. Darkness cloaked the water now, hiding everything but the barest of movement of small waves licking the shore.

He'd imagined the body, or it had been a trick of the light. A floating body couldn't just disappear in a matter of seconds.

He shivered again, not sure if his soaking pants were to blame.

"Da?"

Shaun's eyes were wide and unblinking in the low light.

"I'm okay," Evan said, and shook again. "I'm okay."

He crossed the room and turned on the TV with a trembling hand, finding a cartoon on the next station he turned to.

"You watch for a minute, and Dad's going to take a quick shower."

He left the bathroom door wide open and, after firing up the shower, stripped out of his sopping clothes. Catching a glimpse of himself in the mirror, he saw that his lips were light blue.

The shocking change in temperature brought a rasping breath from him as he stepped into the hot water. Evan let it flow over him, envelope his body in its warmth. Gradually he stopped shaking and the tension in his muscles eased. As the physical strain washed away, his mind began to whir with questions, none he wanted try to answer. Mostly because the solution to almost all of them ended with another question—one concerning his own sanity.

He leaned forward, resting his head against the shower surround. "What the hell's happening to me?"

Shaun's scream rang through the house, and Evan jerked, nearly slipping on the shower floor. He ripped the curtain away and slapped the shower handle off, then jumped from the tub. Shaun's scream came again, louder this time, and Evan ran, launching himself through the doorway and into the living room.

Shaun lay on his side on the couch, his arms flailing at the air, his legs kicking against a stack of pillows. Evan skidded to a stop and knelt, setting him back up into a sitting position.

"What's wrong, honey? What's the matter? Are you hurt?"

Shaun responded with another wail and craned his neck around toward the kitchen. Tears ran in steady streams down his reddened face, and he coughed, choking on his own panic. Evan scanned his small body and saw no bleeding or bruises, although he didn't know how he would've gotten hurt sitting on the couch.

"What's the matter?" Evan asked again.

"D-d-d-da," Shaun stuttered, between hitching cries.

"I'm right here, honey, I'm right here."

Shaun shook his head. "Da!"

Evan wiped away some of the tears and frowned, glancing at the kitchen as Shaun pointed again.

"Da!"

"Okay, okay, I don't know what you're saying, honey."

Shaun glanced around the room through tear-muddled eyes and pointed toward the entertainment center.

"You want the TV off? Was there something scary on the TV?"

He stood, suddenly aware of his nudity, and grabbed a small blanket from a nearby chair. After wrapping it around his waist, he went toward the TV, sure now that something on the program must have disturbed Shaun.

"Dere," Shaun yelled through another sob, pointing again at the TV.

"Okay, I'll shut it off," Evan said, flicking the power switch.

"Dere!"

This time he looked at where Shaun pointed, following his outstretched arm to the iPad lying beside the TV.

"You want the iPad?"

"Na." Shaun screwed up his face in concentration. "Yesh!"

"Okay," Evan said, carrying the device to the couch.

Shaun grabbed it from his hand, flipped it on, and found the flash-card application. The app loaded, and he continued to whimper as he scrolled down the rows and rows of pictures with names beneath them. While he searched, Evan glanced over the couch at the kitchen. There weren't any lights on, and shadows hung beneath the long table and shaded the two doors at its far end.

"Dolldolldolldolldolldoll."

The thick electronic voice spoke from the iPad as Shaun punched the picture of a doll with brown hair, over and over.

"Dolldolldolldolldolldoll."

A shudder ran through his body as Shaun quit hitting the screen and pointed, not toward the kitchen, Evan realized, but toward the basement door.

"Da," Shaun said, his crying tapering off.

Evan tried to form the word but couldn't. The water beads clinging to his skin were drops of ice.

"It's okay, buddy," he whispered, and knelt, hugging Shaun's quaking body close to him. "It's okay."

~

Evan pulled the basement door open and shone the flashlight down the stairs. Panning back and forth, he took the first step, listening.

He'd rocked Shaun to sleep while sitting in his room, humming a tune with words forgotten. Elle had used to sing the song when Shaun was a baby, before the crash, before the cancer, before everything. It was the one thing he could recall from their prior life without feeling the crush of depression. He just wished he could remember the words.

The stairs creaked beneath him as he took another step, the darkness fleeing before his light, only to rush in when he swept it in another direction. He tried not to think about Shaun's outburst, but in his head the voice from the iPad repeated over and over.

The blue shine of the doll's eyes met him when he turned on the landing. The doll stood in the exact same place as before. The basement had a vacuum-like silence to it, a held breath, waiting. Evan strode down the last few steps, faking a bravado without anything to back it up. He flipped on the lights and bent forward, examining the doll's placement on the floor. Were its feet in the same spot as before? He moved around it, trying to recall exactly where he'd left it.

Yes, it hadn't moved.

Evan rubbed his face with one hand, feeling the urge to cry. What the hell was happening to him? He was in a basement, frightened almost to his wit's end, wondering if a doll had walked up the stairs and scared his son.

Anger poured over him. Saturated him.

He wound up a kick and booted the doll as hard as he could. It flew a few feet and rebounded off the wall, coming to rest on its face. Its hair fell in a broad fan around its head. Facedown, it reminded him of the body in the lake.

He reached down, meaning to carry the thing out of the house, to throw it away in the trash bin outside, but stopped. Would that be admitting to some kind of insanity on his part? He straightened, pointing his flashlight at the monstrosity of a clock at the other end of the room, its face taciturn in the beam.

"We gotta get some better lights down here."

Without looking at the doll again, he climbed the steps and shut the door. In the kitchen he grabbed his phone and dialed Jason's number, glancing at the clock to make sure it wasn't too late.

"What's up, man?" Jason answered a moment later. The sounds of a video game in the background filtered through to Evan's end.

"Hey, not much, am I bothering you?"

"Nah, Lily and I are just playing a game."

"Gotcha."

Silence spooled out between them until Jason laughed.

"Ev, you okay?"

Evan sighed and walked into the living room, his blurry reflection in the dark windows looked back at him.

"No, I'm not."

"What's wrong?"

"I don't think we can stay here anymore, Jase."

"What? Why?"

The video game's sound diminished and then was gone with the snap of a door shutting.

"It's not working out well with bringing Shaun across the lake."

"I thought you said he loved the boat rides."

"Yeah, you know, we feel strange here. The guy before us goes missing, and I don't know. I don't think it's safe here for Shaun."

"Safe?"

"Yeah."

"Ev, did something happen?"

All at once he wanted to tell Jason everything: the doll, the body in the lake, his dreams. But what would Jason ask next? Or maybe he wouldn't ask. They were such good of friends that he couldn't ask out loud, but he would wonder, *Is Shaun safe with you?* Stanching the urge to tell Jason all of it, he made his way to Shaun's room, pausing in the doorway to watch him sleep.

"No. I can't explain it."

"Listen, man, sit down for a minute, okay? Do you want to know what I think?"

"No, but I'm guessing you're going to tell me."

"I think maybe you're finally alone with your thoughts, and they're getting to you."

"I'm always alone with my thoughts, they never leave me."

"I know, but that place is different. You're separated from any distractions. You have your writing to focus on now, and you're getting to spend more time with Shaun, and I think it's an overload."

"I like writing, I love being with Shaun."

"I know you do, but this is the first time since Elle that you've had a chance to slow down and realize where you're at. For fuck's sake, man, you're a single father of a child with special needs who lost his wife—you're allowed to feel overwhelmed sometimes."

"But it's more than that," Evan said, turning away from Shaun's room. "I feel like I'm losing it sometimes." It was as close as he could get to the truth.

"And that's perfectly natural. I don't know if you've allowed yourself the time to actually grieve."

"I grieve every day," Evan said. "There's not a moment that goes by that I don't miss her and regret the day of our accident. If I could go back and stop myself from suggesting we go see that movie, we would've never been there at that intersection and Shaun would be fine."

"You can't do that to yourself, there's no way you could've known about the accident or Elle's cancer."

Feeling deflated, Evan sank into the sofa, unconsciously checking the basement door's reflection in the blank TV screen. "I know, it's ..."

"It isn't fucking fair, that's what it is," Jason finished for him. "I'm sorry, man, about everything, but I think a few months to decompress would be good for you, give your mind a chance to recoup some lost ground."

Evan smiled wanly. "Is that a jab?"

"Of course."

"God, I don't know. I wonder sometimes. I wonder if there's someone else that's living our life, the life we should've had, and somehow we got theirs by mistake, like a big cosmic joke."

"I don't know about that, man, but I do know my best friend, and he's the most dedicated, loyal, loving father any kid could want. There's no better hands Shaun could be in. You know that, right?"

"Yeah, but at times I don't feel like it."

"Well, I'm telling you there isn't. Sometimes people are too close to their own lives to see what's wrong or right, but I'm looking in from the outside. You're doing excellent."

"Thanks, I appreciate it."

"You're welcome."

"By the way, how's Lily and Lisa?"

"They're good. Lily's doing soccer this summer. She's all jazzed up about it, broke one of Lisa's plates the other day kicking a ball around inside the kitchen."

Evan laughed. "How's work?"

"It blows, but it pays too well for me to tell the board to get fucked."

Evan smiled and nodded, feeling drained and somewhat foolish.

"Seriously though, man, think about what I said. I'm no psychologist, but you do have one on hand—if you're not using her for something else."

"God. I'm hanging up now."

"Kidding. But if you need to talk about anything, don't hesitate."

"I never do."

Jason laughed. "All right, I got a game to get back to here."

"Yeah, I'll let you go." The image of the doll lying facedown in the basement returned, and he quickly devised a way to fix the issue. "Hey, one more thing."

"Yeah?"

"That doll that's down in the basement, the one with the blue eyes?"

"Doll ... doll ... oh yeah, that's Lily's old doll. My grandma gave it to her for her second birthday."

Evan's heart sank. Thoughts of throwing the thing away evaporated. "Oh, gotcha."

"Why? Does Shaun want to play with it or something?"

"No, no," Evan said, too quickly. The idea of Shaun playing with the thing made his guts squirm. "No, I saw it down there, and it looked strange with the duct tape over its mouth."

Jason's end became quiet, and then he laughed once, dry.

"Yeah, I forgot about that. Lily put the duct tape over its mouth when we were up there staying for a long weekend quite a few years back. She was only six at the time, going through a phase, I think."

"What kind of phase?" Evan asked, the hairs on his arms beginning to rise.

"Oh, you know, kid stuff." Jason laughed again, louder this time. "She said the doll would talk to her at night, that's why she put the tape over its mouth."

Gooseflesh rolled over Evan's entire body, and he swallowed, his throat constricting to a pinhead.

"Anyway, just one of those kid things, imaginary friends and whatnot. She grew out of it."

"Yeah," Evan answered, his voice like sandpaper.

"Okay, buddy, I'll let you go. Call me soon."

"Will do."

"Bye, man."

"Bye."

Evan shut the phone off and sat staring into space for a long time. Shaun rolled over in his bed, and the sound brought him out of the trance. Moving like a ninety-year-old, he crossed the room and flipped the kitchen lights off. He made it only two steps into the living room before going back to the kitchen and propping a chair beneath the basement door's knob.

With the house as quiet as a grave, Evan got ready for bed and turned out the last light, letting darkness cover everything with its heavy embrace.

~

*"I don't want any more chemo," she says, gazing at him through the haze of drugs. "They said it won't do any good anyhow."*

*"But you never know, something could happen on the next round."*

*She smiles at him. "Evan, look at me, I'm wasted away."*

*"No, you're not," he says, unwilling to look at how thin she's become. "You're going to be okay, you're going to make it."*

*She squeezes his hand.*

*"I brought something from home, it's in my bag. Before you leave, I want you to hand it to me."*

*"What is it?" he asks, glancing at the bag that sits near the door.*

*"You'll see. It's what I want."*

*He moves from her, floating, ethereal, not really there, but everything he sees and hears is sharp, like the world is made of shattered glass. Unzipping the bag, he puts his hand inside and rummages around until his fingers touch it.*

Evan came awake, clutching his pillow in two tight fists. His teeth ground together, and tears lay on his cheeks. His breath came out in ragged heaves as he stared up at the ceiling.

"Damn you."

He sat up, steadying himself with a hand on the bed so that he wouldn't tip over, the vertigo of sleep still with him. Shaun's monitor sat quiet, his light snores audible across the hall. Evan stood, rubbing his eyes, and threw on a pair of sweatpants and a T-shirt. The floor beneath his bare feet felt cold, like he was walking on a frozen pond instead of hardwood. Looking into Shaun's room, he gazed at the S shape the boy made below his quilts.

Hints of moonlight illuminated his way through the house. He glanced at the TV and considered turning it on until sleep came again, but the thought of what would be on at this ungodly hour steered him toward the kitchen. He brewed a cup of tea and looked longingly at the last bottle of wine chilling in the fridge, then sat with the steaming cup between his palms. It would be hours before first light, not long enough to drink wine and too long to stare at the wall.

Sighing, Evan slid his laptop across the table and turned it on, opening his Word document once it booted up. The cursor on the screen blinked below what he had written two nights ago.

No. He'd already decided they were leaving today, they couldn't stay here, not anymore. He would find a job close to home, something that could at least pay the bills. He'd find a bank that would loan them enough money to pay off the bulk of their debt. Consolidate, that's what Jason always told him.

His eyes wandered across the room and lit on the basement door, the kitchen chair still propped where he had left it. It looked silly now. Not as much as it would look in full daylight, but silly enough. The screen of his laptop dimmed, and he looked at the words there, imagined the clock down in the dark basement, stolid, mysterious.

Gripping his tea, he rose from the table, removed the leaning chair, and eased the basement door open. Not waiting for his mind to conjure something to be afraid of, he walked down the steps and flipped the light switch on. The basement sprang into view. The doll still lay where he'd kicked it. He made his way to the table and found a folding chair against the end of the nearby workbench. He sat at the table, one hand cupped around his mug of tea, the other flipping through the papers before him.

Most of the sheets contained the detailed diagrams he'd spotted before, their numbers and instructions gibberish as far as he could tell. Deeper in the pile were some handwritten notes. Nearly all of them were illegible, scrawled in erratic angles that spoke of derangement or drug use. Evan had known a kid in college who only wrote poetry when drunk, and then had a fun time the next day trying to decipher his own hand. The writing on the pages looked like drunken messages, and he put several aside before finding one that seemed clearer.

*If this is possible, it will change everything. No more night sweats and nausea. No more running from place to place, job to job. I can fix it all.*

He reread the text, but farther down the page the writing changed into drawings. He held the paper up, examining the doodles. All of them were round and had two lines running through them at different points. Another, smaller circle sat in the middle of the larger one.

Frowning, Evan sifted through more pages of incoherence and found another legible sheet.

*I'll go back and stay inside that night. I won't go out, won't go out, won't go out.*

The writing became larger and larger, until it filled the rest of the paper with erratic slashes that cut through the sheet itself.

Evan set it aside and flipped through the remaining notes. A few more diagrams of grandfather clocks, these looking like they'd been pulled from a book, lay at the bottom of the of the stack. He was about to reorganize the shuffled pile when he saw the imprint of letters on the last page, but he couldn't read them since the writing was on the opposite side. He turned the sheet over and stared at the words traced repeatedly into the paper.

*I CAN SEE THEM.*

Evan dropped the page and glanced around the basement, turning his head to look at the clock behind him. Its face stared back. He stood and walked closer, again mesmerized by the detailed carvings covering its surface. His hand wandered to the trim, tracing the curved lines, their arcs trying to tell him a story. The smooth glass was frigid beneath his palm; he worried for a moment that his hand might stick, but was able to pull it away.

Blinking, Evan turned and picked up his tea, which was cold. Upstairs, he heard Shaun's voice, groggy with sleep.

"Da?"

"Coming, buddy," he yelled, and moved across the room, stopping only once on the landing to stare at the clock before he shut off the lights and went upstairs.

# 11

During breakfast Shaun kept looking at the basement door.

Evan watched him, waiting for another hysterical outburst, but none came. He simply glanced in the basement's direction after every few bites of pancake that Evan fed him, an uneasy look in his eyes. When they'd finished with breakfast, Evan got Shaun dressed and then went through his exercises with him.

By mid-morning they sat in the pontoon, cruising across the lake, fingers of wind that spoke of warmer temperatures combing their hair back. When they walked by Collins Outfitters, Evan waved through the open door to Jacob, who stood chatting with several customers. Jacob waved back, motioning for them to stop in later. Evan nodded, then buckled Shaun into the van and pulled away down Main Street.

They stopped at the same café as before and sat outside at the same table. While Shaun drank his malt through a straw, Evan flipped open his laptop and almost sighed with relief at seeing a Wi-Fi signal come through strong and clear. Not wasting any time, he punched *Abel Kluge, Mill River, MN* into the search engine and watched a few dozen hits come up. Clicking the first one, he read:

*Abel Kluge (1878–1920) was a prominent clockmaker during the early twentieth century. He is well known for his intricately devised pocket watches that wound using a face dial rather than the traditional stem. Although he made great innovations, such as the wristwatch, which would later become popular, his true passion was long-case clocks, or grandfather clocks. It is unclear how many grandfather clocks he made during his short career, but some historians believe the number to be somewhere near one hundred. The dark mahogany that he used to build his clocks is a primary indicator of his style, as is the double pendulum that many of the long cases contained.*

*An emigrant from Hungary, Abel first made a name for himself when he moved to America in 1897. Settling in Chicago with his young wife, Larissa, he began to produce highly sought-after timepieces from a small shop on the north side of the city. His renown grew quickly, and although being rumored as a "man without character," soon Kluge had made enough money to retire, which he did in the winter of 1905.*

*Little is known of his life after moving from Chicago. The small town of Mill River, Minnesota, became his and Larissa's home, and after the completion of a veritable mansion in comparison to the other structures in the town at the time, Abel Kluge receded from the art of clock making altogether.*

*Until his death in 1920, he and his wife lived in seclusion, relying on a small staff of maids and butlers to venture into Mill River for supplies. On November 10, 1920, a member of the staff received no reply from the Kluge's third-floor bedroom, and upon entering, found Larissa seated in one corner of the room, dead. There were no wounds on her body, and cause of death was ruled natural. Besides a small pool of blood on the floor, Abel was nowhere to be found. A subsequent search yielded nothing in the woods surrounding the property. Abel's automobile was present and accounted for, his coat, hat, mittens, and shoes were all found in their proper places in the entry. Temperatures were near fifteen degrees Fahrenheit the night of his disappearance, and after a week the search was abandoned. Abel was officially pronounced deceased a month later. To this day, historians and theorists alike have yet to come to a conclusive answer about what may have killed Larissa Kluge and where her husband may have gone. Some theorize that Abel had a young lover in the nearby town of Mill River and slipped away with her after somehow poisoning his wife. Others contest that he merely wandered away into the night after seeing his wife had died of some natural cause, unable to continue living without her. It is a mystery that may never be solved.*

Evan sat back from the laptop and gazed across the quiet highway, at the lake. He studied where he knew the island was, though he couldn't see it. Coming back to himself, he exited out of the webpage and scanned the other articles. Most repeated what the first piece stated, and he glossed over the words until the last entry. The screen displayed an ornate page from the *Mill River Chronicle*, dated November 13, 1920, and highlighted in the bottom right-hand portion was an obituary. He squinted, leaning close to the screen to read the text.

*Larissa Kluge: 1880–1920. Resident of Mill River since 1905. Deceased Wednesday, November 10, 1920, at her home.*

*Allison Kaufman: 1885–1920. Resident of Mill River since 1885. Deceased Wednesday, November 10, 1920.*

"That's too much of a coincidence, buddy." He looked at Shaun, only partially seeing him. "Two young people in a small town both die on the same day and another disappears?"

Shaun finished his malt with a loud sucking sound. Evan chuckled.

"Was it good?"

Shaun burped a little and smiled. "Ah."

Evan laughed harder. "Ah, like you're satisfied?"

"Ah!" Shaun yelled.

He got up from his chair, still laughing, to kiss him on the forehead.

"You're a card, buddy."

"Car."

"Yep, card."

Evan sat and shot a quick email off to Jason, covering his ideas about the article he wanted to write. He finished it with the facts about Abel and his wife's mysterious deaths.

"And now we wait for Uncle Jason to come through again," he said, shutting his laptop.

Shaun stared at a crow perched on the top of a towering pine behind the café. The crow cocked its ebony head and stared back. Evan watched it for a time before finishing his cooling coffee in a few eager gulps. The sleeplessness of the night before hadn't caught up with him yet, and he didn't want it to. After ordering another coffee to go from the waitress, he glanced at the pine tree again as they got up to leave. The crow was gone.

The sun brightened the day further, warming the air into a promise of summer. When they parked the van at Collins Outfitters, Evan's heart lightened at the thought of his afternoon plans. He carried Shaun into the store and stopped inside the door. A smell of minnows pervaded the air, but other than that, the shop looked clean and tidy, with racks of fishing poles beside coolers, stacks of tackle boxes, and several hangers full of sweatshirts and rain gear.

"Ho! There they be," Jacob said, as he strode into the main area of the shop from a rear entrance. "Good mornin' ta ya both." He shook Shaun's hand and lightly slapped Evan on the arm.

"Good morning," Evan said. "Looked like you were busy earlier."

"Aye, nice fer a change too, been a bit slow round here lately. What are you two fine fellers up ta this mornin'?"

"We came in to have a little coffee and a malt," Evan said, shifting Shaun to his other hip. "Did the twins give you my message yesterday?"

Jacob scowled for a second, then smiled. "Ah, yes. Sorry, boyo, got home late yesterday evenin' and thought 'twas too late ta call. Was on me list this mornin', though."

Evan nodded. "No problem. Actually, Arnold helped me out quite a bit. I'm working on an article concerning that clock that's in the basement at the house, and I was looking for some background information on it. I didn't know if you knew anything else about Abel Kluge and his wife."

Jacob shook his head. "Those boys would know a fair bit more'n I would, all I ever heard was the man was a recluse, and not a kind one at that. No doubt they mentioned Cecil ta ya?"

"Yeah. She hung up on me when I called her."

Jacob laughed. "Oh, that's Cecil all right. She don't come ta town more'n twice a year. Gets some groceries delivered every few weeks. You'll be lucky if ya get 'er ta talk."

Evan knew he was right. Part of him wanted to drive out to the woman's house right then, bang on her door until she let him in, but that wasn't how these things were done.

"We'll see," Evan said, with a smile. "Anyway, we wanted to do some fishing today, and we're going to need some bait."

Jacob's face lit up. "Oh, that'll be great. Sure, I'll setcha up with some minners and crawlers."

"I'm guessing I'll need a license too," Evan said.

"Let's take care of that first," Jacob said.

In a matter of minutes he had the small page filled out for Evan, asking him the occasional question. He then bustled around the shop, gathering a couple of small cartons, filling one with dirt and the other with water. When he'd finished, small, dark shapes flitting against the inside of the minnow container.

"Thanks so much," Evan said.

He tried to walk toward the cash register at the far end of the store, but Jacob tightly held on to the bait and herded them toward the door.

"Get on with ya, can't carry young Shaun here and the bait all at once."

"Jacob, I'm going to pay you," Evan said, reaching for his wallet.

"Three beers," is all Jacob said, winking at him as he walked with them down to the pontoon.

After filling up the boat with gas, Jacob pointed to a small bay down the shoreline and told them about two other spots on the north side of the lake that were always good for a walleye or two. Evan thanked him and then piloted the craft away from shore, waving once at Jacob, who hurried back up the ramp to his store.

They stopped at the island to grab two fishing rods and then set off, eventually dropping anchor at the first spot Jacob had pointed out. Evan sat behind Shaun, helping him hold his rod and cast into the cool water, shaded by an overhanging birch tree. At first Shaun became frustrated as he tried to crank the reel, but soon he got the hang of it. Evan had to slow down his furious pace, otherwise the bait barely touched the water before the boy had it back in the boat.

After some time, he noticed something missing. Doing a mental check, he sat back, still steadying Shaun's hands on the rod. The sun shone down on them from a cloudless spring sky. A few waves rocked the pontoon, and the far-off whine of a boat motor could be heard intermittently. He finally realized he felt peaceful. His mind wasn't clogged with worry or apprehension, and the lack of it had thrown him off. Hugging Shaun close, he kissed his hair, just above his small ear.

"Shaun, are you having fun?" he whispered.

"Fun," Shaun said, yanking the pole back as something tugged on the other end of the line.

"Wooo, you got one, buddy," Evan exclaimed. "Reel it in. Reel it in."

Shaun cranked and fought the fish until it gradually surfaced, flashing and leaping from the water in a shower of droplets beside the pontoon. Evan hauled the fish aboard when it got close enough, and Shaun shrieked with delight, flapping his arms so hard it was a struggle for Evan to balance him and unhook the bass at the same time.

"We're keeping him, pal," he said, putting the fish on a stringer. "Supper."

"Sup-por," Shaun echoed.

They whiled away the time until early afternoon, catching a small mess of fish for a meal. Shaun's head kept dipping on the ride home, and Evan held him tight, smiling as his son fought to stay awake. Evan docked the pontoon and carried Shaun up to the porch, laying him on the most comfortable reclining chair. Shaun grinned at him once and then shut his eyes, exhaustion dragging him into sleep before he could say or do anything else.

While he slept, Evan cleaned the fish on a small wooden table he found to the north side of the house, his eyes shooting to the porch over and over.

*We're both going to have to sleep in the house tonight anyway.*

He threw the fish guts in the woods and took the white fillets into the house to soak them in cold water. The urge to pick up the phone and invite Selena over for supper struck him, and he went so far as to pull her business card out of his wallet. Sliding it carefully into its slot again, he put it back and went to the porch.

Evan lay down on the daybed beside Shaun, the sleeplessness of the night before finally claiming him. The sun and fresh air paired with the low tinkling of the wind chimes became too lulling, and his last thought before he fell asleep was he should've propped a chair against the basement door.

*He barely makes it into the hospital bathroom before throwing up. The vomit courses out of him, sloppy ropes landing in the toilet water. As he heaves he feels the round container in his hand, even though it isn't there anymore; he'd dropped it back into the bag the moment he pulled it out.*

*"Honey, I'm sorry, I—"*

*But her voice is lost in another gagging hack as he doubles over again. When the nausea lets up enough for him to flush and wipe his mouth clean, he leans in the doorway, not looking at where she rests in bed but at the crumpled bag on the floor, at what lies inside.*

*He moves forward, his feet full of lead, his head throbbing in time with the pulse running like a jackrabbit in his chest.*

*"Goddamn you," he says, still not looking at her.*

*He bends, feeling the urge to throw up again, and grasps the bottle, pulling it free. Its contents rattle in his shaking hand. When he looks up, Elle is gone.*

*Instead of her bed, the clock lies on its back upon the floor. Its three glass doors are different; they are rounded and made of the same polished mahogany as the rest of its body. The three cases look like coffins. His mouth falls open, and the pill bottle slips from his hand as he takes a step back—*

*—and watches the middle lid rise, pushed from inside.*

Evan cried out, his arm spasming as he rolled off the daybed. His fist struck Shaun's recliner, pain blossoming in each knuckle. Shaun's eyes leapt open, and he made a frightened sound, something between a shriek and a moan. Evan landed on his hands and knees, panting, his stomach roiling with sick. Sweat hung in beads from his hair and rolled down his forehead. His arms threatened to drop him, and he pushed himself back onto the bed with enormous effort.

"Da?" Shaun asked, his eyes wide as he struggled to sit up.

"I'm okay, buddy, I'm okay. It was a dream." He spoke more to himself than to Shaun, and when he looked up, he saw an expression of concern on the boy's features. "I'm fine, honey, just a dream."

"'Kay?"

Evan's brow creased and his throat constricted. He stood and then sat on Shaun's chair, holding his son's hand in his own.

"Yep, Dad's okay." He summoned a smile, shoving the residue of the dream away, praying that it would fade further. "Are you hungry?" Shaun nodded. "Okay, let's rustle up some food."

~

They ate on the porch, Shaun downing his roast-beef sandwich in wild bites while Evan nudged his around and picked at the few potato chips on his plate.

After lunch they ventured down to the dock, Evan carrying a frying pan, an ice-cream-pail lid, some bubble solution, and a small bottle of dish soap. He set Shaun in his chair beside the beach and began to work, talking to him as he did so.

"You have to be careful not to cut yourself, but you also have to make sure these edges are smooth," Evan said, carving the center out of the ice-cream lid with his pocketknife.

After a few minutes, the lid was only a thin ring, the flat center lying discarded on the dock. "Now, this next part is the real art." Evan poured the entire container of bubble mixture into the frying pan. "You can't put too much or too little dish soap in with it, it's got to be just enough." He squirted the blue soap into the pan, swishing his fingers through it to mix it in. "Then we check it," he said, standing.

Evan set the plastic ring into the pan, submerging it in the substance. After a second he withdrew it, letting some of the liquid drain off. A transparent skin hung in the center of the ring, reflecting the afternoon light in swirling, oil-slick colors.

"Now we see if we did it right."

He checked the breeze, then gently pulled the ring through the air with both hands. A huge iridescent bubble expanded from the hollow cover. It grew and grew until it became the size of a large beach ball. With a deft downward motion, Evan cut the bubble off and set it free. It drifted in a lazy motion toward the lake, its sides wobbling so much that he thought it might burst, but it didn't. It kept moving out over the water, dipping and then rising like a confused bird.

Shaun's face was a portrait of wonderment. His mouth was open an inch, his eyes wider than when Evan had awoken him earlier with his cry. A low breeze ruffled his light hair, and he pointed toward the lake.

Evan had completely forgotten about the bubble, his gaze fixated on the beautiful expression on Shaun's face. When he turned his head, he saw the bubble floated only inches above the water's surface. A particularly high wave rolled toward the island and grazed the bubble's lower half, instantly bursting it.

*That was our life before the accident. Then something came along and tore it apart for no reason.*

Shaun's mouth opened wider, and for a second Evan feared he might cry, but then his eyes shifted to Evan's.

"More!"

Shaun placed his fingertips together in the accompanying sign, the one Elle had taught him, the only one he knew by heart, and then Evan bit his lip to ward off tears.

"More?"

"More!"

"Okay, here we go."

They blew bubbles for hours. When the solution in the pan ran low, he refilled it, to Shaun's happy sounds. The wind changed and began to come from the east, which helped the bubbles travel farther before disappearing. Evan lost himself in the moment, his hands slippery to the wrists. He couldn't make the bubbles fast enough; Shaun's laughter was the ultimate payoff whenever he achieved a truly giant orb. Evan wished the afternoon could last forever—the wind speaking in the pines, Shaun laughing, a smile almost constant on his own face. He wished ... and stopped himself, unwilling to break the spell that surrounded them, an invisible bubble of its own.

Finally, the bottle of bubbles became empty, and a curled line of clouds advanced in a steady wall from the west. The blue sky turned overcast, and the sun hid within the churning, gray folds.

"Time to go in, Shaun," he said, and waited for a reaction.

Shaun frowned, kicking his legs once so that they banged into his chair. Evan tilted the pan toward him so that he could see its emptiness.

"All gone."

Shaun's head drooped. Evan smiled and patted him on the back, then cleaned up their supplies. His eyes kept trying to roam toward the house; he knew they would soon have to go inside. The clouds continued to build across the lake, but he heard no thunder and hoped it wouldn't storm.

Evan fried the fish they caught in flour and butter, seasoning it the best he could with salt and pepper. They ate with relish, Shaun smacking his lips several times, doing it again when he didn't need to simply to get a rise out of Evan.

After dinner Shaun had a bath. Evan washed his hair and scrubbed behind his ears. As he rinsed a washrag, a strange feeling intruded on his mood, a cloud covering the sun. One more bath, another day gone, meal after meal. It was simply a meter, wasn't it? A marking of time until the days were thin, the end near, near enough to touch, to taste. Is that what he was waiting for? The end? For this all to be over?

Evan gazed at his son and stopped him from putting the bar of soap into his mouth, for the tenth time. Shaun splashed the water, and a small runner of drool rolled down the side of his chin. Evan wiped it away, the sight of it more depressing than anything he'd seen in a long time.

"Let's get you out, honey."

~

They sat at the kitchen table working on tracing until Shaun's fingers couldn't hold the marker properly anymore. Evan watched him close, waiting for his attention to stray to the basement door, but either he had forgotten the prior night's incident or he chose to ignore it.

"Okay, time for bed. Big day tomorrow, gotta go to the hospital and do some therapy."

He helped Shaun out of his chair and let him walk to his room, his fingertips barely helping to balance him. After tucking him in, Evan sat on the end of the bed.

"This was a good day, buddy. I had fun."

"Bub, bub."

Shaun struggled with the word, and Evan let him work on it before helping.

"Bubble."

"Bubbow," Shaun repeated.

"Yeah, we had bubbles, didn't we?"

Shaun smiled, snuggling into his pillow. "Moon?"

"Moon?" Evan said, glancing at the darkening window. His stomach sank. "You mean *Goodnight Moon*."

He had forgotten the book at home. How had he missed it? He could even see it sitting on Shaun's bedroom floor. Elle would've never forgotten something so important.

"I'm sorry, buddy, it's not here."

Shaun's face darkened. "Moon?"

Evan opened his mouth to try to explain, but instead the first words of the story came out. He spoke easily and found that he could see every page in the book, the words standing out in bold black and red ink. Shaun's eyes closed as Evan's voice carried him away. He paused at the page about clocks but pressed on, ignoring the shiver that tried to run through him. At last, Shaun's breathing became deep and his arm jerked a little as sleep took him fully.

The creaking of a door opening in the kitchen met his ears.

His head snapped in that direction. He waited, listening to the quiet of the house. With his pulse picking up speed, Evan stood and made his way through the living room to the kitchen, expecting the basement door to be standing ajar.

But it wasn't. He checked all the other doors, and none were open even a crack. He stood in the middle of the kitchen, wondering why the hell they hadn't left today.

*Curiosity killed the cat.*

The words seemed to come out of nowhere, and he shook his head, moving to the counter to make some tea. While the water heated, he watched the light fade from the day, the clouds on the horizon suspended, no closer or farther away than before.

He and Shaun were the clouds. Unmoving, unable to go forward or disperse, static in life. Soon they would both be old, himself in his eighties, Shaun nearing sixty. How would he take care of him then? How would he ensure that Shaun wouldn't be scared if he couldn't come to his calls right away, or if he couldn't remember what he was supposed to do when he got there? What would they do when he couldn't help them anymore?

The thought terrified him. This was the unsaid horror that stalked him each hour, submerged beneath the everyday trials and tribulations, the sadness and suffering. The image of Shaun alone and scared was too much to bear, so he banished it back to the depths of his mind from which it came, to hibernate with fangs of fear ready in its black mouth.

His hand felt cold, and when he looked down, he saw he was holding the basement-door handle. He yanked it back, surprised more by not remembering moving to touch it than by the chill it gave off.

"Basements are cold, that's a fact," he said to the kitchen.

His tea water wasn't as hot as he liked it, but he poured it over the tea bag anyway, then sat at the table with his laptop. His email yielded no new messages, but he remembered he had no Wi-Fi service and couldn't receive anything. He opened his article notes and scanned what he'd already written, and then typed for a moment.

*Abel and Larissa Kluge—dead under mysterious circumstances. Allison Kaufman—died the same day as Larissa, look into death. Cecil Fenz—related to Kluges? Bob's story—notes in basement.*

Evan paused, his fingers hovering over the keys.

*Clock at the center of everything?*

He glanced at the basement door before snapping the laptop shut.

"Nope, I'm tired."

Without bothering to put his untouched tea away, Evan shut the lights off and headed for bed.

But sleep wouldn't come. It seemed drifting off was a magic trick he'd forgotten, a subtle secret of the mind that wouldn't show itself. His thoughts played on a continuous loop, facts and words whirling like a tornado in his skull. After nearly two hours of tossing and turning, he rose and headed to the basement.

"I gotta get that light fixed," he said, traipsing down the unlit stairs until his fingers found the switch at the bottom.

The basement looked the same, and he didn't spare a glance at the doll lying on the floor. Knowing it was silly but doing it anyway, he took a chair and positioned it at the end of the table, not wanting his back to the clock. He sat and ran his weary eyes over the notes. Tonight, the scrawls looked different, Bob's incoherent hand not seeming wild or unruly. In fact, the lines actually appeared to be words, although disjointed and hacked into the page. Evan sifted through them, seeing letters strung together one second, and the next they were gone, lost in a jumble of scribbles.

At the bottom of the pile, he found the words pressed into the paper. Closing his eyes, he ran his fingertips over the ridges, imagining he could read them like braille. *I CAN SEE THEM.*

He shuddered and opened his eyes. What the hell was he doing? Looking through the ramblings of a man who most likely wandered off into the winter night to freeze in some hidden place. Evan rubbed his forehead. God, he was tired. Without thinking about it, he whipped a hand across the sheets of paper in frustration, scattering several to the floor. They landed next to one another like birds alighting to feed.

"I need some sleep, then I can sort this out," he said. "I also need to quit talking to myself."

With that, he stood and reached down to pick up the papers, but his hand stopped inches from the floor. The air around him froze, and all sound stopped. The pages lay side-by-side, their edges almost touching, the scribbles and unintelligible drawings finally becoming clear.

"What the fuck?" he said, stooping to the ground.

He slid two sheets together and saw that they formed the word *BACK*. "No way," he muttered.

He grasped another paper and moved it close to the first two, flipping it different ways, but it didn't fit. Grabbing all of the loose notes from the table, he pulled them to the floor, moving back to give himself room. He swung the papers different directions, matching their edges and then pulling them apart. Moving around the growing spread of pages, he looked at it from different angles like an artist studying a half-finished sculpture. His mind became focused on the task, the basement around him receding, the promise of something just out of reach coming together.

After pushing the last page into place, he stood and observed the four-foot by eight rectangle he'd formed, the mosaic finally complete.

*HIS NAME WAS BILLY AND I KILLED HIM WITH MY TRUCK. HE WAS SIX. I CAN GO BACK I CAN GO BACKICANGOBACKICANGOBACKICANGOBACK.*

Evan staggered away from the papers, his hand coming to his mouth. "Oh my God," he whispered.

# 12

The waiting-room Wi-Fi signal looked strong on his laptop screen.

Evan glanced at a passing nurse who gave him a smile, then lowered his face into his palm. He hadn't slept much the night before. Not that it surprised him. Bob's message still hung like a macabre painting in the hall of his mind. He may have gotten two hours of broken rest in before Shaun woke.

Sighing, he logged on to the Internet and sat still for a moment. Was he really going down this path? A madman had cut the trail before him, he was sure of it. The urge to shut the computer down overcame him, and he went so far as to put his hand on its lid before setting his fingers back on the keys. He typed *Bob Garrison car accident* into the search bar and waited. The results came back with nothing of interest. He tried again, *Robert Garrison Colorado*.

A webpage appeared at the top of the screen, with the title *Bob's Odd Jobs* over it. Evan clicked on it and saw a simple and outdated website with a few pictures of landscaped yards, paintbrushes, and a smiling man with sandy-blond hair in cargo shorts and sunglasses. He read through the description of services and studied the man's photograph. That was him, it had to be. A phone number was at the very bottom of the page, and Evan hesitated only a second before calling it. It didn't ring; an automated voice picked up and told him the number was either disconnected or no longer in service.

He put his phone away and returned to the search engine, typing *Colorado car accidents Billy*. A few dozen hits came up, but most were decades old and none involved any information about a child.

He readjusted himself in the chair and glanced down the hospital's hallway, his brain running too fast for him to examine his thoughts. He saw the arrangement of papers on the basement floor again and pushed the image away, but not before a new idea bloomed in his mind.

With trepidation, he typed *Colorado hit-and-run Billy 6 years old*. The first website that came up made his stomach coil in on itself. *Hit-and-run in downtown Boulder leaves 6-year-old dead*. Evan clicked on the article and began to read.

*A community mourns the loss of a young child today after a hit-and-run accident late Tuesday evening. William Akely, 6, was playing in his front yard at approximately 9 p.m. when he wandered into the street near his home. An unidentified vehicle struck and killed him without stopping. Police say they are following up each and every lead in the case, and are confident that a suspect will be arrested soon. William's mother, Janet Akely, was watching him at the time of the accident, but officials say she momentarily stepped into the house to answer a phone call. A memorial service will be held at St. Luke's Lutheran Church of Boulder on Saturday, June 11. The Boulder Police Department is asking for any and all information in regards to the investigation.*

With a shaking hand, Evan closed the webpages, and sat staring at the opposite wall of the waiting room. He let the white paint invade his eyes until it was all he could see.

"Mr. Tormer?"

He snapped out of his trance and saw that a young Asian woman stood a few paces away, holding Shaun's hands in hers.

"Sorry," Evan said, putting his computer aside. He stood.

"That's okay. I'm Becky Tram. Dr. Netler said you inquired about a PCA?"

Becky had jet-black hair tied back from a round face. Her uniform looked tight in places, as if she had gained weight since she bought it and wasn't willing to give in to a larger size. She smiled, revealing a set of very white teeth and dimples in her plump cheeks.

"Oh, yes, nice to meet you," Evan said, holding out a hand for her to shake.

"You too. And this little man did awesome today," Becky said, guiding Shaun to Evan.

Evan grinned and pulled Shaun up, to hold him on his hip. "Did you?" he asked, tickling Shaun's neck.

Shaun laughed and kicked his feet.

"Yes, he did great. We worked really hard, so he might be tired. Have you been doing small motor skills with him lately?"

"Yeah, we've been doing tracing and some therapy putty from time to time."

"Great. I can tell you work with him at home since he's versed in most of the stuff we do."

"He has a great PT and OT staff back where we live."

"Well, he's doing wonderful, lots of echolalia today too. So, were you thinking of regular PCA hours, or once in a while?"

Evan shifted Shaun to his other hip. "Probably just from time to time. I'm home with him now, but I thought it might be good to set something up in case I needed to go somewhere."

Becky nodded. "Absolutely. My schedule is pretty open for the summer, and I could probably do almost any day of the week except for Mondays. Did the front desk give you my résumé?"

"They did, it looked great."

"Good. Yeah, I've been doing PCA stuff for about six years now, and it works really well with my OT. I'll eventually be full-time here, but not until they have an opening."

Evan's eyes glazed slightly. "Would you be able to come out tomorrow?"

"Sure, what time?"

He blinked. "How about one? Shaun usually takes his naps in the afternoon."

"That sounds great. Where do you guys live?"

"The Fin."

Becky's cheerful face lost some of its color, but she recovered immediately. "Okay, sure, I know where it is. My dad has a boat he'll let me use. I'll be out a little before one."

"Perfect," Evan said, shaking her hand. "We'll see you then."

~

Even with the sun straight overhead, Evan was cold. As they crossed the water and the Fin materialized, the notion to pack and leave as soon as they got there became more and more appealing. What were they staying for? The possibility of a story in a magazine? At what cost? Visions of a floating body and the doll standing on the basement landing flashed through his mind, and he pressed the heel of his hand against his forehead. That could've been his imagination, just circus acts in the old brainpan.

*Shouldn't you be worried about that? The cost for staying might be your sanity.*

Lack of sleep paired with stress could do weird things.

*Shaun saw it too.*

But he could've been asleep and dreamed it, or seen something on TV that scared him, Evan retorted. The voice didn't answer, letting him stew in his own thoughts until they reached the island.

The afternoon passed in a lazy blink of an eye. The sun arced overhead, and Shaun napped. Evan sipped on coffee, maintaining a steady caffeine buzz that pushed him through the day. He cleaned a little, puttering around the house, ignoring the basement door as much as he could. When Shaun woke up, they sat by the lake's edge, watching the afternoon rays walk across the waves.

When they returned to the house, Evan surprised himself by pulling out the business card with Selena's number on it. He stared at it for a while, and eventually drew out his phone and punched in the numbers before he could stop himself. The rush of adrenaline from calling her both frightened and soothed him. It was as if he'd just woken up, the day a haze of motions and words until then.

"Hello?"

Her voice startled him, and he nearly fumbled the phone, realizing he had no plan of what to say to her.

"Hey, Selena, it's Evan."

"Hi, how are you?" Warmth flooded her voice.

"Hi, um, good. Say, I didn't know if you'd be in the neighborhood this evening. We were going to have a pizza and thought you might like to stop by."

Once the words were out of his mouth, he wanted to bring them back, wanted to reverse and not have called her at all.

"You know, I was thinking of going for a paddle in a bit. The exercise should justify some pizza, right?"

He smiled. "Absolutely."

She laughed, tinkling crystal. "I'll see you two in a while."

"Sounds great."

"Bye."

"Bye."

He ended the call, a surge of excitement rushing upward from the base of his stomach. Immediately a blade of guilt sliced through it, cutting it into pieces that withered and deflated. He walked past the couch on which Shaun rested, watching cartoons, and stepped onto the three-season porch. The cooler air pushed against him and hummed through the screens. He sat in a chair that gave him the best vantage of the lake.

"I'm sorry, honey," he said, so low he barely heard the words. "I don't know what you would've wanted." He laughed and rubbed at his eyes, the moisture in them beginning to sting. "What you really wanted, I guess we never talked about it much. We were always too busy with Shaun and each other to discuss it."

Evan spun the heavy ring on his finger a few times, noting how well it still shined. He could see himself in its reflection, as well as a distorted image of the room around him.

"I know you want me to be happy, but this still seems fast. It's like everything came at me at once, and I don't know what to do." He swallowed, needing to go on. "I'll be alone if you want me to, I can do it, no problem. I know you said—"

His face crumpled and he breathed out a long, hot sigh. "I can wait until we're together again. Let me know what you want."

A breeze picked up and streamed across the porch, pushing at his hair. For a minute he stared at the lake, the water dull blue, capped with streaks of burgundy where the sun glanced off the waves. While he watched, the constant touch of the breeze caressed his face. The wind chime sung, its sound lighter than he'd ever heard it before, the air picking out its own melody. He sniffed and looked through the screens, expecting her to be there, smiling at him, but nothing so dramatic happened. The breeze finally slowed, then stopped, and the pines became still again.

"Okay," he said. "Okay."

~

After Selena arrived, they ate dinner. Evan was surprised and amused at how much the psychologist could eat. As the meal wound down, Selena noticed him watching her, a half grin on his face.

"What?" she said, through a mouthful of pizza.

He shook his head, the smile still tugging at his lips. "Nothing, just wondering how many times you'll have to paddle around the lake to burn all that off."

A mock indignant look crossed her face, and she balled up a napkin to throw at him. Evan laughed and dodged it. This caused Shaun to giggle and look back and forth between the two grown-ups.

"You need to teach your dad some manners, Shaun," Selena said. "Tell him women don't take kindly to weight jokes."

Evan laughed. "Oh I wasn't making fun of your weight, just how much you ate."

Selena raised her eyebrows. "Well then, I'm thoroughly offended." With a quick movement, she reached out and snagged one of the two remaining pieces of pizza. "Maybe this will help me feel better."

He shook his head and, still laughing, shot Shaun a silly face.

They cleaned up dinner, and Evan found a dusty game of Yahtzee in the closet off the living room. They set up the game at the kitchen table and began to play. He and Selena took turns helping Shaun hold the shaker cup and counting the numbers on the dice. Evan noticed a warmth in his chest every time he watched Selena's long fingers grasp Shaun's hands and guide them to pick up the dice. The guilt tried to return whenever he registered it, but then he would think of the breeze caressing his face on the porch.

*It might only have been a gust of wind.*

Yes, and it might not have.

When Shaun couldn't hold his head up anymore, Evan helped him to bed. Before he could offer to read a story, the boy had drifted off, his eyelids twitching.

"Already dreaming," Selena said from behind him.

Evan turned and nodded before kissing Shaun on the forehead. He followed her back to the kitchen and walked to the fridge.

"Want a glass of wine?"

"What the hell, I had about seven pieces of pizza, right?"

"You know I was kidding," he said, pulling the last bottle of cab out of the fridge.

"Mmm-hmm, sure," she said.

Her eyes danced and she smiled. Evan poured them each a glass, handing Selena hers as he sat at the table. They sipped in silence for a while, and amidst the pleasant quiet, he wondered if everything he'd experienced on the island truly had been an overactive imagination on his part. With Selena sitting across from him and Shaun sound asleep in his bed, he very much wanted to believe that was the case.

"What are you thinking?"

Evan glanced at her and shook his head. "I'm not going to answer that question from a psychologist."

She smiled, but became sober again. "Sorry, it seems that you're distracted a lot of the time."

"You're right, I do get sidetracked, always have."

"It's not a bad thing, you know, it's usually characteristic of a creative mind. You mentioned you're a writer, right?"

He chuckled. "I wouldn't call myself a writer. I've had one article published and written a few others." He shrugged and sipped his wine.

"It's nothing to scoff at."

"It's nothing to do cartwheels over either."

"Well, you do have more responsibility than most people, you know?"

He nodded. "It's funny. I never think of it that way. Shaun's been like he is for over four years. It's our life now, I'm used to it, as much as anyone can be. Sometimes I think about what things would be like if we hadn't gotten in that crash, how life would be now, but it's really a waste of time, right? The past, I mean."

She smiled. "That was almost poetic."

"Almost."

"It's scary, isn't it?"

"What's that?"

"Being the only one he counts on every day. I can see it in the way you talk to him sometimes."

"What scares me is what would happen if I weren't around anymore. I have things set up for my best friend to take care of him, but ..."

"But the thought of him being here without you—"

"Terrifies me, yeah. I can't think of anything more frightening." he swirled his wine and watched the red liquid spin. "Sometimes I wonder if other people know how good they have it. They take life for granted until a car comes along, or cancer, or a million other things that happen." He shook his head. "I know I did."

"Everyone does," Selena said. "Until it happens, you don't worry about it, unless you have a disorder, and I've seen my share of those. Some patients I've treated can't leave their house for fear of something happening to them, can't go to the grocery store without worrying someone has poisoned all the fruit."

"Yeah, the old saying always comes to mind, if everyone put their troubles in a pile, you'd grab yours back."

She nodded. "Very true."

They drank in silence for a while, then Selena asked, "So how long are you planning on staying here?"

"I don't know, we were thinking at least until fall, maybe longer. We'll see." Evan watched her take a drink of wine. "How about you? Sticking around for the foreseeable future?"

"I think so. I have a steady client base, not too busy, not too light. It fits around everything else I like to do."

"What else do you like to do?"

"I like to hike, and obviously canoe. If it's rainy, I read."

"And fishing?" he asked, with a smile.

Selena's face grew somber. "I haven't since my dad passed away."

"Would you like to go sometime? With Shaun and me?"

She considered it for a moment, tilting her head so that her long hair swayed in a way that he liked.

"I think that would be nice."

Their eyes held for a beat, and before Evan could look away, Selena did, glancing at the floor.

"So what are you writing about now?"

He licked his lips, his eyes skimming over her shoulder, to the basement door. "Here, let me show you."

He led her down the steps, holding her hand in the dark—completely on the pretense of avoiding a fall, he told himself—and turned the lights on in the basement. It was nice having someone with him down here; the air felt better, lighter. When Selena spied the clock at the far end of the room, she stopped, transfixed.

"Whoa."

Evan kept walking toward it. "I know, it's pretty impressive, right?"

"I don't know if I'd call it impressive. 'Weird' might be the word."

"Definitely weird. Come here, let me show you the sides."

Grateful that he'd cleaned up Bob's message the night before, he brought her close to the clock's intricately carved case and let her examine it.

"Wow, it looks like writing or something."

"Good, I'm glad you think so too. I was beginning to wonder if it was just me."

She studied the clock from all angles, peering up at the looming structure as she walked to its other side, her stance almost like she expected the timepiece to topple forward at any second.

"So this is what you're writing about?"

"Yep, and I've already started digging into things a little bit. Seems it's got a fairly dark history. Its maker disappeared the same night his wife died, in its presence, over ninety years ago, and I think another person did too, but I'm not sure yet."

Selena took a few steps back, bumping into the worktable and causing one of the brass weights to roll toward the floor. Evan reached out and caught it before it could fall.

"Sorry, it's really ..." She searched for the word, bringing her hands up before her. "Odd."

"Yeah, I'm excited to delve into the story a little deeper." he paused, glancing at Selena and then the clock. "You wouldn't want to come with me somewhere tomorrow, would you?"

"Where?"

He cleared his throat. "To the house where it came from."

Her eyes grew large for a moment, and she tilted her head again. "Oh, wow, why?"

He had to smile at her discomfort. "I want to take a look around, get a feel for the place if I'm going to include it in the article. We might even find something interesting there."

"Do you have permission to go inside?"

"No, but from what I gathered, there hasn't been anyone living there for a long time. At the very least, I want to see the outside. I'm going out there tomorrow afternoon."

Selena gave the clock another look, and then turned her gaze to him. "This is important to you, huh?"

He nodded. "I think the article might get my foot in the door with a magazine in the cities. I—"

"What?"

What the hell. If not now, then it would be later. "I lost my last job after borrowing some money that wasn't mine, to pay for my wife's treatments. I paid it all back before they even knew it was gone, but they caught it in the accounting office and let me go a few weeks back."

He waited for her reaction, and when she only nodded, he continued. "I never did anything like that before, and I don't plan to ever again, but it was what I had to do at the time. If I sell this article, it might help get our lives back on track. We need this."

Selena watched him for a time, her eyes running over him as though she were inspecting the clock again.

"You think I'm a criminal," he said.

"No, I don't. I think you're a sweet man who loved his wife very much."

His throat swelled, and he nodded, looking down at the floor.

"I'll go."

A smile pulled at his mouth, and he tried to restrain it from becoming goofy without much success. "Great."

"Now, can we go back upstairs?"

"Sure."

He followed her toward the kitchen, throwing one last look at the clock before killing the lights.

# 13

Evan hoped for sunshine but received a sky full of clouds instead.

The day dawned gray and unyielding, the lake's surface coated with a thick layer of fog that obscured everything in a soupy haze. Sometimes it sounded like a boat passed only yards from the island, but Evan knew that fog distorted noises, giving sounds hallucinatory qualities. It hadn't rained yet, but the sky threatened it, hovering close, with rounded bellies of thunderheads nearly skimming the treetops.

They spent the morning inside, away from the cool air and clinging mist. Evan practiced letters with Shaun and helped him pronounce several short words until he said them correctly. A few minutes to noon, the fog began to lift, but the clouds remained, their cover tainting Long Lake an icy color of ash.

"It's supposed to be warm, Shaun," Evan called out as he readied lunch. "This is springtime, not fall, buddy."

Shaun peered at him from the kitchen table, not sure if he should smile or frown at his father's statement. Evan laughed. For the first time since they'd been there, his spirits were fairly good. After seeing Selena off the night before, a sunset glaze coating the dark lake as she'd paddled away, he'd slept well. No dreams jerked him awake, and when he rose, the cloaking fatigue he'd worn the days prior didn't follow him out of bed.

"Tuna sandwich, my boy," he said, sliding the plate onto the table. "Your absolute favorite." At least it had been before the accident. "There you go, buddy."

He guided Shaun's hands toward his mouth, not helping him as much as he normally did. A small amount of tuna and mayonnaise fell out and landed on Shaun's shirt, but he didn't notice. He took another generous bite and chewed, watching Evan with large eyes.

"Eat?"

"Yep, we're eating, buddy."

"Eat?"

"Oh, you want me to eat? I will after you're done."

As Shaun finished his last bite, the sound of a boat motor neared, becoming louder and louder, and Evan walked to the window overlooking the lake. A small red boat coasted to a stop beside the dock, and Becky Tram tied a mooring rope to the supports before climbing out. She wore jeans and a windbreaker, with a hat pulled down over her dark hair.

"Your friend is here, Shaun. Will you be okay if she stays and Dad goes to town for a bit?"

"Yesh."

"Really?"

"Na."

Evan frowned. "Well, which is it? Yes or no?"

Shaun smiled and turned his head to the side but kept his eyes on Evan. The expression looked so funny, Evan burst out laughing.

"You're a card."

A knock came from the door, and he went to let Becky inside. When he opened the door, the young PCA stood on the stoop, a little out of breath.

"Hi, Becky, nice to see you."

"You too, Mr. Tormer."

"Call me Evan," he said, leading her inside.

"Wow, this is really nice."

Evan watched her turn in a small circle, her eyes roaming the walls and floors.

"Thanks, it's actually my best friend's place. We're watching it for him."

"Hmm," Becky said.

"Hi," Shaun said.

"Hi, Shaun," Becky said, walking over to the table. "How are you today? Good?" Shaun reached out and tried to touch her face. "Are we going to have fun this afternoon?"

Evan let Becky and Shaun get reacquainted before leading her on a brief tour of the house.

"And what's through those doors?" Becky asked, pointing to the master bedroom and basement when they reentered the kitchen.

"The master bedroom and basement. You won't need to go in there," Evan said, tapping a notebook on the kitchen counter. "Here's my cell phone, and here's Selena's number in case of an emergency. If you need anything, call and I'll come right back. I shouldn't be gone for more than a few hours."

"Don't worry, we'll be fine. We're going to do lots of stuff, right, Shaun?"

Becky knelt next to Shaun's chair. He kicked his feet with excitement and smiled. A sudden anxiety gripped Evan, a cold fist inside his chest. An overwhelming urge to stay blanketed him. He frowned, trying to trace where the feeling came from, but as swiftly as it appeared, the dread vanished.

He shook his head, waiting for something else. Another warning? Premonition?

"Evan, are you okay?"

He glanced at Becky, who still held Shaun's hands in hers. Her eyes looked cautious. How long had he been standing there?

"I'm fine, gathering my wits. Not much to gather, though."

Becky laughed politely at the joke.

"Okay, you be good," Evan said, stepping forward to kiss Shaun on the forehead. "And like I said, you need anything, definitely call."

"Will do."

He stopped at the door to don a sweater and grab his laptop. He knew if he looked back one more time, he wouldn't leave. With the feeling of plunging out of an airplane, he shut the door behind him and jogged down the hill, toward the lake.

~

Evan glanced at the van's dashboard clock and looked around the vacant park for the third time. Wind buffeted the vehicle, making it rock on its springs. The street he parked on had no traffic, and the only buildings in sight were a row of townhouses and one small apartment complex on the corner. Dead leaves from the previous fall skipped down the sidewalk, their hides raw and brown, ready to crack and break apart with the spring's moisture. Other than the breeze and pressing clouds, he was alone.

The door to the van opened, filling the vehicle with cool air.

"Shit, you scared me," Evan said, relaxing as Selena smiled and climbed into the passenger seat.

She wore a blue knitted hat that contrasted her brown hair nicely, along with smart-looking slacks and a short coat.

"Sorry, couldn't help myself," she said, still grinning.

"Yeah, you look sorry," Evan said, putting the van in drive. "Did you really eat lunch out in this weather?"

"Well, no, not today, actually. But I almost always do when it's nice. I love that park. Barely anyone comes there, it's so peaceful."

"I could've picked you up at your office."

"I know, but I like to walk, and it's not that far from my building."

Evan guided the van through the streets of Mill River until they rode south out of town. He couldn't help look out his window at the lake, seeking the island.

"You doing okay?" Selena asked.

He brought his eyes back to the road. "Yeah, I'm good."

"Worried about him?"

"Is it that obvious?"

"Yes." She smiled and lightly touched his arm. "I'm sure he's fine. You said the PCA was highly recommended, right?"

He sighed. "Yeah, she is."

"Then they'll have fun while you're off ghost hunting."

He had to smile. "I hope we don't run into any ghosts."

"You said we're going to an abandoned mansion, right? All those places are haunted, don't you watch TV?"

"You believe in ghosts? A learned woman of psychology?"

"Sure. There's too many people telling too many stories for it not to be true."

"Collective hallucinations."

"Not a chance." She looked at him. "What do you think?"

He remained quiet for a long time. "People are haunted, not buildings. There's things inside that they can't let go of, and that changes them, usually not for the better."

They drove in silence after that, with only the rush of a passing car to break it. A dirt road appeared on the right, and Evan slowed, reading the street sign.

"Wicker Road," Selena said, as they turned onto the narrow drive. "I've never even noticed this before."

The road ran straight for nearly a mile. A band of thicket not yet fully greened lined each ditch, the tops like clutching fingers bared to bones. A small farm appeared on the right, its buildings derelict, paint faded to gray, doors at odd angels.

"Nice neighborhood," Selena murmured.

Wicker Road curved once to the right and then dead-ended in a tangle of brush and mature pines. Evan slowed the van and panned the small turnaround before the forest. A break in the woods opened to the left, and he eased the vehicle forward until they were even with it.

A lane extended in a line through the heart of the forest. Hunched trees with bowed trunks bent over the narrow drive, creating a gloomy archway large enough for a small car to pass through untouched. Evan glanced at Selena and raised his eyebrows.

"Really?"

"Oh yeah," he said, cranking the wheel toward the lane.

Dry branches scraped against the van's body, at times emitting a shriek like nails on a blackboard. He grimaced each time an especially loud screech came from outside, imagining what the paint would look like once they got through. After a minute of slow travel, the encroaching trees retreated and a low structure appeared.

"Shit," Evan said, stopping the car.

Climbing out, he walked to the edge of the plank bridge running across a small, but swift-flowing stream several yards below. Tentatively, he stepped onto the bridge, waiting for it to moan or crack under his feet. It felt solid.

"You're not really considering that, are you?" Selena said, her head poked through the open window of the van. She rolled it up as Evan climbed back inside.

"I think it's fine. It looks sturdy anyway." He glanced at Selena and couldn't help smiling at her beleaguered expression. "If we break through, it's a short fall."

"Oh, in that case, let's go."

He eyed the bridge one last time, then gunned the engine. The van rocketed forward onto the planking and sped across without a bump. Evan grinned out of the side of his mouth but didn't look at Selena. He heard her draw in a breath to say something, but she stopped.

The forest thinned and then disappeared completely, a clearing expanding into a level field, in the middle of which sat a three-story house. A rounded turret graced the front of the building, with black windows set in each level. The top had broken off at some point, leaving the turret with an unfinished look. The rest of the house appeared church-like, its walls smooth, with high-set windows in the shapes of circles and ovals. The siding was dark and rain-beaten and missing boards in a few places. Rotting shingles lay on the ground near the entrance beneath its towered front.

Evan pulled the van within thirty yards of the house and put it in park. The gray clouds above the building seemed to be only feet from the roof.

"You really know how to show a girl a good time," Selena said, looking through the windshield.

"It was either this or the movies," he said, grabbing his notebook from the center console.

They walked across the empty yard to the front door. The porch sagged beneath their feet, and nail heads poked through the wood, waiting to snag clothing or flesh. The oak door stood solid in its frame, with only a small peephole in its surface. Evan stopped before it, resisting the urge to lean forward and peer through the little glass eye. What if something was looking back? He shuddered.

"You're serious about going inside?" Selena asked.

He nodded. "I want to look around, and it doesn't seem like anyone would mind. There wasn't even a gate across the driveway."

He watched her give the house a look and cross her arms.

"You don't have to come inside, you can wait in the car."

"No thanks, I guess I'll take half the blame when we get caught for breaking and entering."

Evan turned the handle on the door, and it swung open without a sound, revealing a dim entryway.

"See, no breaking, just entering."

Selena rolled her eyes.

He stepped inside, smelling the mustiness of the air, the damp scent of rotting wood and paper. Although dark, he could still make out the space they stood within. The entryway stretched toward another room, much larger than the one they stood in now. The place looked gutted. He didn't see furniture or other adornments anywhere. Bland paint curled away from the walls in revolt, and somewhere, he heard a slow drip of water. Plaster and insect carcasses crunched beneath his shoes.

"Charming," Selena said, behind him.

Evan soaked in the atmosphere, imagining the house as it must have looked decades ago. It would have been impressive, especially for the time it was built. They made their way into what looked to be a large dining room with high oval windows set in each wall. An animal nest of some kind lay in one corner, and the house creaked around them with a nudge of wind.

"Apparently clock-making was a good gig back in the day," Evan said.

What could only be a kitchen branched off to the left of the dining room, and straight ahead a stairway ran up and turned toward the second and third levels.

"If we fall through the floor in here and get trapped, no one's going to find us, you know," she said.

He smiled. "That reminds me of a Care Bears episode, did you ever watch them when you were a kid?"

Selena shook her head, trying to avoid crushing any more bugs beneath her shoes.

"This little girl tricks a couple of boys into coming to an abandoned house to look for treasure," Evan said, as he put his weight on the first stair. "They fall through the stairs and end up in this little room in the basement. The girl comes to look for them after the Care Bears tell her she should, and they rescue the boys."

"Well, if we fall through, we'll pray for Care Bears then."

"Shaun likes the Care Bears," Evan said, almost to himself.

The stairs held them as they climbed to the second floor. A hallway with over a dozen rooms branching from it consumed the level, and Evan barely paused before continuing up. A rickety wooden railing leaned toward them as they neared the third floor, and he had to push it out of the way for them to pass. At the top of the stairs, a single door stood closed, with only a dark bathroom taking up the space to the right, the single leg of a claw-foot tub poking into view.

"This is their room," Evan said. "This is where they found her."

He couldn't keep the excitement out of his voice. Reaching out to the doorknob, he found that his fingers trembled when he touched the cold metal. Without waiting any longer, he turned the handle and pushed, the door swinging open with a squawk.

The room was enormous, taking up most of the third floor. Stained hardwood floors that would've been luxuriant ninety years ago were dark with water and time. The walls, once covered with some sort of decorative paper, lay bare, studs showing through the plaster like bones peeking from torn flesh. A ring of windows lined the far wall in the round shape of the turret, which made up that part of the room, and only one was shattered. A single painting, its image obscured by the damp conditions, hung on the left wall. Evan walked toward it, checking the floor as he did.

Selena let out a small gasp behind him. He turned, sure that one of her feet had fallen through or some type of animal startled her. Instead she faced the right wall, with one hand close to her mouth. Evan started to ask her what was wrong, but he followed her gaze and stopped dead in his tracks.

The shadow of the grandfather clock was on the wall.

Fear bred of impossibility rushed through him, starting in his chest and flowing outward like cold water running through his arteries.

"What is that?" Selena asked, her hand still close to her lips.

Evan walked forward, forcing away the shock. As he neared, he saw that the shape on the wall matched the clock's outline perfectly. The height and width were both right. The edges of the shadow weren't crisp lines but faded, elongated, and jagged. Reaching out, he stretched toward the dark silhouette.

"Evan, don't," Selena whispered.

He looked over his shoulder and saw Selena's sculpted eyebrows bunched together. She shook her head.

"Don't."

"It's okay," he said, and placed his hand on the rough wall.

Nothing happened. He almost expected something to, but his fingers merely skimmed the dusty surface, making a rasping sound. He studied the shadow for over a minute before stepping back to take in its full form again. This was where the clock had stood years and years ago.

"It looks like it's scorched," he said, the resonance of his voice hollow and weak in the large room.

"Scorched? Like there was a fire?"

He frowned and leaned forward, rubbing the edge of the stain with his fingers. They came back with only dust on them.

"There's no soot coming off it, though I don't know if there'd be any left after ninety-some years."

"That's really creepy," she said, sidling up next to him.

Her shoulder brushed his, and a tremor of heat raced down his arm. Ignoring the sensation, Evan stepped forward again and traced the outline.

"Have you ever seen pictures of Hiroshima and Nagasaki after the atomic bombs were dropped?" he asked.

"No, why?"

"The heat and radiation were so intense that the shadows of objects were burned into walls behind them."

Evan stepped back, still looking at the dark striations along the edges of the shadow, their lines like brushstrokes of midnight. He stared at the center of the shape until Selena touched his arm.

"What does this mean?"

"I don't know. This isn't what I expected to find."

"What did you expect?"

"I'm not sure. Something, but not this."

He walked away from the spot, pausing to examine the floor in one corner before moving to the windows. The view of the forest and field surrounding the house was breathtaking, but something looked off. It took him a few seconds to realize what it was. The grass and trees closest to the house were dead. In an almost perfect circle around the building, the foliage looked brown and dismal. When they'd entered the house on the ground level, the effect hadn't been noticeable, but from a higher vantage point, it became obvious.

Tearing his eyes away from the spectacle below, Evan moved along the wall, trying to process the clock's shadow and the lack of growth outside. His shoulder caught something hard as he walked, and when he turned to look, he saw that the corner of the painting had snagged his shirt. He unhooked the cloth, expecting the painting to shift, but it didn't. He reached out and tried to move the picture, but it stayed firmly in place.

"Glued or something."

He looked closer at the painting, with its running lines that once might have been a graceful depiction of something in nature. A hole sat in the middle like a black eye forever watching the room. Evan put his finger against the hole's edges. It looked as though someone had shot the painting with a gun.

"What?" Selena asked. She stood by the doorway gazing longingly back down the stairs.

"I said this picture is glued or—"

His tongue stilled as his eyes hovered on the lower right side of the painting. He reached up and, with care, rubbed the spot with his thumb.

"Evan, I don't mean to sound like a wuss, but I'm starting to get a little freaked out. Can we go?"

He nodded, his eyes still locked on the words etched in the painting. "Yeah, let's go. I think I got all I need here."

Even in the wan light, the name stood out in ink that hadn't suffered the span of years. He read it one more time to be sure he wasn't seeing things, then turned toward the doorway, giving the clock's shadow one last look.

# 14

"Yay, Shaun! You did it."

Becky clapped her hands and watched Shaun's face light up as he looked at the finished puzzle before him.

"Yay!" Shaun said.

"You did great. Okay, what's next? Should we have a snack?"

He slapped his hands down on the table and grinned.

"Oh, be careful not to hurt yourself. I'll get us a snack."

Becky rose from the kitchen table and moved to the fridge, her gaze wandering to the gray light outside. The clouds hadn't released a single drop of rain, but they hadn't abated either. If anything, they looked darker. With a quick glance into the living room, she continued toward the refrigerator.

The house didn't seem so spooky after being in it a while. She'd almost turned back before getting to the island, her childhood fears becoming more pronounced as the boat pushed her closer and closer to the Fin. As kids, she and her friends had floated near the island on inner tubes and rafts, daring one another to set foot on land. There had been a running wager: fifty dollars to whoever actually did it. No one ever collected on the bet, and now she couldn't remember who, if anyone, had held the money.

Shaking her head and smiling a little at the memory, Becky picked up a cereal bar from the counter then pulled the fridge door open and scanned the contents. She grabbed a juice box for Shaun, then paused, her hand hovering over a half gallon of chocolate milk.

*No, that's why Greg isn't with you anymore, remember?*

She sighed and settled for a low fat yogurt instead.

A gloom, which had nothing to do with the weather or her location at the moment, descended over her as they ate at the table. She stabbed her spoon into the yogurt as though it were the culprit of her unhappiness.

"Men are shallow, Shaun. Don't grow up to be shallow, okay?"

Shaun swallowed his bite of cereal bar, his eyes large. "'Kay."

"You're such a sweetie, you know that?"

He smiled, his teeth covered with bits of the bar. Becky laughed and helped him with a sip of juice.

A dog whined behind the basement door.

Becky froze, her hand trembling enough that the straw pulled away from his lips.

"More?" Shaun asked, signing the word too.

"Shhh, hold on," Becky said.

She stared at the door for almost a minute, sure that she'd been mistaken about what she heard. The Tormers didn't have a dog—at least, Evan hadn't mentioned it.

"Do you have a dog?" she asked, her eyes still on the door.

"Da," Shaun said, pointing at the dog in the puzzle.

"Yep, that's right. Do you have one? Downstairs?"

Shaun's brow furrowed, and he looked at the puzzle. "Da?"

The whine came again, this time farther away from the door. It filtered up through the floorboards beneath their feet. The keen of it raised the hairs on Becky's arms, bringing to mind images of an animal hurt or dying. Was that why Evan said she wouldn't need to go downstairs? Because he had a mistreated dog down there?

She stood, the sound of her chair sliding across the floor akin to the wailing below. A part of her wanted to stay upstairs, but another part, larger and kinder, couldn't stand the sound of an animal in pain.

"I'm going to be right back, okay?" Becky said, placing a hand on Shaun's shoulder.

Thoughts of what she would do if she found a beaten or abused pet cascaded through her mind. She would have to call someone, that much she was sure of. She would never turn a blind eye to a child being neglected, and she couldn't ignore a pet in the same situation.

Shaun made an agitated noise behind her, but she didn't turn. Her hand already lay on the doorknob, which was cold. She wrenched the door open, waiting for an injured dog to come racing past her and into the kitchen, but the stairs stood empty. Darkness clung to the steps, and she could barely make out a platform farther down. Her hand found a switch inside the stairway, but when she flicked it upward, no light bloomed below. At that moment she nearly shut the door. She hadn't heard anything really, and Evan seemed like a nice man who loved his son, not the kind that would lock away a tortured dog.

As she began to shut the door, the dog whined again down in the dark. The sound was so full of anguish her heart ached. She could already feel its fur beneath her fingers and its grateful tongue licking her face.

Becky stopped on the landing, only then realizing she'd traveled down the stairs to get there. The black of the basement looked like swirling ink before her eyes. She'd never encountered darkness so thick. Not even when her cousins locked her in a closet when she was six. The gap beneath the door had let a little light in, enough to spur hope of getting out.

But now, her breath was trapped in her chest. She stepped forward, finding the next stair with her outstretched foot. Her hands groped before her, and she imagined what she would do if something reached out and touched her fingers. She would die, she knew it in her heart. There would be no scream, or even time to register the pure terror; she would simply drop, dead as a swatted fly.

Instead of the slimy touch of something unimaginable, her hand brushed a wooden post. Following it down, mostly for support, she felt the edges of an electrical box, and after an excruciating beat, the switch flipped up, coating the basement with dim light.

Becky stood motionless on the steps, her fingers pressing the switch up as though it might snap down on its own. A doll stood near the bottom of the stairs, its lifeless blue eyes gazing across the room. If they'd been trained on her, she might've screamed, losing all will to venture further. A few boxes and an old desk sat to her right, but the object at the far end of the space was what held her attention.

The biggest grandfather clock she had ever seen stood there, its hulking three-towered bulk taking up most of the wall. Its black finish looked like fabric cut from a midnight sky, and its face seemed to stare at her, pinning her to the spot on which she wavered.

"Puppy?"

Her voice sounded weak and small. The word died so quick in the basement air she wasn't sure she'd even said it.

"Hello? Are you hurt?"

A quiet whimper came from the other end of the room, and Becky squinted beneath a makeshift worktable set up in front of the clock. Shadows cloaked the area, and she couldn't see if anything lay there.

"It's okay, I'm not gonna hurt you."

She waited for the jingle of a collar or another noise, but none came. She moved down the last few stairs and onto the basement floor. The air was definitely cooler down here, and it smelled. What was the smell? Something sharp and acrid but organic. She'd smelled it before.

Blood.

"Are you hurt?" Becky said, forcing herself to walk toward the table.

She ignored the sensation of being watched, and completely struck down the idea that the clock was the one watching. A clock watching. She nearly let out a strangled laugh through her tightened throat but cut it short.

The dog whimpered again, and she tried to make out its form under the table. A dark shape lay there, but it looked wrong somehow.

An overwhelming urge to backpedal to the stairs hit her like a bat to the head.

*You should run.*

Instead, she took another step forward and squatted by the table to examine the darker shadow. Becky placed her hands on the floor and leaned forward, trying to make out the shape of the dog.

Something wet touched her fingers, and when she looked down, she saw why the form beneath the table looked so strange.

The pool of blood that she'd thought was a dog rolled toward her, a black puddle moving like quicksilver. Becky pulled her hand up, revulsed, her face crumpling. She opened her mouth to scream—she had to, there would be no getting around it now—

but the dog whined again, louder this time, and she realized where the sound came from.

From inside the clock.

"No," she gasped.

Her muscles, the ones she'd meant to work on and tone up for Greg so he wouldn't leave her for someone thinner, shook, and her attempt at standing resulted in falling flat on her ass. Her air left her, and all at once she was a child again, lying on her back beneath the weeping willow she'd been climbing until a branch broke and released her to the cruel arms of gravity. A small amount of air whistled into her lungs, and it was this sound she thought she heard as she tried to crab-walk backward. But when her breath heaved back out, the noise continued, drawing her eyes upward.

The three bare light bulbs were slowly unscrewing themselves.

"No," Becky said, this time getting some force behind the word, like an admonition to the turning bulbs.

The bulb closest to the stairs dropped free of its fixture, winking out like a falling star before exploding in slivers of glass behind her. Becky yelped and stopped moving backward, a painful spine of glass poking into her palm. She watched in horror as the next bulb in line finished unscrewing and plummeted to the cement floor.

Darkness moved in closer, like something alive and ready to pounce the second the light vanished. Far away, she heard Shaun call out for her upstairs. Her arms shook, trying to hold her upper body up. Tears slid down her cheeks, but it was like watching someone else cry. The last light twisted with agonizing slowness, drawn out by an unseen hand, but it wasn't this that held her attention.

Becky stared ahead, her eyes bulging as the grandfather clock's middle door swung open, and the last light bulb fell, shattering on the floor.

# 15

Evan slowed the van to a crawl and read the fire number poking from the bushes beside the country road.

Checking his notes, he saw the number matched, and turned the vehicle onto the driveway. No tar or gravel covered the drive, unlike most of the other homes he'd passed on the way out of Mill River. After dropping Selena off in front of a low office building a short distance from the park, he'd taken Main Street north, leaving the quaintness of town behind for the truly rural feeling that only wilderness can bring. The road wound around massive stands of pines, their reaching branches forever green against the marbled sky, and beside Long Lake at times, before the water ran out and the vegetation of spring took over completely.

It hadn't taken long to find Crux Drive, and Evan kept checking the clock, not wanting to be gone from Shaun more than a few hours. He'd actually driven past Cecil Fenz's driveway at first, because there was no mailbox at the head of the trail. Now, as he bumped through the dense woods, the gray light from above dimming further amongst the budding trees, he wondered if the directions on his phone were correct. The narrow drive twisted twice, hard, like a bend in a river, before straightening out again. The van traveled up a short hill, and then the cover broke, a yard and house coming into view before him.

The house surprised him, not only because it was such a contrast to the one he'd just left but because it didn't look like the home of a recluse. It was two stories and wide, a covered front porch adorning its front. The roof drew his eyes upward, with its slatted tile shingles and curved peaks. The eaves were delicately carved, ornamental wood, and it became apparent when he parked the van close to the house that the designs were constellations. A small garage stood next to the house, humble in its low shape, and a tilled patch of earth, nearly fifty yards square, sat beyond the garage, neatly placed stakes marking rows in the dirt.

Evan shut the van off and waited for a moment in the quiet. He looked for some movement behind the opaque windows or a sign that he'd been spotted, but none came. The painting in the Kluge mansion floated in his mind's eye, and he breathed deep a few times, calming the nervous tension that hummed inside him. He grabbed his cell phone and climbed out of the van.

The cool afternoon air bit into his neck as he walked up the steps and across the porch, his feet thunking on the boards. He wished it would rain and get it over with; for some reason, the feeling of waiting for it to happen was almost too much. He raised a hand to knock on the front door, but a voice filtered out from behind it, startling him, his knuckles still inches from the wood.

"What do you want?"

It was the same voice from the phone but with an edge to it. Evan wondered if there was a gun pointed at him right now.

"My name is Evan Tormer, I called you a few days ago. I just have some questions."

"Go away, you're trespassing."

Even though the words sounded menacing, he could still hear a strange lilt to the woman's voice, something cultured, foreign.

"Please, I won't take much of your time."

"You'll take none of it. You'll get in your car and go while you still can."

The metallic click of a cocking gun met his ears. The fear of being shot by this strange woman in the middle of nowhere became overridden by the questions that plagued him, and before he could stop himself, he spoke.

"This is about your mother, Bella."

Evan waited, the threat of rain no longer a concern, but the anticipation of a bullet punching through the door became almost too much to take. The seconds ticked by, agonizing in their unending length, and then a new sound came from inside, one that surprised him. Several locks snapped, and the door cracked open enough for him to see a gray eye surrounded by parchment-like skin peer out.

"Who are you?"

This time he heard a touch of curiosity in her voice.

"I'm looking for information, information about a grandfather clock. It was built by Abel Kluge. I know your mother knew him."

The eye studied him, ran up and down his frame before the door slammed shut. The hope growing in his chest flickered and died. But before he could decide whether to call out to her again or give up, another snap came from the door and it opened fully, revealing the woman standing there.

The top of Cecil Fenz's head barely came to his shoulder, though it wasn't because of stooping or a bent spine on her part. She stood straight, dignified, with her shoulders thrown back, not rounded as he'd expected. She had silver hair, the color of the clouds over the house, which draped down her back in a ponytail. Her face had small features with articulate eyebrows that reminded him of the precise carvings in her eaves. She wore a painter's smock and gray slacks. In her right hand, she gripped a large revolver, not pointed at him, but not at the ground either.

"Speak fast and clear, and if this is any kind of trick, things will not end well," Cecil said.

Evan didn't doubt her a bit.

"I'm staying at the house on the island, the Fin. The clock is in the basement. I started off wanting to write an article about it, about its history, but now ..." He shifted and glanced into the woods surrounding the house. "Now I need to know."

Cecil studied him for another moment, then let the gun point fully at the floor. "It'll rain soon, come inside before it does."

She stepped aside, and Evan moved past her, into a comfortable foyer lined with paintings on each wall and wooden benches. Cecil shut the door and locked it.

"I haven't had another person in my house for five years, and it would've been more if the electrical panel hadn't shorted out." Cecil walked past him, her slippers slapping against the wood floor as she went. "I pride myself in being able to fix most things. Saves money, saves time." She gave him a disdainful look over her shoulder. "Saves conversation."

"I'm sorry to intrude," Evan said, following her into a warm kitchen with floor-to-ceiling windows and a long breakfast bar at its center. "I got your name from the twins in town, Arnold and Wendal—"

"Peh!" Cecil swung her hand through the air in a violent motion. "Insolent old men have nothing to do besides meddle in others' affairs and rest their sagging bottoms in chairs all day."

Evan couldn't help but smile at the old woman's vehemence. She turned on her heel and went to an industrial-looking stove, where she banged a pan onto the top and began to heat water.

"You like coffee?"

"Yes, that would be great."

"Good, because coffee and wine are all I drink, and it is too early for wine." Cecil's hand's worked fast in the cupboards and drawers, but her eyes remained on the clouds outside. "But I may regret that later."

Within a few minutes, she handed him a cup of coffee the color of tar poured from a brass pot that chugged merrily on the stove.

"This is the only way to make coffee, everything else is barbaric."

Her slight accent became more noticeable, and Evan paused, his cup halfway to his mouth.

"You're French?"

Cecil shot him a glance and then drank a sip of coffee. "Half. My mother came from France, my father was English, but born here." She looked around the kitchen and shook her head. "The kitchen is no place for talk. Only gossip and food is made in kitchens."

She led the way out of the room through an archway that opened up into a sitting room with an elegant glass table over ten feet long and several overstuffed leather couches. Every wall in the room held at least two pieces of art, and all had the same sublime look to them, their colors meshed and flowing in brushstrokes both bold and gentle. Evan studied the painting closest to him, a beautiful scene set beside a waterfall with stones of all colors bathing in its swirling pool. A boy lay on his side, dragging a flower in the flowing water, his eyes on the sky above him.

"I call that one *A Day's Dream*, for nothing like it could exist in this world," Cecil said, as she settled into a comfortable-looking chair.

"You painted this?"

"I painted everything in this house. Call me egotistical, but I like my paintings more than anything else I've seen."

Evan took a drink of his coffee and felt a disconsolate wave wash over him, knowing that he'd been drinking swill labeled as "coffee" up to this point in his life.

"That's amazing," he said, then took another sip.

Cecil nodded. He set his cup down on the glass table and sank into the couch nearby. He folded his hands, then refolded them, not knowing how to begin. Cecil saved him the trouble by speaking first.

"So you've seen it."

It wasn't a question but a condemnation.

"Yes, I happened on it as soon as we moved in."

"'We'?"

"My son, Shaun, and I. We're house-sitting for a friend who owns the island."

Cecil said nothing, only watched him.

"I didn't know what to think at first."

"And you still don't, that's why you came here, correct?"

"Yes."

Cecil sighed and looked down at her coffee. "My mother came from a village outside of Paris. She spent her first fifteen years there before her father shipped her off to America, to a better life." Cecil made a disgusted look, then continued. "She moved in with her aunt in Wisconsin, a cruel woman who drove her out of the house almost as fast as she'd taken her in. My mother wandered. For a while she worked as a pastry chef's assistant in a small bakery, until he died of a stroke. After that, she begged for change and rode short distances on a railroad. But after almost being raped and killed, she took a job cleaning and cooking at the house you've no doubt just come from. That's the only way you would've known my mother's name."

Evan nodded. "The painting."

"That was her true calling, the art that made several men from her country famous. She spent every free moment either drawing or painting on anything she could find. Her hand was true, and her mind had an inner vision most others can only dream of."

"Apparently she passed her gift on to you," Evan said, motioning to the walls.

Cecil shook her head, slowly, deliberately. "I received but a fraction of what she possessed. If you could've seen her work, if you could've seen that painting in the room before—"

She stopped, her small face crinkling with lines.

"What happened there?"

His initial excitement at opening up a channel for answers wasn't as strong. Something dulled it, clouded over it like the weather outside cloaked the sky.

"To understand what happened, you must first understand what Abel Kluge was."

"What was he?"

"A madman, and a cruel one at that. If he hadn't needed a maid that could also cook when my mother came calling, he would have turned her away, battered and bruised, no matter. He was not unfamiliar with women looking like that anyway, since he sometimes administered beatings to his wife as well as the rest of the staff."

Evan waited, not knowing what to say, and decided not to say anything, in hopes that Cecil would keep talking.

"You see, Mr. Tormer, work was scarce in the early 1900s, and an employer that paid steadily was even more of a rarity. The staff at Kluge House got room and board, pay, and Abel's knuckles if he became displeased with any of them." Her eyes trailed to the window and grew distant. "I have no doubt my mother would have died there had she not met my father."

"He worked there too, I'm assuming?"

Cecil turned back toward him and dipped her chin once. "Yes, he was the groundskeeper and the head butler. He and my mother fell in love shortly after she arrived there, and they began to make plans to leave the awful place as soon as they could afford to, but the money didn't ever seem to add up and they were forced to stay."

Cecil finished her coffee and scooted forward to the edge of her chair, pensive, staring into his eyes. Evan could see the old woman was working something out inside her head.

"I suppose that woman was the final piece of the bizarre puzzle assembled in that home," Cecil said quietly.

"Allison Kaufman," Evan said.

Cecil half smiled, without humor, and he decided it was a terrible thing on her tired features.

"I see you've been somewhat successful in your research, or deductions."

"It was the only thing that fit," Evan said. "Two people die and one disappears on the same day in a small town? Not likely."

Cecil shook her head, like a pendulum. "Not likely at all. If Abel Kluge was a madman, Allison was his equal. She was orphaned young and grew up in a small church south of Mill River. No matter how strict the nuns were back then, they were no replacement for parents. She turned to mischief at an early age— stealing, drinking, even prostitution before she met Abel. From what I know, she showed up at the gates one day, long, brown hair most of the way down her back, eyes conniving. Something about her must have flipped a switch in him, for she was immediately given a room, and was his mistress within days."

"Right in front of his wife?" Evan asked, taken aback.

Cecil gave him the half smile again. "Oh yes. By then, Larissa wasn't much more than a husk of her former self. He'd hollowed her out with beatings and mistreatments for so long, I'm not sure she even realized what was going on."

Cecil sat back in her chair, her spine still rigid, as if the telling of the history wouldn't let her relax.

"But Allison, on the other hand, put up with nothing from him. In a matter of months, most of the staff answered to her as the lady of the house. My mother told me some nights the staff was unable to sleep, for the sounds of their carrying-on in the upstairs bedroom would filter down through the house, sounds of sex, pain, hissing, screaming. I shudder to imagine what really went on in those rooms."

Cecil paused, pursing her lips while her eyes found the painting over Evan's shoulder.

"My mother and father lived in constant fear of them, for Allison only heightened the violence and mistreatments that went on there. In fact, it appeared that her cruelty rivaled Abel's in many ways. My mother said that more than once a servant was randomly called to her room, strapped down, and then whipped within an inch of his or her life, as Abel and Allison took turns behind the leather strap."

"God, why?" Evan said, feeling a lurch of revulsion in his stomach.

"Because they were able to, Mr. Tormer. I assume it made them feel powerful, as we crush a spider that crawls onto our pillow. They were merely full of hate and needed someone to unleash it on. But fate, it seems, is the great equalizer. Nothing in this world goes unnoticed, no deed, good or bad, remains unbalanced. Less than a year after coming to Kluge House, Allison became sick. It was soon clear she had the consumption."

"Tuberculosis."

"Yes. It was still a very prominent disease in those days, taking bloody bites out of the population whenever it could. No one knows how Allison caught it or why no one else became infected, but it sealed all three of their fates."

Evan's heart picked up speed. A picture formed in his mind, the room that he and Selena had stood in rearranging itself into a scene he could almost touch.

"He built the clock for her, didn't he?" Evan asked, knowing he was right.

"Yes. My mother told me he was completely devastated by her prognosis, which deteriorated each week, so he started to work in the basement of the house. He spent hours upon hours down there, and the staff was forbidden to enter, to see what he slaved over day and night. When he wasn't working, he was at Allison's bedside, watching her, or contacting every doctor within six counties to come and see her condition. But there was nothing anyone could do."

Cecil grimaced as though tasting something bitter.

"The day Allison fell into a coma, he had four men haul the clock up from the basement. One of them was my father. That clock ... No one wanted to touch it, for anyone could see it was an evil thing, unnatural and ugly even in the light of day. They placed it in Abel and Larissa's bedroom, against the wall."

"I saw where it stood, there was a shadow still there."

"I don't know what that is, but it is no shadow. That night the staff lay awake in their beds, with a storm roaring outside the windows and Abel's voice coming from upstairs, chanting words that weren't words. Near morning, the storm broke and a single scream came from the room—Larissa's last sound on this earth.

My father ran to the room, gripping a pistol, ready to do what needed to be done if Abel had finally gone too far, but when he burst inside, it was already too late. Larissa and Allison were dead, and Allison's hair had gone completely white."

The entire room seemed to shift a little, and Evan swallowed, trying to push away the image of the long, white hair in the dustpan.

"But what chilled his blood more than anything, my mother told me much later, was that clock, sitting there against the wall, all of its hands running *backward*."

Evan blinked. "Backward?"

"Yes."

"But what was he trying to accomplish with it?"

"Only he and God know that for sure, but one night when I was very young, I heard my father and mother speak of that morning in whispers they thought I couldn't hear. My father said he was sure that Abel had tried to reverse Allison's condition somehow with the clock."

"Reverse? Like turn back time?" Evan said.

He noticed his voice sounded far away, like it came from another room in the house, and the words in Bob's shaking hand kept surfacing from the deep tidewaters of his mind: *IcangobackIcangobackIcangoback*.

"Like I said, Mr. Tormer, he was a madman, and there is nothing more dangerous than a lunatic in love."

"But how did they die? The article I read said there weren't any marks on Larissa's body and only a small pool of blood on the floor."

"Of that, we know the same. There weren't any weapons present, nor was there any trauma done to either of them. It seems Abel may have sliced himself on the center pendulum, for they found a small amount of blood on its edge and inside the clock."

Evan let the information soak into him. The coffee had elevated his senses and sharpened his thoughts, but the harder he tried to assemble the facts into something cohesive, the more they swam into a blurry jumble like Bella's painting in the room. As if reading his mind, Cecil spoke.

"She told me it was a field of flowers, daisies." Cecil glanced at him. "The painting. She'd given it to Abel and Larissa before Allison arrived at the house, perhaps to put her and my father in better favor."

"Did it?"

"No, but Abel knew talent when he saw it, and hung it in their room nonetheless."

"It was glued to the wall—why did he glue it to the wall?"

Cecil cast her eyes downward, grimacing again. "It wasn't, it was simply hung there. But the morning after my father found them, it was stuck in place like someone had welded it."

"That doesn't make any sense," Evan said, rubbing his forehead.

"Has any of this tale made sense, Mr. Tormer?"

"Please call me Evan—and no, it hasn't." He looked at her. "But I believe you."

"I appreciate the sentiment, but I can't say I'm glad you came calling today. I prefer to forget the things I've told you, and you would think I'd be able to at my age, but I don't—I can't." Cecil stared hard into his eyes. "That abomination in your basement isn't natural, Mr. Tormer. It is a man-made cancer that poisons everything it touches. My father was the first to enter that room, the first to see, only moments after, what happened there. I was seven when he died of some strange disease the doctors had no name for. He simply withered away, a black ichor spreading beneath his skin until he looked burned from within. I can still hear the agony in his voice as he died, intertwined with my mother's cries."

Cecil's eyes jittered slightly, and Evan wondered, not for the first time, if he'd made a mistake coming here. The woman before him, so stolid moments before, now looked unhinged.

"She went insane after my father passed, slowly, one day at a time. I cared for her, and she told me these things before she lost her mind completely." Cecil's jaw stiffened, the muscles bulging beneath her thin skin. "And do you know what? She still painted every day, but the only thing that ever graced her canvas after my father died was that fucking *clock*!"

Evan stood and bumped the glass table with his knee, spilling his half-empty cup of coffee. On the transparent table the liquid looked like blood, running in lines toward Cecil, who vibrated with a manic energy in her chair, watching him with blazing eyes.

"Destroy it, Mr. Tormer. Break it, burn it, do whatever you must before it takes everything from you like it did to me!"

Evan opened his mouth, but the only thing that came out was a small moan, barely audible even to his own ears. Then he turned and walked for the door; he had to get out of the house. His nerves were wound into a bundled heap of utter panic that urged him to run. He glanced over his shoulder, sure he would see Cecil following close behind him, her knurled hands raised like claws overhead. But the kitchen and archway were empty.

The cool air was a blessed welcome against his skin, and he slammed the door shut behind him and finally gave in to the pleadings to run. He jogged to his car, and after climbing inside, took deep, cleansing breaths and waited for the boiling anxiety to abate. After a minute it did, but when he reached to start the van, he noticed his hands still trembled.

An electronic chirp issued from the backseat, causing his slowing heart to stutter again. Evan twisted, fumbling for the computer case and dragging it onto his thighs. When he opened the laptop, the strong Wi-Fi signal in the upper right-hand corner caught his attention. He glanced at the house again, then lowered his eyes to the email that had caused the signal of new messages. The first email was from Jason. Evan clicked on it, the mere sight of his friend's address a comfort.

*Ev, I spoke to Justin about the article. He said that's not something he's looking for right now, but he'd be happy to hear any other ideas you have. Sorry, man. Hope you and Shaun are well. Call me soon. – Jason*

He reread the words several times and his shoulders slumped. A different idea? After everything that he'd learned?

*But what have you learned?*

The voice sounded snide and superior.

*You found the ravings of an obviously insane man and brought up some of the town's oldest, dirtiest laundry. Sordid affairs and possibly murder, but to what end? You're going to solve a mystery that's over ninety years old? Oh, wait, I see, there's something else you're digging for. That little idea that came into your mind the moment you read the article about the hit-*

*and-run, and now the old bat in the house said the words that have been percolating in that fucked-up brain of yours out loud. You think it's possible? You really think it is? Then if you do, you're more disturbed than ever.*

"Shut up," Evan growled, gritting his teeth.

His phone chimed from the center console. He jerked in his seat as if it were a biting snake. A slightly familiar cell-phone number graced the display.

"Hello?" he answered.

A short puff of breath came from the other end, and then silence.

A cold dump of adrenaline entered his system, flooding his veins with a cocktail of weakness and dread.

"Becky?"

"Ahhhhhhhhhhhhhh."

Becky's voice came out less than a whisper, like dead leaves sliding on concrete. The sound rolled a wave of goose bumps across his skin.

The call ended, leaving him with dead air in his ear.

Frantically he punched the number into the phone and waited. It went straight to voice mail.

"Shit!"

He dialed Becky's number again while slamming the van into drive. As he rounded the turn and headed down the driveway in a flurry of dust, he threw a look at the house, barely noticing the curtains beside the front door shift back into place.

# 16

Evan held the pontoon's throttle wide open.

The steely water reflecting the sky rose in short waves that the craft burst through and surged over. The wind, mostly calm before, now pushed and tugged at his shirt, causing him to shiver with each gust. He hadn't been able to reach Becky again on the hurried ride back to town, and he'd lost track of how many times he'd hit the redial button.

The Fin grew and grew on the lake's choppy surface, and Evan strained his eyes, squinting against the wind to see the house through the trees.

No fire. That was good. Becky's boat was still tied to the dock. That was good too—she hadn't run off and left for some strange reason, and she hadn't taken Shaun anywhere.

*Please, please, please let him be okay.*

As the details of the island became clearer, he saw that two figures waited on the beach, one seated and the other standing a short distance away.

"Thank God," Evan said, relief washing over him in a warm wave.

He saw Shaun's small form nestled in his chair. The boy was moving, but something was wrong. Shaun wasn't wearing a coat, or even a sweatshirt, and his feet dangled down low enough that the washing waves rushed up and covered them. Becky stood a few steps away, staring at Evan as he approached.

"What the fuck?" Evan said, cutting the motor down to guide his way to the dock.

He drifted the last few yards and let the front end of the craft bump into the planking. In two strides he stood on the dock, and looped a rope around the pontoon's railing. Then he was moving again, anger filling the void left by panic.

"What the hell's going on here?" he asked, hurrying past Becky to where Shaun sat.

His anger flared brighter when he saw the blue tinge to his son's lips and they way he shook from the cold.

"Fucking shit," Evan said, peeling off his long-sleeved shirt before unstrapping Shaun from his chair. "What do you think you're doing?"

He tugged his shirt over Shaun's head and picked him up. Shaun shivered and pressed his face into Evan's neck. When he turned back toward the water Becky still hadn't moved.

"Hey, I'm talking to you," he said, as he stepped before her.

Becky's half-lidded eyes stared across the lake, toward town. Her lips hung apart, revealing her teeth clenched together, her jaw muscles contracting over and over.

"Becky, are you okay? Are you hurt?" he said, moving closer. "Why did you come down here?"

Shaun shivered against him, and Evan hugged him tighter. With a shaking hand, he reached out and touched the woman's shoulder.

"Becky, come back to the house—"

Her head snapped around so fast Evan expected to hear her spine break. Her eyes were wide, unseeing, looking through him, and her lips peeled back from her teeth even further, in a rictus. Evan yanked his hand back as though touching a hot burner.

"Ahhhhhhhhhhhh."

The sound came from behind Becky's teeth, and her tongue darting wildly between the gaps in them. With slow movements, he retreated up the hill, clutching Shaun.

"Da," Shaun said, into Evan's neck.

"It's okay, buddy, it's okay."

He kept walking backward, his eyes locked on Becky, who continued to stare at the spot where they'd been. "I'll be right back," Evan called down to her, and jogged to the house. Once inside he set Shaun on the couch and began to pile blankets on him.

"What happened, honey? Did she hurt you?"

Shaun gazed at him, his teeth chattering while another shiver coursed through his small body. Evan dug into his pocket for his phone, wondering who he should call. Becky's employer at the hospital? The police? An ambulance?

The sound of a boat engine starting made him look up from his phone.

"No way," he said, walking to the front door.

Becky wasn't standing in her spot near the lake anymore. She was in her father's boat, and as he watched, she cut a short swath and turned the craft toward the opposite side of the lake, accelerating more and more.

Evan stepped out of the house. "Hey! Becky! Becky!"

His yells did nothing to slow her. She piloted the boat away, a V of water gliding in the wake, her back turned toward him. Soon the craft was only a speck dotting the gray waves.

Evan shut the door and walked to the couch, his eyes unfocused. "Let's get you in the tub, buddy."

After checking Shaun's body for marks and welts of any kind and finding nothing, Evan gave him a bath, warming him up. As Shaun splashed and played in the soapy water, he kept replaying Becky's behavior in his mind. What the hell had happened? When he'd left that afternoon, she'd been a normal young woman, capable and trustworthy. What could possibly alter someone so much in a matter of hours?

"Ow?"

Evan came back to himself and realized that the water in Shaun's bath had begun to cool. "Sorry, honey. Let's get you out of there."

After drying him off, Evan set him on the couch, rewrapping him in the blankets again. He sat and stared at his son for a long time, taking in his features. Shaun looked back, grinning from time to time. It was like seeing glimpses of Elle behind a fluttering curtain when he smiled, her lasting gift to him.

"You got your mom's smile, you know that, buddy? I'm so glad I still get to see it." Tears filled his eyes. "I'm sorry I left you." His voice became hoarse, the horrible ideas of what could've been flowing through his mind. "I didn't think anything would happen. I'm sorry you got cold, I'm so sorry you got cold."

"Ky?" Shaun said, his brow furrowing.

"I won't cry," Evan said, wiping at his eyes before leaning forward to kiss him on the brow. As he sat back, he glanced over the back of the sofa.

The basement door was open a few inches.

Evan stood and took a step toward it, waiting for it to fly open all the way, pushed from something behind it. But it stayed motionless. Had it been closed when he left? Yes, he was almost sure.

"I'll be right back, honey," he said over his shoulder.

After grabbing the flashlight from the kitchen, Evan went to the basement door and opened it fully. He flicked the flashlight on, then went down the stairs, playing the light off the treads and walls. Reaching the bottom, he flipped the light switch on, but nothing happened. He tried a few more times, toggling the switch up and down, as fear rose in his guts. Evan illuminated the doll, still facedown where he'd left it, and swept the beam around the space. Nothing looked out of place. He pointed the flashlight at the ceiling, panning it across each of the dark light bulbs. It looked like they'd all blown.

He moved down the last few steps and stopped, turning in a circle. Slowly he swung the beam toward the clock, its darker shade already drawing his attention. It was as he'd left it. Knowing more of its history didn't make him any more comfortable in its presence. Someone once said fear was the result of not understanding something. Standing in the cloying darkness with the clock only feet away, Evan didn't agree.

"Hello?"

The sound of his voice startled him. He hadn't meant to speak. Now he waited, stomach churning, dreading a response.

Silence.

"Da?" Shaun called from the living room.

"Be right there, buddy," he yelled, then turned and headed back up the stairs.

~

Evan made dinner for Shaun and then called the hospital and told the woman in the PCA department about Becky's strange behavior.

"I'll check to make sure she made it home okay," the woman whose name he thought was Marissa said.

"Could you please give me a call back after you talk to her?" he asked, feeding Shaun a bite of hot dog.

"I will, sir."

The phone rang fifteen minutes later, and Marissa told him that Becky had made it to her parents' home and that her father said she wasn't feeling well. Marissa apologized for Becky's behavior and said she would take it up with their administrator.

"That's not necessary, I was just concerned about her. Thank you for calling back."

Evan held the phone for a long time, almost expecting it to ring again, but didn't know why. He wanted to call Selena, but the idea of smothering her with his problems made him put the phone down.

*You took her on a great first date, fella. She'll definitely want to run right out here and have dinner again really soon.*

He smiled.

After putting Shaun to bed, Evan went down to the basement. First, he replaced the dead bulbs with new ones he found in the entryway closet, and made a point of fixing the one going down the stairs. When he unscrewed it and looked at the filament inside, it appeared whole and unbroken. But then again, you never knew with light bulbs. Next, he walked around the basement, telling himself that he wasn't searching it. Searching would mean he was looking for something, and if he was looking for something, what was it? Every so often his eyes would stray to the clock, and he would avert them as Cecil's words came flooding back each time he did: *Destroy it, Mr. Tormer. Break it, burn it, do whatever you must before it takes everything from you like it did to me!*

All at once he remembered the email from Jason. His heart sank, and he stopped moving, standing in the glow of the newer and more powerful bulbs. What point was there to keep digging on the story? Justin didn't want the article. Any effort he made after this would be solely for his own interest.

*And what interest is that?*

Evan found a broom standing against the far wall and began to sweep, something to do while he thought. Maybe Jason didn't explain the central idea well enough to Justin. The article could be excellent, possibly a serial story spread out over several issues of *Dachlund*. If Justin could hear what he'd learned today, there would be no way he could turn him down.

Evan paused and nodded to himself. With few more sweeps, he gathered up the small pile of dust and dirt he'd accumulated into a dustpan and carried it upstairs to deposit in the trash. As soon as the basement door was shut, he brought his laptop to the table and opened it. After only a few minutes of searching his email, he found Justin's office number from the previous time he'd published with him. Normally Jason handled the in-between area of selling an article to the editor in chief, sometimes joking about being his agent, but now there was no choice. This was different.

Evan punched in the number on his cell phone and waited until Justin's voice mail picked up. Clearing his throat, he waited for the beep.

"Justin, this is Evan Tormer. Sorry to bother you, but Jason mentioned you wouldn't be interested in the article about the clock, and I wanted to let you know that I came upon some interesting information today. If you would hear me out, I'd really appreciate it." He licked his lips before continuing. "There's a story here, Justin, something really odd. Give me a call when you can."

Evan left his cell phone number and ended the call, feeling powerful somehow. Maybe it was going over Jason's head, even though his best friend had been the one to introduce him to Justin. Maybe it was being proactive in some small way. He didn't know. All that mattered now was getting the clock running again.

He froze in mid-movement, his hand hovering above the laptop's lid. Had he just thought that? Getting the clock running again?

The article, he needed to get the article running. A cold channel coursed through his stomach like an icy spring river breaking free of winter's grip. It was like the thought hadn't been his, but that was stupid. He'd experienced strange ideas and images drifting off to sleep at night and then coming to, the obscure and peculiar thoughts completely alien to him. But this was different; he was wide-awake.

Evan shook his head. "Long day, lots of activity, that's all."

He closed the laptop and stood, putting the computer away before noting the time. It was late, and he needed sleep. He would tackle this again in the morning.

*Weren't you planning on leaving the island only a short time ago?*

"Shut up," he muttered, and flipped the light off in the kitchen before heading toward his room.

He stopped in the hallway and pushed open Shaun's ajar door. Shaun lay on his side, his light hair sticking up against his pillow. Evan walked into the room and knelt beside the bed, held the soft fingers poking from beneath the quilt.

"I won't ever let you get cold again," he whispered. "You're all I have left. I know I haven't said this before, I don't know why, but Mom didn't want to leave us, honey. She tried, she tried really hard to stay, but she couldn't, and I couldn't do anything to help." His voice shook. He didn't understand where the wellspring came from, only knowing he couldn't stanch it. "I wish we could all be together again, and that this had never happened to you." He traced a finger down the pale scar on Shaun's head. "I dream about it sometimes, our life without everything that happened. Someday we'll be whole again, I promise."

He stroked Shaun's hair one last time and stood, hearing the slight creak of his knees. "Good night, son."

Evan slipped out of the room, closing the door only a little, and got ready for bed. It was early in the morning when sleep took him, and the last coherent words that he thought while drifting off were *tomorrow will be better*.

# 17

Dawn was like something out of a vacation pamphlet.

Sunlight streamed across the lake, coloring the water with shining blazes that hurt the eye when directly looked at. The air held a humid quality that spoke of summer heat, the kind that drove people to the beach and drink beverages from coolers packed to the top with melting ice. The foliage became greener, more alive after the gray of the day before. Evan soaked it all in, his spirits lifting despite waking in a cold sweat that morning.

He didn't remember the dream, only the terror. He came awake to his heart thudding like a dual bass of the metal bands he used to listen to in high school and his legs rubbery, as if he'd run a long distance with something chasing him only a few steps behind. But the morning stripped the feeling away almost at once. After a cup of coffee taken on the porch, the strength returned to his legs, and by his second cup, with Shaun stirring in the other room, he felt completely normal.

As he helped Shaun get dressed, he grasped the boy by his shoulders and peered into his upturned face.

"How about we go fishing again today?"

Shaun grinned but gave him a querying look.

"Fishing, like we did the other day."

His mood dimmed a little when Shaun motioned to the TV in the living room.

"No, not TV. Lake—we're going to go out on the pontoon."

"Pun," Shaun said, raising his arms so Evan could carry him.

"How about boat?"

"Boat!"

"That's good, buddy. Boat, we'll go out in the boat today."

Evan took Shaun to his chair at the table, now washed down from the sand and dirt that had clung to its feet from the night before, and began to make breakfast. As the eggs sizzled in the pan, his attention kept returning to his phone. After dishing up his and Shaun's plates, he finally gave in and dialed Selena's number, amused that he now had it memorized. She answered on the second ring.

"Good morning."

Her voice sounded bright as the sunshine outside, and he smiled, a flutter like a trapped bird tickling his stomach.

"I wasn't sure you'd answer after the wonderful time you had yesterday."

She laughed. "That was nothing compared to my Monday."

"Good, I hope you weren't too put off."

"By an old, creepy house? No, not at all. You should hear the things that people tell me on a day-to-day basis, some of it would make you cringe."

"I bet."

"So is that the only reason you're calling me this morning? To see if I had a good time yesterday?"

Evan chuckled and moved Shaun's plate closer to him.

"Actually, Shaun and I were going to go fishing, and I thought you might like to come. Maybe bring back some memories?"

The line grew quiet, and Evan sat, his spirits falling.

"I'm sorry, I didn't mean to overstep my bounds."

"No, it's not that at all, I'd love to come. It just caught me off guard, that's all. It's the anniversary of my dad's passing."

"Oh God, I'm so sorry, I didn't—"

"It's okay, you didn't know. It's weird that you asked today, that's all. But I can't really think of any better way to spend the day. I always take it off, so I'm free."

"You're sure? You don't have to."

"No, I'll be out within an hour. Fishing's always better in the mornings, you know."

Evan smiled. The girl knew her stuff. "We'll see you soon."

"Bye."

"Bye."

He set the phone down and helped Shaun with a large bite of egg.

"Selena's going to come with us. Is that okay?"

Shaun chewed and stared at him with large eyes that almost always seemed to ask a question. How much did he understand?

Evan scooped up another bite of egg, and Shaun coughed, his eyes widening as he opened his mouth and made a gagging sound.

"Shit, are you okay?" Evan said, leaping to his feet.

All at once the kitchen was too hot, cloying and close. Shaun struggled in his chair and gagged again, spewing out the chewed eggs in a gelatinous clump that fell onto his pants legs.

Terror gripped Evan and he became immobilized by it, crushed in a palm that showed him a future alone, with two graves to visit instead of one.

"Shaun!"

He broke free of the paralysis and unbuckled the chair's straps. Shaun coughed again, a strained, ragged sound that came from deep in his stomach.

*Out of air, he's out of air!*

A barrage of first-aid posters and Red Cross handouts flooded his thoughts as he leaned Shaun forward and slapped his back with a solid whack. Air flew from Shaun's lungs, and to Evan's relief, he gasped some back in. His airway wasn't totally plugged.

Picking him up from the chair, Evan clutched Shaun to his chest, his arms threaded beneath his son's, hands locked over the boy's sternum. Trying to maintain a semblance of control, Evan pulled one, two, three times in rapid succession. With each movement, a thin stream of air jolted from Shaun's lips and he gasped a little back in. A small amount of vomit dribbled out of his mouth when Evan pulled again, and he stopped, sweat coating his entire body.

Would this be how it ended? With a bite of egg and his lack of memory of the Heimlich maneuver? Would this be the day he feared above all others, the day when Shaun would slip away from his frantic grasp, somehow slighting all his measures to keep him safe?

"No," Evan grunted, his eyes tearing up with moisture born of panic and premature grief. *"NO!"*

He spun Shaun over and laid him on his back, kneeling beside him. Shaun heaved in a little air and then gagged, coughing out streams of spittle and mucus.

"Open your mouth, honey, open your mouth," Evan said, forcing his fingers past his son's spasming teeth.

He swiped an index finger to the back of his throat, searching for an obstruction but feeling nothing. Another pass came up empty.

Evan fell back on his ass, pulling Shaun into his lap.

"Open your mouth, Shaun, open it!"

Trying to ignore the wavering alarm of his voice, he pried Shaun's mouth open and looked inside, ready to reach in and grab any soggy chunk of egg that might be there.

Several white strands poked up at the back of his throat, their bright color catching the light.

Evan's face contorted as he reached with two fingers and managed to grab the hairs. With a revulsion so pure it bordered on horror, he pulled the white hairs out of Shaun's mouth, watching their length extend far, much too far, into his son's throat.

"Uhhhhh," Evan moaned, and instantly remembered Becky's incoherent mumblings down by the beach.

He pulled and the hairs kept coming, impossibly long, stretching, catching the natural light of the room until they seemed to shine with a glow of their own.

Just when he thought his arm would not be long enough and he would have to re-grip the hairs, they slid free of Shaun's mouth and hung suspended from the tips of his fingers, limp, like pale parasites. With a cry of revulsion, Evan flicked them away, knowing, somewhere in the deep cellar of his mind where all morbid thoughts were birthed, that the hairs wouldn't fly free of his fingers. They would wrap around his hand, entwine themselves to him, and begin to slither toward his own face, seeking the wet darkness of his mouth.

But they did detach from his fingers. After an almost graceful flight, they landed in a coil on the kitchen floor and flattened there, unmoving. He looked down at Shaun, who breathed fully and deep, tears running from his eyes in streams that tracked sideways toward his temples.

"You're okay, honey, you're okay," he said, clutching his son close in a hug.

The sound of Shaun's heavy but easy breathing was like music to Evan's ears, and he relished it the only way a person who knew the loss of something precious could.

"Da," Shaun sobbed, and Evan held him tighter.

"I'm right here, buddy, you're okay, you're fine."

He rocked him as if he were an infant, for what seemed like hours, his eyes straying to the white hairs from time to time, which shone like threads of snow in the morning sun.

~

"Are you okay?"

Selena's soft voice brought him out of his fugue, and he blinked, sitting up straighter in the pontoon's seat. The sunlight glared off the water, and he felt it tightening the skin on his face. He'd have to be careful not to get burned.

Burned. Burn it. Destroy it.

"I'm great," Evan said, and tried to smile. "Thinking."

"You were miles away."

"Yeah, busy morning."

*Of pulling white hairs that couldn't have been there out of your son's throat—out of his stomach.*

He shook his head, silencing the voice.

"Do you want to talk?" Selena asked, setting her rod against the pontoon's railing.

"You keep trying to do your thing, don't you?"

"Can't shut it off."

"No, I'm fine."

"Is it the article? Is that what's bothering you?"

Shaun kicked his legs out and squealed with delight as the pontoon drifted over a wave. Evan watched him for a moment before he answered, telling himself he wasn't waiting for him to begin choking again.

"Yeah. I got an email from my friend saying the editor wasn't interested in the story."

Selena frowned. "I'm sorry. Is there any other magazine that might buy it from you?"

He shrugged. "Maybe. I'm giving it one last go with him, see if I can convince him it's worth printing."

"So the mystery woman you went to see yesterday wasn't a dead end?"

"No, no, she wasn't."

Evan related the events at Cecil's house to her, as the boat drifted in a lazy line parallel to the nearby shore. When he'd finished, Selena sat quiet, not looking at him for a while.

"And you think she was telling the truth?"

"Definitely. Even if everything she said was made-up, she still believed it. Plus all the pieces seemed to connect."

Selena picked up her rod and twitched it up and down, and Evan once again admired her skill, which outdid his own.

"Is there another interest you have in all this?" she asked, not looking at him.

*Yes.*

"What do you mean?"

"I mean, you seem somewhat fixated on the story. I'm wondering if it has any significance to you other than the article."

"No."

*Liar.*

"I think it's an incredible mystery that no one's heard before."

*You think it can do something impossible, you think it can turn—*

"And one that could secure a future for Shaun and I if someone would pick it up," he said, fighting the voice into silence.

"Okay, I was curious, that's all."

She tipped back in her seat and propped her feet up on the pontoon's rail, giving him a great view of her legs. She glanced at him, the dark sunglasses doing nothing to hide the meaning of the look. Evan turned his head away, hoping the blush on his cheeks would be hidden by the heat of the sun.

The sound of a boat motor drew their attention to a nearby point of land, and a few seconds later a large craft appeared. As it neared, Evan heard the engine slow and saw the familiar form of Jacob at the wheel. The Irishman raised a hand in greeting and steered toward them.

"Oh God, it's him," Selena said in a low voice.

Evan looked at her, surprised. "You know Jacob?"

"Unfortunately. He screwed my dad out of a land deal years ago. He was really rude and cruel about it too. I'm sorry, I can't stand him."

With that, she turned away to fish off the opposite side of the pontoon. Evan was at a loss for words but had no time to ask any more questions, as Jacob idled his Lund sideways to them a dozen yards away.

"Mornin', boyos! I thought 'twas you over here. How're we doin' this mornin'?"

"Great, how about yourself?" Evan said. The awkwardness of Selena's words still hung over him.

"Oh, not bad, not bad. Sorry bit of tragedy back in town, though."

"Oh yeah, what happened?"

"Young gal by the name of Tram died at her own hand last night."

A strange humming filled Evan's ears, as if his head had been thrust underwater. The pontoon lurched sickeningly beneath him, and his gorge rose like an elevator. Jacob said something else, and Evan had to struggle to keep his head up. He felt like lying down, even on the moving floor of the boat.

"Are you all right, son?" Jacob said, throwing his boat in gear for a moment, to keep even with them.

"Yeah," Evan managed to say. Shaun squealed loudly, the sound cutting through the hum of Jacob's motor and into Evan's eardrum. "I'm sorry, I missed what you said before."

"Oh, I jest said the poor gal must've been disturbed fer a time."

"How?" Evan asked, the breath in his lungs hot, way too hot.

Jacob shifted his eyes in Shaun and Selena's direction. "I'm not sure it's proper for present company."

"It's fine," Evan said, with more of an edge to his voice than he meant.

Jacob looked doubtful but spoke above the rattle of the motor. "Word is she climbed out onta her parents' roof and fell headfirst onta the drive. I suppose it could be an accident, but that's not what people're sayin'. Horrible business. I know her father quite well. Tragic, so young."

Evan nodded, his stomach almost boiling. It was all he could do to keep the vomit from racing up and out of his mouth.

"Well, I jest wanted ta say hi. Sorry ta come bearin' such awful news. You have a good day. Catch me a fish, Shauny!"

After a final wave, Jacob gunned the engine and raced off across the lake, spangles of water flying up from his boat's prow and catching the sun like dropped jewels. Evan set his rod down and propped his face in one hand. His arm shook, and he thought he still might lose the battle to keep his breakfast down. He needed to rest and forget yesterday, forget the glassy stare in Becky's eyes and the sound that came from her mouth.

"My God," Selena said. She faced him again, her rod tied up and propped against an empty seat. "That was the girl who did PCA work for you yesterday?"

He could only nod.

"You said she acted really strange when she left?"

"Yeah," he croaked.

Raising his face from his palm, he gazed across the lake to where the island sat, a dark clump rising up out of the water like a tumor. He felt unhinged. Everything looked lurid and fake in the sunlight. He wanted to step out of the pontoon and tear a hole in it all, rip open the water, slash the sky so he could look beyond and see the dark, clicking gears that drove everything in a mockery of life.

"The hospital said she was safe, that she didn't feel well but was safe," Evan said. "I let it go at that, didn't give it another thought."

"Look, you can't blame yourself for this. I'm sure there's an explanation. People who do things like this usually contemplate it for a long time before carrying it through. I'm guessing you'll find out that she was a deeply disturbed person."

Evan tried to recall anything that Becky had said or done before her episode that would fit the criteria of a demented mind.

*She went in the basement, that's all it took.*

He wrapped up his fishing pole and made sure Shaun was secure in his seat.

"I think we'd better go home."

Selena pressed her lips into a thin line and moved around Shaun, to where he sat. She knelt near his feet and placed her hands on his thighs.

"It wasn't your fault, Evan. You had no idea she was capable of something like this. I'm just glad Shaun is okay. Someone who's that troubled couldn't possibly be a good caretaker. I know you feel responsible in some way, but you're not. Take it from a professional—I've dealt with multiple people who were suicidal, along with surviving family members and friends of those who killed themselves. Every survivor has the same guilt. They ask themselves, could I have done something different? Could I have prevented it? The answer is almost always no. If someone means to kill him- or herself, they find a way. Period."

Evan looked down at her, her hair tossing in the light breeze. Her pretty face was upturned to his.

"I told her not to go down in the basement," he whispered.

Selena leaned back from him.

"But she did. Something happened to her down there, I know it."

"It's only a clock, Evan. I think you've become so embroiled in the research you're putting merit in these wild claims. That woman you spoke to is probably senile, and if she isn't, maybe her memory isn't as good as she says. An inanimate object can't make people kill themselves, it's not possible."

Evan looked away from her and stared across the lake.

"Yeah," he said.

Selena cupped a hand around his neck, guiding his face back to hers. When he looked at her again, her face was very close, the dark lenses of her sunglasses reflecting the blue sky. Then her lips were on his. He had no time to react or pull away, even if he'd wanted to, the sweet taste of her breath in his mouth as she leaned into the kiss. It was surreal but so right. He couldn't do anything but succumb to the pleasure of another person so close, who wanted to touch him, to care for him.

When she broke away, a small smile played at the corners of her mouth. Her lips were red, full, and wet, and for a moment he couldn't take his eyes off them. An alien lust flooded him, something he hadn't encountered in years. He wanted her—it was undeniable. All of the restraint he'd held like a shield before him crumbled with that one kiss. If Shaun hadn't been a few feet away, he would have been unable to stop himself from seizing her by the shoulders and pulling her to him again. He would've dragged her down to the floor of the pontoon and had her there in the middle of the lake. And he could tell she would have wanted him to.

"Sorry, I had to do that," she said, breaking him from the vivid fantasy.

He stumbled on his words for a moment, his face flaming hot again. "Thank you," was all he could say, which earned him another smile.

"It's such a beautiful day and Shaun's having so much fun, could we stay out a little longer? This—"

Selena paused, looked down and then back up at him.

"This is the first time in all the anniversaries since my dad's been gone that I'm enjoying myself."

Thoughts of Becky's suicide tried to hem in his mind again with clouds of angst, but he pushed past them, taking in the way Shaun laughed and stared at the birds flitting by and the pleading look on Selena's face.

"Sure, let's troll for a bit, see if we can catch lunch," he said, and started the motor.

# 18

That evening, Evan was dozing when the phone rang.

He had kicked back in a chair beside the sofa on which Shaun had fallen asleep for his afternoon nap. They'd caught enough fish for lunch, and after returning to the island, he fried a batch of fillets, along with sliced potatoes and mushrooms. Shaun ate an amazing two helpings, and was only outdone by Selena, who managed three. They spent the afternoon lazing in the shade, the sun traveling in a slow arc almost directly overhead. The pines whispered gentle secrets to one another, and a sense of peace settled over him. It was a welcome contrast to the earlier horror of the morning. Whenever he began to hear Becky's sickening moan, he remembered Selena's comforting words. Becky must have been disturbed before she came to the house; there were no other possibilities. He held on to the thought until Selena departed in the old canoe, a sense of sadness washing over him as he watched her paddle out of sight.

He hadn't meant to fall asleep in the chair, and only realized it when his cell woke him, its buzzing dance bringing it dangerously close to the edge of the kitchen table. Rubbing the sleep from his eyes and shaking the feeling that his head had been filled with lead while he slept, Evan picked up the phone, not bothering to see who the caller was.

"Hello?"

"Evan?"

"Yeah."

"Hey, Evan, this is Justin Baker over at *Dachlund*."

For several seconds he stood in place, wavering with the unsteadiness of waking. It took Justin asking him if he was there to sink home whom he was speaking with.

"Yeah, Justin, hey, how are you?"

"Good, good. Say, I guess I'm a little confused here. Refresh me on which article you're talking about."

"The one Jason sent over to you, about the clock, the grandfather clock."

"It's not ringing any bells, no pun intended."

Evan laughed. "It's the one about the clockmaker and his wife, how their deaths were mysterious and this clock is one of the few remaining relics from their life."

"You know, I'm not seeing it here, Evan. I haven't gotten anything from Jason since the last time you did that opinion piece on special education, which was excellent, by the way, really well received."

"Thanks, I appreciate it," Evan said, frowning as he sat at the table. "So you're sure nothing about a clock came through?"

"Nope, but it sounds interesting. Why don't you zip me an overview of your idea, what kind of spread you had in mind, that type of thing, and I'll let you know if it's something we'd want to print."

He was silent for a time, processing what Justin said. "That sounds great, I'll do that."

"You still have my email?"

"Sure do."

"Good. Well, looking forward to it, Evan. I'll talk to you soon."

"Yeah, absolutely," Evan said, and ended the call.

He stared at the blank screen of his phone for over a minute before turning it back on again. Hitting Jason's number, he went through all of the scenarios that would explain the email he'd gotten the day before that didn't involve his best friend lying to him. He came up with nothing.

"You have an uncanny way of calling when I'm taking a shit," Jason said.

"Why did you lie to me?" Evan said, anger suddenly rushing through him and venting in his voice.

"What?"

"You heard me, Jase, why did you send me that email saying Justin wasn't interested in the article when you never even sent it to him? I just got off the phone with him, so don't try to bullshit me."

The quiet on the other end of the line broke with Jason's sigh, a deep, deflating sound that could've been something breathing out for the last time.

"I'm sorry, man. Let me say that right off the bat, I didn't mean to mislead you."

"You sure have a funny way of being honest then."

"I know, I know. Listen, hear me out. This is hard enough for me to talk about, let alone jump right into, and it wouldn't have boded well for what I wanted to do for you and Shaun."

"You're making zero sense, Jase."

"Okay, fuck. You had to go and want to write about that fucking clock, didn't you?"

A familiar shiver ran through him. "What about the clock?"

"It has nothing to do with the clock. It's my grandparents, they—"

"What happened?" Evan asked, the blistering anger becoming more of a flicker.

"They died over a decade ago, and that's what I wasn't completely honest with you about. I wanted to help you two, I wanted to get you back on your feet again, man. If I'd told you, you might not have wanted to bring Shaun there."

Evan's mouth was dry, the saliva gone, replaced with sand. "What happened to them?"

"That's just it, I don't know. No one knows for sure. I told you they died within a matter of months of one another, when they actually died on the same day."

A building apprehension overcame him, a missing piece of something about to drop into place, and he didn't want to hear it. He pulled the phone away from his ear and almost ended the call, but instead pressed it back to his head.

"They don't know if it was foul play or not," Jason continued. "They never found my grandma, it was like she got erased from the face of the earth. A fisherman found my grandpa in the lake. He'd drowned, but the police didn't know whether or not he'd had any help doing it. They brought up all kinds of theories: my grandpa killed my grandma and then drowned himself, my grandma killed my grandpa and then left the country. It was all horseshit. Neither one could've done that to the other.

They were married for over forty years, you don't do that to someone you love."

*Oh, you'd be surprised what people do to the ones they love, Jase, you wouldn't even believe it.*

Evan shook his head, his stomach rearranging itself into his chest as he remembered the outline of the floating man. "What do you think happened?"

"I have no fucking idea. Maybe somebody boated in and killed them. But there wasn't anything missing from the house, no sign of forced entry, nothing. My grandparents had lived in Mill River for almost all their lives, people loved them. No one local would want to hurt them."

The strange looks from some of the people when he'd mentioned where they were staying started to make sense—the Fin, that place of secrets, the cursed island. He could almost hear them whispering amongst one another, their voices growing more and more quiet as the years passed but never forgetting.

"Why the hell didn't anyone say anything about it to me in town?" Evan asked. "And why didn't Jacob tell me, since he was such a good friend of your dad's."

Jason laughed with no humor. "Jacob wasn't only a good friend of my dad's, he was best friends with my grandfather after Dad passed away. I actually thought he might say something to you, but he's like everyone else up there, close lipped about anything that might mar the image of the perfect tourist town. They prefer to talk behind backs. You should've seen the looks we'd get when we stayed there."

Evan placed his forehead in his free hand. "Holy shit, Jase, you should've told me."

"I know, I know, but I thought you'd refuse to bring Shaun there, even though it happened years and years ago. I thought you'd turn down my help."

"I don't need your *fucking* help!" Evan said. "You think I need my hand held? I've suffered more than you'll ever know in your perfect little world, brother. You should focus more on your fucking expense account and less on us."

Silence fell over the line, not only Jason's end but Evan's also. He opened his mouth to apologize, but Jason spoke first.

"Yeah, well, I just wanted to help."

It was Evan's turn to sigh. "I know, man, I'm sorry. We appreciate all you've done for us. It's—"

Evan almost told him about everything that had happened, the things he'd seen, or not seen, Becky. But a dam lodged in his throat, blocking it like something physical.

*A hair.*

"It's been a challenge, and I think you're right about slowing down to adjust. We need this, I need this. I'm sorry."

"Me too. When you started talking about the clock in the basement, I knew you'd be asking questions around town and what happened with my grandparents would come up for sure. That's why I tried to throw you off."

"Why didn't you tell me all this when it happened? I knew you were upset and everything, but I had no idea something like this was going on."

"We were in the middle of college, man. We were young, and I was scared and ashamed. My dad was already gone, and my mom wasn't the most supportive. I'm just lucky I had Lisa and Lily to focus on. I didn't know what to think back then, and I still don't now. I tried to glaze over it, tried to go on vacations up there with the family after a while, but it wasn't right anymore. I couldn't feel good there."

*Something didn't let you feel good here, my friend.*

Evan let the gap in conversation stretch. He didn't know what else to say. The sense of betrayal had given way to unease, and something else. Even though it sickened him, he recognized it for what it was: intrigue.

"I'm glad you got ahold of Justin. The clock story sounds good, he'll print it."

"Thanks. I'm sorry, I really am, Jase. I didn't mean it—"

"Save it, you sound like a whiny little bitch."

Evan couldn't help but laugh. "So I have your blessing to write it."

"Yeah, make it good. Maybe I'll put a bug in Justin's ear about finding a full-time position for you there."

Evan smiled. "Thanks, Jase. You're my brother, you know that?"

"Sure do. I only want the best for you guys."

"I know."

"Good. Give Shaun a hug for me, and try not to call when I'm taking a shit, okay?"

They both laughed and hung up. Evan sat staring at the wall, through it. The slight glow of knowing his and Jason's friendship was still strong paled in comparison to the numerous questions that grew from the new knowledge. He stood and made his way to the windows overlooking the dock and the lake beyond. He half expected to see the floating form of a body there. Instead, the water rippled and the pine boughs bent, while the wind chimes tinkled in tones that didn't sound pretty anymore.

Shaun stirred on the couch, and Evan went to him. Sitting beside him, he stroked his son's hair as he opened his eyes.

"Hi, honey, good sleep?"

Shaun smiled and yawned, stretching his arms over his head.

"Let's get you up and do some exercises."

For the next hour they worked on balancing and range-of-motion routines. The strength in Shaun's arms surprised him at one point, and he actually lost his grip on his small wrists. This brought about a shocked look on Shaun's face before he erupted in a series of excited shrieks. Evan clapped his hands over his ears in mock dismay, which only caused him to yell louder.

"You're getting too strong, son," he said, once Shaun became calm again. "Can you say 'strong'?"

"Strog."

Evan smiled and reached for the iPad to run through some flash cards, but he stopped. Putting his hands on Shaun's, he looked into his son's eyes.

"Do you like it here, Shaun? Should we stay?"

"Stay?"

"Yes, do you want to stay? We'll leave if you say so, right now, buddy. You tell me. Give me a sign."

He put a palm against the boy's cheek and waited. Shaun's eyes roamed across his face for some guidance.

"Stay?" Shaun repeated.

Evan dropped his hand into his own lap and nodded.

"Let's go down to the lake."

~

They watched the sun set behind the trees, its burning orange coalescing into a deep red, and then it was a purple bruise hidden behind a wispy crop of clouds. A floatplane roared into view near dark, its flashing wings close enough to see lines of rivets in its aluminum hide. Evan watched Shaun's face turned toward the whirring prop, and for a moment he imagined that the truck had not slid through the stop sign. He imagined the white line of scar evaporating, leaving smooth, unblemished skin and an undamaged brain beneath it. He watched the wonder in Shaun's features catching the last light of the day, and when he turned his head to issue an excited yell, Evan almost expected full sentences of questions to come out of his mouth instead.

"You can ask me, buddy," he said, holding one of Shaun's hands as the plane touched down on the lake, its skis slinging up jets of water. "How does it fly, Dad? How can it land on the lake?"

Shaun vibrated in his chair, his head turned away as the plane slowed before taxiing toward the right, out of view.

"You can ask," Evan whispered.

# 19

That night, after Shaun fell asleep, Evan began working on the clock.

He went downstairs with his laptop, intending to make some notes and begin an outline to send to Justin. Sitting at the worktable, he cleared a spot, moving the diagrams and Bob's scribbles out of the way. It felt natural to write in the presence of the clock, an inspiration whenever he glanced up from the screen.

Soon he found himself staring at the clock more and more while typing less and less. Its obsidian luster deepened further under the glow of the new light bulbs. The four hands on its shining face were still, but he could imagine them moving. He could see the shortest one buzzing around faster than the other three, like a fly caught under glass. The longest would move slower, placid in its surety. All of them spinning backward.

Evan jerked at the cold touch of the encasement's glass, and only then realized he'd stood and moved in front of the clock. Dropping his hands to his sides, he saw the places where his fingertips had brushed the pane, the fine lines of his fingerprints visible like road maps. The strange symbols and hash marks in place of numbers shone. Now that he looked closer, he saw they were separated into ten groups. Ten, not twelve.

Frowning, he turned and grabbed the chair near the table and pulled it before the clock. When he stood on the chair, his head came slightly above the clock's face. Yes, the symbols were definitely in groupings, with small spaces defining their outlines. Evan reached out and placed an index finger on the group at the twelve o'clock spot. He traced the raised markings, trying to ignore the shaking of his hands. The brass was colder than the encasement, and he shivered. Dropping his hand away, he leaned in close to the face, the grin of the crescent moon looking even more gruesome at this distance.

Something in the center of the group caught his eye: a minute O that looked incongruous with the rest of the cryptic figures around it. It took another moment for the rest of the shape to come into focus, and then suddenly it was there.

A zero was buried within the grouping.

Evan pulled back, blinking. Had that been there the entire time? No. Maybe. He looked again and saw in the spaces between the symbols, a clear path cut through, forming the number.

"How did I miss that?" he whispered.

He waited, staring at the spot, for something to change or the zero to disappear, consumed by the nonsensical etchings again, but it didn't. It remained. With trepidation, he focused on the next distinguished cluster. Sure enough, a one hid in its center. A two could be seen in the next, a three in the one after. All of the numbers were buried in the negative space between the cast symbols. He counted up to nine before coming back to the zero at the top.

"It's like a fucking rotary phone," he said.

The idea struck him as funny, and he laughed. Harder and harder, he shook with giggles as his legs grew weak beneath him. He stepped down to the floor and steadied himself on the worktable until the laughter began to taper off to chuckles and snorts. Evan wiped his eyes and looked back at the clock, expecting the numbers to be gone, hidden once more in the strange calligraphy.

They weren't. Apparently, once seen, you couldn't un-see them.

"Curiosity killed the cat and nothing in the world could bring him back."

Evan swallowed, not liking the sound of his voice in the basement. He needed to get to work, enough messing around. But as he turned away, his eyes snagged on the four hands of the clock, now pointing at distinguishable numbers. He froze, feeling as though he stood at the edge of a bottomless cavern, his toes encroaching on empty air. Which way to step? Onto solid ground, or into the emptiness?

*You know why you're down here and not upstairs punching away at Justin's outline, just like you know why you haven't left this island like any sane person would have by now. You know.*

*Dispense with the self-serving lies. I am the self, you can't bullshit me.*

Hating the voice inside, Evan noted the placement of the clock's hands and took in which numbers they pointed at. One, nine, one, nine—1919. He tried to remember if he'd bumped the hands. No, he hadn't. He rubbed his face, swiping at his eyes, which were much too tired all of a sudden.

How many people had been around the clock over the years? How many curious fingers had touched, prodded, spun the hands? A warmth glowed in the base of his stomach, the same as earlier that day on the boat when Selena kissed him. Excitement. The possibility of something impossible. He opened his mouth as though to speak, to chide himself out loud, and then shut it.

The idea, hidden beneath the dark waters of obscurity over the past days since finding Bob's notes, rose from the depths, becoming clearer and clearer. For a moment he tried to refuse it, to push it back below to where it would return to the indefinable shadow it once was, but instead, he let it come fully into view. The enormity of the possibility, along with its insanity, almost floored him. Evan gripped the back of the chair and slowly slid into the seat, the strength leaving his legs.

*Once seen, it can't be unseen.*

Evan looked at the monstrosity standing indifferent against the wall.

"He tried to go back, back before she got sick."

He didn't know if he spoke of Abel or himself. His jaw worked soundlessly, and if the lights were to wink out, he knew he would die, crushed by the immensity of the concept that now breathed—*pulsed*—with life.

"I can go back."

Bob's words spoken aloud should have chilled him, but they didn't.

Evan shut his laptop, went to the diagrams at the far end of the table, and began to read.

~

When he awoke hours later in his bed, it was to the sound of a pistol cocking. A very round, very cold circle of steel pressed into his cheek, and he saw the outline of a man standing over him. Evan's heart went from a normal beat to a full racehorse gallop in less than a second. Adrenaline rushed through his recumbent form, and he trembled beneath the light blanket that covered him.

"You yell, I kill you and then your son, you understand me?"

The man's voice was low and unsteady. It wavered as though he were shaking too, but Evan couldn't feel any vibration through the barrel of the gun.

"Yes," Evan said, his voice a sleep-filled croak.

The man leaned over him, and the pressure of the gun increased. He wondered if the intruder had changed his mind and would pull the trigger in the next second, sending him on to whatever waited. The bright thought of seeing Elle flared, extinguishing as he imagined Shaun waking to a single gunshot, frightened beyond anything he'd known before as a strange man entered his room to end his life. The worst part would be Shaun wouldn't know what was happening or why. This thought kept Evan still, waiting for the man either to speak or to let down his guard enough for him to launch an attack.

"Where is it?"

So it was a robbery.

"What?" Evan said. The barrel pushed so hard against his cheek, his teeth ached.

"The clock, the fucking clock," the man said, his voice coming out in a rasp.

"Downstairs," Evan said, readying to fling his hand up and roll his body at the same time.

The gun drew away, and the man stepped toward the door. Evan saw his arm reach out for the switch. Light flooded the room, and he found himself looking at a late-middle-aged Asian man with close-cropped dark hair. His eyes were narrowed against the glare of the sudden light, and his mouth was a hard line drawn at the bottom of his face. The revolver in his hand was so large, it seemed like a prop out of an action movie. Evan sat up, careful not to make any movements too fast.

"What do you want?"

The man's mouth quivered. "I want to see it."

"You can have it, as long as you don't hurt my son."

The man grimaced and stepped forward, leveling the gun at Evan's forehead.

"What did you do to her?" he asked. A tear slid free of his left eye and caught the light before rolling out of sight under his jaw.

Evan brought his hands up to his shoulders and leaned back. "Who, who are you talking about?"

The man's lips moved, but his teeth remained locked together. "Becky, my daughter. What did you do to her?"

Evan's mouth dropped open, and he took in the likenesses of the man before him and the young PCA—the same color hair, the same cheek bones.

"I didn't do anything to her."

"Bullshit," Becky's father said, thrusting the handgun forward.

"I didn't. When I came home, she was acting strange, and before I could talk to her, she left in the boat."

Another tear traced the same course as the first one, and Becky's father wiped it away. "She came home from here almost catatonic. She barely said hello and then threw up in the upstairs toilet. We put her to bed, and in the morning—" His voice rose like a roller coaster before the big drop. "I found her broken on our sidewalk. My baby girl, gone. Do you get that?" He tilted his head, as if speaking to Evan in another language. "Do you understand having someone ripped away from you for no reason?"

*Yes, I do.*

Evan remained quiet, still not knowing if the other man would pull the trigger or not.

"Please don't hurt my son."

Becky's father blinked and licked his lower lip. "She left a note, but it didn't explain anything, no reason why. But she must've been up all night writing, while my wife and I slept. She wrote 'clock' over and over and over on a piece of paper until there was no white left anywhere, only the word ground into it with ink."

A cold clarity gripped Evan. He should agree with Becky's father, tell him there was something wrong with the clock, that it was *unnatural*. He should go with him down to the basement to destroy it, and when Becky's father wasn't looking, take the gun from him and kill him.

Evan shook his head. No, he hadn't just thought that. He didn't want to hurt the man any more than he wanted Becky's father to hurt them. The uncharacteristic blood thirst receded, and he gazed into the gun's unblinking eye before looking at the man who held it.

"I'm sorry about your daughter, I really am. I called the hospital after she left to make sure she got home safe. I was worried but—"

*But you were too fixated on the idea to really care, too enamored with Selena and—*

Evan closed his eyes, cutting the voice off mid-sentence. He spoke with slow care, his words metered out with the truth he felt. "I'm sorry, I can't say how sorry I am, but I didn't do anything to her."

Becky's father watched him with his dark eyes. "Get up," he finally said, motioning toward the door with his gun.

Evan swallowed, hoping his legs would hold him. He stood and walked out of the room, Becky's father following him. The surreal quality of the light and sensation of clinging sleep made him wonder if this all was a dream, a nightmare that was a little too real. They moved down the hall and across the living room. The darkness outside the window was thick.

*The night will never end.*

"Where's the basement?" Becky's father said.

"The door on the right," Evan said, pointing.

"You first."

Evan could smell the other man's cologne or shaving cream, and pulled open the basement door. He flicked the light switch on and started down, hearing Becky's father several steps behind. Panic still gripped him, but it was separate now, detached in a way that made him feel sleepy. He wanted only to go back to bed and lie down, pretend this all was a dream that would fade with the light of morning.

They stepped into the basement after Evan turned the next switch on, and he moved to one side, giving the other man a clear view of the clock. Evan watched his reaction, waiting for an outburst, either tears or maybe a crazed battle cry, but Becky's father did nothing. He stood motionless, taking in the clock's wide-shouldered encasements, its black shine. For a moment he thought the man might be transfixed, hypnotized by the sight, but then he was moving, walking in a straight line toward it, his eyes never leaving it. Evan took a half step toward the stairs, trying to judge whether he could make the turn and race up the treads, out of sight before the gun would go off. He needed to get Shaun out of the house and into the pontoon, away from this man whose grief was driving him to things Evan was sure he would never even consider normally.

He glanced at the stairway and then back to Becky's father as he set the gun on the table and bent to pick up something from the floor near the workbench.

*This is your chance. Go while he's not looking, get Shaun safe and then call someone to get this man some help.*

All of his thoughts ceased when he saw what Becky's father held in his hands.

The can of mineral spirits looked old, the top holding a slim layer of brown rust, and cobwebs first stretched from its handle and then broke, floating back to their tethers on the wall. Becky's father held the can at arm's length, then spun the cap off.

"Tessa's always after me to stop smoking," he said, digging in one front pocket. "Now I'm so glad I haven't, because I don't see any matches down here."

He drew out a silver lighter, the refillable butane kind, and pivoted toward the clock. Before he turned, Evan saw a manic smile stretched across his lips.

Evan ran.

He didn't wait to see if Becky's father would actually go through with what he intended. He didn't try to talk him out of it. He ran. A solitary pain lanced through his heart as he realized his chance to make things different, as insane as it seemed, would be a pile of ashes soon, possibly with the rest of the house. He almost stopped and turned back, a powerful pull trying to lock his feet to the stairs.

*You're giving up the chance to save Elle, to save Shaun from the disabled life he is cursed to lead. You're running away again.*

The last words came in Elle's voice, and he stumbled, nearly falling into the kitchen. Evan grunted and continued to move, shoving away everything else besides the need to get to Shaun.

He stepped into the kitchen and ran across the floor, for the first time noticing the chill on his bare legs.

*Wait around, it won't be cold for long.*

He nearly brayed insane laughter at that.

*Hope you have good homeowner's, Jase. 'Cause this one's gonna catapult the old premium!*

A loud bellow came from the basement, followed by a metallic clang.

Evan slowed and then stopped, breathing with his mouth wide open, listening over the pounding of his blood.

Silence. No *whoompf* of the clock igniting, no crackle of flames eating wood in burning bites. Serene quiet. He gulped down air, trying to slow his heart and the racing thoughts in his head. What the hell happened? All this buildup and no fireworks? The feeling of laughter came again, and he squashed it, because he knew if he started now, he might not stop.

Shaun's snores came from the partially open door of his room. Cold sweat formed on Evan's back, and he shivered as a bead ran down the groove of his spine. Still no sound from below.

*Get Shaun out of the house, that's your only concern right now.*

He nodded and took a few steps back the way he'd come, stopping to listen every other second. Nothing. Afraid that he would see the shiny barrel of the handgun appear in the doorway at any moment, Evan walked closer and closer to the stairs. With a quick movement, he poked one eye around the doorjamb and then drew back.

The stairway was empty. As silently as he could, he moved down the first two treads, ready to run back at any sign of approach from below. Another step. Another. Evan stopped at the landing and peered around the corner, mimicking the move he'd used at the top of the stairs.

The basement was empty.

The absence of Becky's father startled him more than if the man had been inches away, the gun pointed directly at him. He blinked, searching the floor and corners. Where was he hiding? Evan moved from the safety of the stairwell and took the last steps down. The cold cement leeched heat from the soles of his feet, sending frigid runners up through his calves. He scanned the boxes to his right, the sewing area, the table—everything was where it should be. He knelt, making sure the other man hadn't crouched beneath the worktable. Only shadow and dust lay there. He walked forward, a new, unnamable fear falling over him like a wet sheet.

Turning in a circle, he looked at every possible hiding place. Outside of Becky's father being a professional contortionist, the options were limited. He opened each of the cabinet doors above the workbench to quell the need to be sure. After making his way to the end of the bench, he stopped, staring at the glass encasement below the clock's face. A man could hide in there. Definitely.

Evan walked around the table and approached the clock, his hands blocks of ice at the ends of his arms. The air in the basement seemed to have dropped several degrees, feeling more like a meat locker with each passing second. With one hand, he reached out and touched the brass knob on the center door and tried to turn it. It wouldn't budge. He tried harder, the flesh of his fingers turning white with effort. The knob squawked and then turned, and the door opened. A waft of air smelling of dust brushed past him as he leaned in closer. The pendulum and its surrounding darkness were all he could see. No man, no gun, nothing but shadow.

Evan stepped back and shut the door, a thought striking him. He'd heard the mineral-spirits can hit the floor, but where was it? Where was the spilled thinner that should've assaulted his nose the moment he walked down here? He bent his knees again and looked under the table, sure he would spot the can on its side. Evan stiffened, one hand braced against the cement for balance, his neck craned down, his eyes wide—

—as he stared at the mineral spirits can in the corner beside the workbench. His mouth opened, and a word tried to come out. Instead, it stayed on his tongue and resounded in his head.

*No. No. No. No.*

Evan stood, the unreal quality of a dream surrounding him as he walked around the length of the table and moved to where the can sat. Bending down, he touched the cap, tight with rust on its spout, the cobwebs clinging to its top, unbroken.

Dizziness washed over him, and he staggered away from the corner. The basement swayed as if though rested in the middle of a titanic teeter-totter. Evan moved with it, the unreality of everything compounding at once. His mind strained at its bindings, stretching them, forced by the incongruence of what he'd seen.

"It didn't happen, it didn't happen, I'm not here right now," he said, taking the first step on the stairs.

The pleading sound of his voice scared him; it was hollow and detached, the voice of an automaton going about its commanded task. He shut off the lights with a swipe of one hand and trudged up the stairs, his left forearm sliding along the wall to keep him upright.

The air in the kitchen smelled wonderful compared to that of the basement, and he hauled in several deep lungfuls before turning off the last light and shutting the door behind him. Evan moved through the house on numbed feet, the feeling growing steadily up his legs, as if he'd stepped on bed of Novocain syringes.

Without thinking about it, he stripped his bed of blankets and pillows and laid them down in Shaun's room, only inches from his bedside. He collapsed onto the floor, the blankets barely padding the hardwood, but the relief of being next to Shaun more than offset the discomfort.

One of Shaun's hands dangled off the bed, and Evan reached up to place it back under the blanket but stopped. He held it in his palm, closing his eyes as he did. He fell asleep that way, as the darkness in the east bled to gray.

# <u>20</u>

Evan sipped his coffee and watched Shaun across the table.

The simple act of feeding Shaun his morning cereal grounded him, anchoring his mind in the normal, keeping his thoughts from returning to the night before. Evan clamped a hand on to his forehead and rubbed his temples. Nothing had happened last night, nothing. There was no gun, the mineral-spirits can wasn't moved, there was no man. He sighed, rubbing his bloodshot eyes before draining the rest of his coffee.

"Wawee?" Shaun asked.

"What, honey?" Evan said, sitting forward.

Shaun furrowed his brow and tried to point toward the bedrooms. "Wawee?"

Evan glanced in the direction and then turned back. "I don't know what you want, buddy."

Shaun's eyebrows drew down, and he struck the cereal bowl with one hand, causing the spoon to fly free. Milk and soggy flakes spattered the table, and a few dollops landed on Evan's thigh.

"Shit! Stop it, Shaun," he said, grabbing Shaun's flailing arm.

"Wawee! Wawee!" Shaun cried, tears beginning to run down his cheeks.

Evan stood and hugged his son's arms tight to his body.

"Shhhh, honey, stop, you're going to hurt yourself. Don't, don't, don't."

The boy continued to struggle, but his movements became less frantic, and gradually he lapsed into simply crying.

"I know, buddy, I know it's hard. I'm sorry I can't understand sometimes." Evan looked at the kitchen counter and saw the iPad there. "Do you want your iPad? Flash cards?"

He grabbed the slim case and held it out to Shaun. Shaun shook his head.

"Na."

"Okay, okay, buddy." He set the device down, and his shoulders sagged. "Let's just get ready to go."

~

They left the island in the pontoon half an hour later, the day warm but muddled with shining silver clouds in the sky. Evan began to steer toward the little marina on the mainland, but a thought struck him like a hammer.

*A boat.*

If Becky's father had really come to the house last night, he would've come in a boat. Evan scanned the shoreline on the west side of the island. No crafts jutted out into the water, and from what he could see, none were pulled up into the woods.

"Let's take a little side trip, buddy," he said, turning the pontoon south.

They cruised over the calm water, around the end of the island, the little clearing with the fire pit coming into view after a few minutes. When they rounded the heavily wooded southeastern side, Evan let out a breath he didn't know he was holding. Small waves lapped against rocky shore. He could see no boats anchored along its edge. To be sure, he throttled up and cruised the entire length and turned left, until he could see their dock again.

A strange relief came over him, followed by a layer of fear on its heels. Not seeing a boat made him believe that nothing had happened the night before, but the absence of one confirmed the cold inkling that had been with him all morning.

*You're going crazy.*

That's what'd been happening since they arrived. All the unsettling occurances, they were all in his mind.

He looked at Shaun, who was enraptured by the approaching land as he always was. What would happen to Shaun if he lost it completely? He would have nowhere to go. Evan's parents lived in southern Florida and didn't have the capabilities to care for Shaun, and he had no other close relatives, since Elle's parents were deceased. There was only Jason and Lisa, and although Jason meant well, he wondered if his best friend could care for Shaun in the way he deserved.

Stop it, he chided himself. Just stop. He wouldn't lose Shaun, and he wasn't going crazy. It had been a dream, a horrible and realistic dream, but a dream nonetheless. There were no other explanations.

*Ghosts.*

The word floated through his mind, wrapped in absurdity as well as a niggling fear.

"Ghosts," he said, tasting the word while feeling foolish at the same time.

*So you don't believe in ghosts, but you believe in time travel?*

"How about a dream, Shaun?" he said, drowning out the voice's annoying musings. "How about that's what it was. No more fried food for Dad before bed."

Shaun looked at him and smiled. The simplicity of joking out loud did wonders for him, and he breathed in the fresh air, feeling better. Or maybe it was putting distance between them and the island.

Evan focused on the approaching dock and shut all other thoughts off.

"Too much thinking never does anyone any good," he said, in a bravado he didn't feel.

Shaun didn't respond, and Evan wondered if he would agree if he could.

~

After dropping Shaun off at the hospital for therapy, Evan drove through town, not entirely sure where he was going. He found himself back at Collins Outfitters, and sat looking at the side of the building for over a minute before he climbed out and headed for the door. Arnold and Wendal were at their customary posts, and Evan realized their seats had been empty when he and Shaun came through earlier.

"Morning," Evan said.

Arnold nodded. "Morning to you, young fella."

"Going to be hot today, you think?"

"Oh, yeah. It's hot every day now that the snow's gone."

Evan laughed, struck by how normal the conversation seemed, in contrast with what had happened the night before.

*The dream.*

"You get ahold of old Cecil out there?" Arnold asked.

A little twinkle in his eye told Evan he already thought he knew the answer.

"Actually, I did," Evan said, satisfied at the startled look both the twins gave him.

"You're kidding?" Arnold said.

"Nope. She even let me come inside."

"Well, I'll be a monkey's uncle. That's the first I've heard of her talking to someone besides the grocer or repairman." Arnold eyed him up and down. "You must've had a silver tongue to charm that old biddy."

"Something like that. Is Jacob in, by chance?"

"Oh yeah, the old mick's in there somewhere."

"Thanks."

Evan moved past the twins, through the door of the building. He wanted to stop and go back, to tell them both off for not having said anything about Jason's grandparents, for they surely knew about what had happened. Well, he couldn't fault Wendal for not saying anything. The dark humor made him smile a little.

"What's so funny, boyo?" Jacob said, standing behind a counter.

"Nothing. How's it going today?" Evan reached out and shook the older man's hand.

"Goin' well, goin' well. Didn't see ya come in with yer boy this mornin'."

"Yeah, he's at his therapy now." Evan watched Jacob nod and then begin to unpack a box of spinner lures. "Jacob, I know I owe you a beer."

"Three, I think," Jacob said, giving him a smile.

Evan didn't return it. "But could we go get some coffee in lieu of those? I need to speak with you about something."

Jacob looked at him for a moment, and then nodded. "Okay, boyo, what's this about?"

"Jason's grandparents." He watched Jacob's face fall a little. "I know about everything."

Jacob sighed, looking down at the glass top of his counter. A boy no older than seventeen, holding a stack of fishing vests, came out of the back room behind Jacob and paused, his eyes going from his boss to Evan.

"Nate, why don't ya watch the store fer a while," Jacob said.

"Sure thing, Mr. Collins."

"Come with me, Evan," Jacob said, heading through the doorway behind the counter.

Evan followed him, smiling politely at Nate as he went by. The room behind the counter held several tall shelves stocked with boxes of fishing gear of all sorts. Jacob led the way through the stacks to a gray steel door with a cartoon taped to it. Jacob opened it and beckoned Evan inside.

"Me office," Jacob said, closing the door behind them. "Ignore the mess, will ya?"

The office was spacious, with two wide windows overlooking the lake. Dark paneling lined the walls, and several massive fish were mounted here and there, their taxidermied eyes glaring in glassy stares. Jacob's desk had piles of papers and photos littering both ends, with a clear path down to the wood in the middle. The air smelled of sweet tobacco. Evan sat in a threadbare chair in front of the desk, while Jacob rummaged below it on the other side.

"I know it's early, but it's noon somewhere, me father used ta say," Jacob said, standing with a can of Budweiser in one hand.

Evan almost said no, and then sat forward, taking the ice-cold can from the older man. "Thank you."

"I keep a little stocked at the back of the fridge," Jacob said, pulling another can out. "Keep it fer emergencies, mind ya."

"Is this an emergency?" Evan asked, opening his beer.

Jacob's eyes darkened. "No, but it helps." He snapped his beer open and took a sip, pulling the corners of his mouth tight as he swallowed. "Me wife'd kill me ass if she knew we were drinkin' in here. But what she don't know won't hurt me."

Evan said nothing and drank. It tasted good and felt great on his parched throat.

"I suppose Jason told ya the nasty details?"

"He did."

"Then ya know how much I cared for Daniel, his granddad."

Evan remained silent, and Jacob continued, looking down at his beer.

"When Ray passed away, Daniel and Maggie were devastated, as was I. I took food out ta them from time ta time, jest ta help out. When I saw Daniel startin' down the road of depression, I took him fishin'. It was all I knew ta do ta ease the pain. We'd spend hours in the boat, and even though he'd be away from Maggie most of the day, she didn't mind so much once Dan started comin' back around."

Jacob took another long drink from his beer, and set it down but kept his fingers wrapped around it.

"I guess in a way we did some replacin' of sorts. He became me best friend, and I became somethin' like a son ta him."

"Why did you lie to me when we first came here and I asked if you knew Jason's grandparents?" Evan said. The earlier anger diminished when he saw how affected Jacob was.

"I didn't want ta scare ya away." Jacob rolled his tongue around in his mouth, as if tasting something bitter. "Lots a rumors fly around this little town. People gab when they shouldn't, make up parts where they've lost the story, and soon ya have shit rollin' around town that's nothin' like the truth." Jacob looked at Evan, his eyes sad but sober. "I didn't want ya gettin' scared off by a bunch of ghost stories."

*Ghost.*

"What do you mean?"

"After Dan and Maggie passed, all kinds of things were said. Superstitious bunkum, all of it. I tried ta quell it. It made me madder than a shaken hornet, but people will talk, as they say."

Evan sipped his beer and looked past Jacob's shoulder, to where the island sat on the lake. "What do you know about the clock?"

Jacob finished his beer and set the can down with a *thunk*. "Ugliest stack of sticks I've laid eyes upon. Dan bought it at auction when the title dispute fer the Kluge property was finally resolved, got it as a project ta fix on." Jacob laughed once, a short bark, and shook his head. "I asked him, 'Dan, why would ya want a feckin' clock that don't work?' and he jest said it was valuable."

"When did he buy it?"

"About a year before they passed, I suppose."

"And did Daniel seem different after he bought it?"

Jacob eyed Evan, wariness on his features for the first time since they'd met. "This fer yer article?"

"Yes, and out of curiosity."

*Curiosity killed the cat.*

Jacob paused and then pulled another can of beer out of the fridge beneath his desk. "Evan, I like ya, boyo, but I won't tolerate Dan and Maggie being misrepresented. Follow?"

"I follow. I just want to know."

Jacob stared at the desk. "He became a little distant after buyin' the clock. Maggie told me once that sometimes he'd spend most of the day down in the basement, tinkerin' away. You see, he bought that thing in several pieces. Someone had partially dismantled it durin' the years, maybe tryin' ta do the very thing that Dan was." Jacob shrugged. "Either way, Dan was no clockmaker, but he was smart and good with his hands. He got it mostly assembled, showed it ta me one day before we went out on the lake."

"Did he mention why he was so dead set on getting it running again?" Evan asked.

"No, but I will say this: I wouldn't call it frantic, but he was obsessed with that clock. Talked about it from time ta time, but I could always tell it was on his mind. Sometimes he'd go twenty minutes jest starin' out at the lake while we fished, not sayin' a thing, jest lookin' at somethin' I couldn't see."

*I can go back.*

Evan finished his beer, and saw that his hand trembled. Jacob seemed to notice it too.

"You okay, boyo?"

Evan set the empty can down on the desk. "Yes, I haven't been sleeping well lately."

This was definitely the truth, what with armed men coming into the house at night and then disappearing without a trace. Evan sighed with the weight of the memory. It was still fresh in his mind, but with the bright lake beyond the window and the taste of beer on his tongue in Jacob's snug office, it was far away— someone else's problem.

"What do you think really happened out there?" Evan asked, nodding toward the island.

Jacob's brow crinkled, and the darkness returned to his eyes. "I don't know, boyo. No one but Dan, Maggie, and the good Lord do fer sure."

"If you had to guess."

Jacob fell silent for over a minute, and then turned and stood, looking out the window at the impressive view beyond. His voice floated back over his shoulder, disembodied and thin.

"I never knew a couple who loved one another as well as those two. Dan would've died fer Maggie, and she fer him. And maybe that's jest what they did."

Jacob turned back to Evan, and he saw a glaze of moisture on the older man's eyes, like windows after a mist.

"All superstitions aside, you mark me words, boyo. Somethin' right terrible happened on that island, and I thank God above I don't know what it was."

# 21

Evan almost drove straight to Selena's office, but thought better of it and went grocery shopping instead.

It wouldn't have done to show up at her business with beer on his breath, no matter what time of day it was, and noon was still a couple of hours away. He pottered around the grocery store like a much older man, forgetting why he went to an aisle, only to realize he was staring directly at what he needed.

After leaving the store, he drove to the hospital and waited in the car until Shaun's appointments were over. He watched people come and go, watched them walk across the parking lot to their vehicles, some laughing, some somber. He wondered about their lives, who they were, whom they loved, why they were here. He'd done it many times before, especially when his dreams were still attainable and his life hadn't been taken apart and rearranged into something unrecognizable. He remembered Elle telling him his people watching was a result of being a writer at heart. *You want to know because you want to tell their stories, or make them up,* she'd said. He had no interest in writing about other people now; he merely wondered if they'd suffered more or less than he had.

Inside the hospital his mood rose the moment Shaun came into view down the long, sterile hallway, this time guided by a heavyset therapist with blond hair and a permanent smile. The thought that Becky Tram would never walk down these halls again caused the strength to drain from his legs. She wouldn't get married or have children because she was now lying on a cold metal tray somewhere in town, a mortician standing over her trying to figure out how to put her head back together.

Evan bit back the sick that tried to rise into his mouth and smiled as he picked Shaun up. The woman related the events of the therapy session and commented on how strong Shaun was. Evan smiled and nodded at the right times, then thanked her, feeling like a marionette with invisible strings.

Since it was almost tradition, they went to their café and sat outside after ordering a banana split. Evan hadn't brought his laptop with him, and he didn't miss it; anything to do with the clock brought up too many uncomfortable questions. Instead he focused on Shaun, who was watching a group of boys approaching on the sidewalk. They were maybe twelve or thirteen, and their laughter and talk seemed to flow from one to the other—boy-speak that most adults couldn't understand. Evan gazed at his son.

*Do you know that you're different? Can you tell? Do you long to be free of your chair and constant fatigue? Do you have an inkling that there's more to all of this?*

The thoughts pulled a knot tight in his chest, and he had to look away. He noticed that the waitress bringing their banana split and coffee was struggling with the door leading onto the patio. Evan stood and walked over, opening it for her.

"Thanks," she said, smiling.

"Here, I'll take that for you."

The waitress smiled again, giving him the ice cream and coffee cup. "Thanks, I just started, and I haven't got the hang of carrying food through here without spilling it yet."

She let out an endearing, nerdy honk of laughter as Evan took the food from her.

"No problem," he said, as she disappeared back inside.

He heard the laughter of the boys on the sidewalk, along with sounds Shaun made when he was happy or excited. Turning, he saw the group of boys standing on the other side of the low, decorative fence that separated the café's patio from the sidewalk, a few feet from where Shaun sat. The largest of the boys, who had a wild shock of black hair and a sunburned forehead, was pulling faces at Shaun, his tongue hanging out wildly as he rolled his eyes back in his head.

"Ahhhhh, does the retard like it?" the boy said, and screwed up his face while mimicking Shaun's sounds. "Ahhhhhh!"

"He probably thinks he's looking in a mirror, Davey," one of the other boys said, and the entire gang broke up in shrieks of laughter.

A boiling sensation flowed over his body, as if a powerful UV lamp had been turned on only feet away. A savageness unlike anything he'd ever experienced before blinded him, and all he felt was the flow of air over his skin as he moved. There was a panicked shout that echoed on the building fronts, followed by a yelp of pain, and when he blinked, Evan saw one of his hands wrapped firmly in the big boy's dark hair. The other hand held the scalding coffee a few inches from his face.

The rest of the boys stood several steps back, their faces pale white in the brightness of the day, eyes wide and staring. Evan expected them all to start screaming or calling for help, but they were transfixed by what was happening before them. The shock of what he'd done dissipated almost at once, and the rage returned full force as he remembered the mocking sounds that came out of the big boy's mouth. He pulled Davey closer, yanking at his hair so that the kid's head jerk around.

"Listen, you little fucker, my son was in a car accident and has brain damage. He's gone through more in the last three years than you probably ever will in your life. Now if you don't want me to burn the fucking skin off your face with this coffee, you'll get moving. You got me?"

"Yes, sir," Davey squeaked. His voice sounded so high that he could have sung soprano.

Evan released his hair, giving him a little shove that he hadn't meant to but couldn't help. The boy rubbed his head where he had gripped him, his eyes full of tears and absolute fear. There was a beat, and then the whole pack of kids ran, the bottoms of their shoes kicking up dust from the sidewalk as they pelted away. They never looked back, and Evan watched them round the corner and disappear like a herd of prey running from a predator.

Shaun's sobs brought him back, and he looked at his son, who stared at the ground where the banana split lay facedown, rivers of melting ice cream flowing away through the cracks in the patio blocks. Evan closed his eyes and sat, then held one of Shaun's hands. He surveyed the street and saw no one, silently thanking fate that they were the only customers outside at that moment.

"I'm sorry, honey, I dropped it."

Shaun gazed at him, his eyes rimmed with tears.

"D-d-drupa."

Evan nodded. "I'll get you another one. To go." He picked up his coffee as he stood.

~

They arrived at the island around noon, the sun finally making its first appearance of the day overhead. A sickening sensation flowed through Evan's stomach as he tied up the pontoon and carried Shaun to shore. Had he really meant to grab that kid? To burn him? No, he couldn't have actually gone through with it— but he wondered. A second more without restraint, he might have. He might have tipped the cup and let the steaming liquid stream over the kid's already burned forehead and drizzle down his cheeks, red streaks appearing like tracks of fire on his skin as the coffee did its work.

He shook his head. No, as much as it would've been satisfying to hurt the boy, he couldn't have done it. Grabbing his hair had been a step too far; even laying a finger on the kid's shirt would land him in court these days. He stopped, standing still on the dock for a second, his hands full of grocery bags. What if little Davey told someone, or one of the other boys said something to their parents? Would they be able to identify him?

Of course. He and Shaun were probably the talk of the town because they were living on the island, and with Shaun's disability, there wouldn't be much room for mistaking who he was.

He moved to the shade where Shaun rested in his chair, anxiety constricting his lungs. He dropped the groceries and sat, crumpling more than easing down. When he looked out across the lake, he expected to see a boat topped with red and blue lights approaching, stern-faced men in uniforms at its helm.

*Get a grip.*

He hadn't hurt the kid, not really, only scared him, and the little shit deserved every second of it. Maybe next time he would think twice about teasing someone with disabilities.

A little heartened by the thought, he pulled his phone out and dialed Selena's number, then ended the call before it could go through. Glancing at Shaun, he saw his eyes flutter and close, only to open again.

"Let's get you inside, buddy. Dad could use a nap too."

After laying Shaun in his bed, Evan hauled the remaining groceries into the house and put them away. He'd bought the makings for lasagna, one of Shaun's favorites, and wondered if Selena liked it too. He reached for his phone again, to call her, and once more stopped himself, feeling needy and pathetic.

"Take a nap, you need it," he mumbled out loud, and went to the couch.

The sun faded behind a layer of clouds, and the cool, gray light that filled the house was soothing. Evan looked down the hallway, making sure that he could see where Shaun lay, and put his head on a pillow. He fell asleep like toppling into an abyss before he could adjust himself into a more comfortable position.

~

He awoke to the feeling of soft fingers stroking his hair. As the vestiges of sleep left him, Evan thought it was Elle waking him in the morning, as she sometimes used to do. She would draw him out of sleep by dragging her fingertips through his hair and then trailing them down his shoulder and onto his stomach, where they would do a few slow circles before traveling farther south. Then she would pause, stroking his upper thighs with maddening restraint. He would be fully awake by then but still feigning sleep, a smile on his lips, waiting, waiting for her hand to slide over and ...

Evan opened his eyes to find Selena standing next to the couch, her fingers brushing his hair. He started, his heart leaping and then jigging in an insane rhythm. She stepped back, her eyebrows drawing together.

"I'm sorry, I didn't mean to startle you."

"Ah, it's okay," Evan said, clearing his throat.

"I wouldn't have come in, but the door wasn't shut completely and came all the way open when I knocked."

He cleared his throat again and sat up, acutely aware of the straining bulge in his jeans. What the hell had he been dreaming about? He crouched over his erection, hoping she hadn't noticed.

"That's fine." He frowned. "I'm sure I shut the door tight."

He traced back through his actions before lying down, and couldn't remember if he had or hadn't. Evan rubbed his face and looked around. Shaun still slept, although he'd turned over and one arm dangled out of bed and into the shadow below it. Something could grab him like that. Grab him and pull him under the bed if it wanted to. He shuddered, blinking at the sun that now sat above the mainland.

"What time is it?" he asked.

"Four o'clock."

"Oh, wow, we've been sleeping for four hours."

"Well, you must have needed it," Selena said, turning away from him.

Evan began to rise off the sofa and paused, her words striking a nerve. Elle used to say that whenever he overslept on a weekend or when Shaun would sleep sometimes for five hours or more right after his accident. Even the way Selena said it reminded him of his wife, the caring tone telling him he could've slept all day if it pleased him. Brushing off the déjà vu, he stood, thankful that his arousal had dissipated enough for him to move normally.

"I thought I'd drop by and check on you guys, make sure you were doing okay today."

"We're good, thanks. I appreciate it," he said, moving toward the kitchen. "We got back around noon from Shaun's therapy—"

He halted halfway across the threshold of the kitchen, his eyes widening as he stared at the floor.

Three watery footprints trailed across the linoleum.

Evan swallowed and jabbed his fingers into his eyes, rubbing them, sure that sleep still clung to the lids and made him think he saw—

But when he opened them again, the footprints were still there. Their forms were drying, beginning to shrink, becoming baby prints, but still very much real. He knelt and reached out, touching one of them. His finger came away wet. He heard Selena move closer and step into the kitchen behind him.

"And then what'd you guys do?" she asked.

Had his feet been wet when he put away the groceries? No. His shoes might've been, but he'd taken them off at the door, like he always did. His sock-covered feet were dry. Besides, the shape of the tracks couldn't be denied. They weren't shoe prints. Whoever had walked into the kitchen had been barefoot.

"What are you looking at?" Selena asked.

"You didn't come into the kitchen, did you?" he asked, without taking his eyes off the small puddles.

"No, I shut the door and came over to wake you. I probably should've just let you sleep."

His jaw worked for a moment, and then he grabbed a dishtowel that hung off the nearby counter.

"No, that's fine. I needed to get up anyway," he said, swiping the tracks away with the towel.

He felt the cool water soak into the fabric, and it repulsed him on some base level. Evan stood and opened the trash lid, then tossed the towel inside, glad to be free of its touch.

"Are you all right?"

He turned and saw the concerned look on her face, maybe the way she looked at a client who sat, no doubt, on a heavily padded leather love seat in her office.

"I'm fine, just a little wonky from the nap."

"'Wonky'?" she asked. "Are we British now?"

He shook his head and chuckled, the laughter feeling good after the touch of the dishtowel. "Yeah, what of it?"

Selena smiled. "Oh, nothing. I always liked British guys, their accents are a turn-on."

He blushed but couldn't help returning her smile. "I'm half English."

Selena giggled and tilted her head in a way that made him want to go to her, put his fingers in her hair, and pull her close. Their eyes locked for a second, and time stretched out like pulled taffy, elongating while their gaze welded solid. Selena finally dropped her eyes, smiling again, this time to herself.

"Do you mind if I use your bathroom?" she asked.

"No, go ahead, the loo's down the hall, on the right," Evan said, in his best English accent, which wasn't very good.

She laughed again and disappeared into the living room. Evan walked out to the kitchen's boundary and turned around, expecting the tracks to be back on the floor, but it was dry. He sighed, rubbing his forehead. What the hell was happening to him?

Hallucinations? He hadn't imagined the wetness of the towel. Was there any other explanation?

An idea came so quick and clear to his mind, his head almost snapped back with its arrival. He had the urge to slap his forehead, like a character in a classic comedy show. The grocery bags—he'd set them right where the tracks had been. There were cold items in there, things that would cause condensation. A little moisture had leaked out and only *looked* like footprints.

The explanation felt so good, so right, that he almost sagged with relief. That was it, definitely and most assuredly. He pulled a chair out from the table and heard the wind chimes outside spring into life, as if slapped by someone passing by. At the same time, movement to his right drew his eyes to the wooded backyard.

A dog crawled across the grass, its front legs straight and jerking with effort to drag the rest of its body, which slouched low because of its missing hind legs.

Evan rounded the table, hearing a chair flip over with his passage, but it sounded dim and distant as he pressed his face against the window like a child peering into an exhibit at a zoo. The dog looked like a golden lab, its fur almost orange in the afternoon light. Its head drooped below its shoulders as it moved, its concentration held on the edge of the woods. Its hips swayed back and forth, the bleeding nubs twitching with effort to move legs that were no longer there.

"Holy shit," Evan gasped, his breath fogging up the window and obscuring his view.

He wiped the moisture away, leaving a streaky haze at eye level. The dog stilted its way over a hump in the lawn and then, after one baleful look at the house, slid itself behind a large pine tree.

"What are you looking at?"

He jerked, his stomach constricted so he couldn't get out the moan that ached to be free of his lungs.

"Dog," he said, his mouth forming the word without conscious effort.

"What?" Selena asked, coming to his side.

"There's a dog outside. Shit, it needs help, it's injured."

Evan moved around Selena, to the counter, where he knew more towels lay neatly tucked inside the lowermost drawer. He pulled three or four out and dashed through the living room to the outside door, not bothering with his shoes before plunging outside.

The air was warmer than earlier, and the sun looked too bright in the now-cloudless sky. A small stick cracked under his foot as he ran around the side of the house, but other than that he heard no sound. How the hell had a dog gotten onto the island, much less one without rear legs? A collage of images including spinning boat propellers and glistening bone shot through his mind. Evan ran to where the dog had vanished from view, trying to decide what action to take when he found the poor creature. Could he stanch the flow enough to get the animal across the water and into town? Was there a veterinarian in Mill River that would be open now?

An oily patch of blood glistened on several blades of grass, and the sight made his scalp pull tight, halting all other thoughts. He slowed his pace and traced the two drag marks with his eyes. The faint sound of the house door swinging shut echoed across the yard. He walked in a straight line, stepping around a few globs of coagulated blood, all the while searching the trees ahead for the golden fur he knew couldn't be too far away. The tracks led down through the quiet trees, never deviating left or right. His throat tightened against the thick smell of blood. There was a lot of it, pools of black here and there, reflecting the thick canopy of branches overhead in monochrome flashes. The ground leveled off, and he could hear the slow beat of waves against the shoreline. If the dog got confused and waded into the water, it would certainly perish. Evan picked up his pace and then slid to a stop, turning back the way he'd come.

The drag lines curved a little and then stopped beside a towering pine tree. A few specks of blood dotted the ground and then disappeared, as if the dog had paused here and then ... what? Evan hurried around the base of the tree, sure that he would find the hump of matted fur barely breathing on the other side—but there was nothing. A sound drew his attention back the way he'd come, and he saw Selena making her way toward him, her face full of questions.

A horrifying thought came to him, and he froze, watching Selena approach.

"Do you see it? The blood?"

She frowned and looked at the ground, then returned his gaze. "Yes, how could I miss it?"

He nodded.

"What the hell happened to it?" she asked, stepping beside him.

"I don't know, but its back legs were gone." He heard her surprised intake of breath.

"But where is it?"

They moved out in an expanding circle, keeping the last sign of blood at the center. Evan walked all the way down to the lake before coming back to the pine. He stared at the ground and knelt, touching the blood with one finger. It was sticky, and a bit of sand came up with it. He rubbed his finger against his pants legs and looked at Selena, who appeared shaken. Her hair hung in damp strands next to her face, and her cheeks, normally full of color, were slack and pale.

"Maybe it made it all the way to the lake," she said.

Evan shook his head, still staring at the bare spot of ground on which the last drops of blood lay. "There would've been something, blood on the rocks, and if it drowned, it should still float." He tore his gaze away from the earth and looked at Selena. "Was Shaun still sleeping when you left the house?"

"Yeah, I checked on him before I followed you."

"Let's go back, and I'll call animal control in town, maybe they have a list of missing pets."

She nodded and turned toward the house. Evan stood a moment longer, listening to waves lap on the shore, the smell of blood no longer strong but still in the air, before following her through the trees.

# 22

"Thanks very much, I appreciate your help."

Evan ended the call and looked to Selena and Shaun at the kitchen table. Shaun sucked on a glass of orange juice through a straw, while Selena cupped a mug of tea she hadn't took a drink from yet.

"Well?" she asked, as he sat in a seat opposite them.

"Nothing. No golden labs, or any dogs for that matter, have been reported missing in the last week. They said if we saw it again to call them and they'd send someone out to take care of it," Evan said, rubbing a dark stain on the table with his finger.

"Someone must have dumped it here then," Selena said. "Threw it out of a boat as they were passing by." She made a disgusted face and cupped her tea tighter.

"Yeah, that's what I was thinking. Horrible."

"Do you think it's still alive?"

Evan recalled the amount of the blood on the ground and how the animal had moved, jerking and lunging forward as though determined to get into the woods. It was on its last legs. He closed his eyes and forced the black humor away.

"No, I don't think so."

No one said anything until Shaun finished his orange juice with a loud sucking sound as the straw vacuumed up the last vestiges of liquid. Shaun sat back, belched, and looked at Evan.

"More!"

Evan glanced at Selena, and they both burst out laughing. Shaun smiled, delighted at having caused the outburst. He signed with his hands and yelled again.

"More!"

Evan stood, the laughter pealing out of him. "You need to eat dinner first, buddy."

He tousled Shaun's hair as he walked by and opened the fridge to begin the process of making supper.

Selena chuckled a few more times and then took her cup of tea to the sink. Her hip brushed his thigh as she walked by, and a ripple of pleasure rolled up from the point of contact. He cleared his throat and pulled the hamburger and cheese from within the fridge.

"Stay for dinner?" he asked, as she poured the tea out and set the cup down.

"You know, I better not. I heard there might be rain tonight, and I've been out on the lake in storms before. It's not pleasant."

He was about to say, *You can stay here tonight,* but cut it off with a self-conscious effort. His mind immediately pelted him with versions of how the night would go. How he would make up the couch for himself and give Selena his bed. How she would come to him in the night, silent and ethereal, covered with only a blanket, and ask him to join her.

He swallowed, realizing she'd said something he hadn't caught.

"Sorry, what?"

She smiled a little. "I said, maybe tomorrow or the next day, though. I shouldn't be busy."

"Sure, no problem. I'll walk you out."

Selena said goodbye to Shaun before they moved to the door, Evan maddeningly aware of how close her skin was to his. Should he try to kiss her? Would that be too forward? She'd already bridged that particular gap, so he didn't think she would shrink away, but did he really want to? His emotions seemed caught on a bungee cord. One minute he would be tight, bound by thoughts of Elle in cords of guilt, and in another he would be free-falling, recalling the gentle breeze that had seemed to caress his face that day on the porch when he'd asked for a sign. Elle would want him to be happy; she'd even said so.

That was enough to kill the urge to try anything physical with Selena. Instead, he opened the door for her and waited as she stopped by his side.

"Tomorrow?" she asked.

"Tomorrow."

She leaned in, and for a second he readied himself either to commit toward her or to pull back. Caught in his indecision, he stayed still as she placed her lips on his cheek and kissed him lightly before stepping back.

"Get home safe," he said, a huskiness in his voice.

She smiled over her shoulder and walked toward her beached canoe. Evan shut the door and touched the place where she'd kissed him. It burned a little, and he could still feel the softness of her lips there.

Moving back into the kitchen, he clapped his hands together, startling Shaun, who grinned at him.

"Let's make some la*scag*na, Shauny!" he said, intentionally mispronouncing the word as his mother had done when he was a child.

Shaun laughed, and Evan began to cook.

~

He recited the last page of *Goodnight Moon* and glanced at Shaun, whose eyes were closed and mouth was open a crack. He breathed deep, in slow measures that never failed to make Evan feel at ease. Sleeping. He couldn't get hurt while he was sleeping, couldn't fall or tip from his chair, couldn't choke on food.

*Or hair.*

Evan grimaced. "Night, honey, I love you."

He kissed Shaun's scar, feeling the puckered flesh there, soft but ridged where his head had been split open like an egg. He left the bedroom, not closing the door all the way, and walked to the kitchen, already knowing where he was headed.

The basement was cool, and for once Evan welcomed it. The air outside the house had taken on a thick and heavy feeling as a single thundercloud approached from the west. Maybe the rain would wash the air clean. Maybe it would wash away the blood outside. The thought slowed him as he was about to sit at the worktable. He could see the poor animal limping, its awkward movements disturbing and strange.

Something clicked in the silence of the basement, startling him. Evan turned toward the sound, toward the clock. He stepped forward and set his hand against the side of the closest encasement. Maybe the humidity in the air caused its joints to shift.

*Maybe it knows you're close.*

He shivered and stepped back, focusing on the work he'd done the night before.

The schematics and diagrams had seemed impossibly complex, but the more he looked, the easier they were to read. After several hours of toiling the night before, he judged that the clock was almost completely back together.

Evan started working again. Untangling the weight cables had been the most challenging aspect of the repair so far. Someone had yanked and pulled on the cables until they'd become a snarled mess. The timing mechanism itself didn't look damaged, but the one thing that stood out was an extra rocking switch mounted under the chime hammer. The switch wasn't listed on any of the diagrams, and when he'd tried to flip it back and forth, it wouldn't move a bit. All he could gather was that it would need to be flipped after the clock was fully reassembled and wound, which would be soon.

*Wound.*

The word made him freeze in place as he hung the last of the three brass weights on its cable. He would need to wind the clock, and for that he'd need—

"A key," he said.

A small sliver of panic lanced through him. He hadn't seen a winding key on the table, or inside the clock for that matter. Evan finished hanging the weight and sifted through the papers on the table, picking them up and setting them aside with care. After scouring the table, he searched under it. Nothing. He opened the clock door and half crawled inside, running his fingers along the base. He bumped the pendulum with his shoulder while standing, causing the chime to utter a muted bong. It sounded ominous, a single drumbeat in the middle of an uninhabited jungle. Licking his lips, he stepped back and closed the encasement door. His eyes traveled up its length, to the very top, where the two carved points—*horns*—came together.

Evan grabbed the chair and pulled it close to the encasement, and stood on its seat. The top of the clock was level with a small trim piece that ran its entire edge. Nothing but cobwebs and dust lay on its surface.

"Shit," he said, stepping down from the chair.

His gaze fell on the three holes at the bottom of the clock's face. Three holes that would accept a single, specially made key, which wasn't here. A black anger began to flow through him. Even if he put the clock completely back together, he would have no way to make it work without the key.

He raised a fist, sure in that moment that he would smash it through the glass door, pull out all the work that he'd done in the last two nights. Destroy it, burn it.

Slowly his fist fell to his side, and tears flowed into his eyes like rain filling cisterns during a storm. Why? He pulled the chair close to the table and dropped onto it. Why? Fate had brought them here, he knew it, for one single purpose: to go back.

"It wasn't supposed to happen," he croaked. "We weren't supposed to get hit, Elle wasn't supposed to die." He ground his teeth together. "We're supposed to go back and fix it."

Evan sniffed once and wiped his palms across his eyes, smearing the tears away, disgusted. He stood and opened the encasement door again, making sure that the long chime rods were securely in place.

*It's ready, and the key has to be here somewhere.*

He started by searching every drawer and cabinet in the workbench and found nothing. He pawed through boxes of fabric and knickknacks that lined the opposite wall. He crawled from one end of the basement to the other, his face inches from the cool floor as he tried to spot the shape of a key lying somewhere.

*Somewhere.*

Evan tramped up the stairs, a sheen of sweat standing out on his face. The palms of his hands were dark with dust and dirt, but he barely noticed the smudges he left on the kitchen counter and drawers as he sifted through their contents. Towels, silverware, pens, pencils, pots, pans—everything went on the floor.

When he finished with the kitchen, he continued in the living room, pulling the cushions from the couch and looking behind the entertainment center. The front closet held only an old rain slicker and an ancient tackle box. He dumped the tackle out and left everything in a heap on the closet floor, finding nothing.

His room didn't take long since there weren't many places for a key to hide. As he pulled the last drawer in the bedside table open, a growl left his throat, sounding more animal than human.

He banged the door open and moved to the far end of the house, not pausing before walking straight into the master bedroom. Evan strode to the bed and flipped up the mattress and box spring to look beneath them. He dropped both and went to the closet, pulled the double doors open, grunting upon seeing the empty space.

One place left.

He went to Shaun's room, his eyes casting back and forth as he walked, thinking that the key could be sitting in plain sight, and had been the entire time they had been there. He pushed through Shaun's door and slowed, seeing his son's thin body beneath the blanket, the rise and fall of his chest, a shadow clinging to the opposite side of his head, the side with the scar.

An overwhelming sense of defeat crashed into him, and he stumbled with its weight. In slow motion, Evan fell to his knees beside the bed. His head hung down, chin against breastbone. He'd been a tornado until that point, sure that the key must be somewhere within the house. Life couldn't possibly be that cruel, but it was, he knew it was. And he also knew that—

"It's not here." Evan lifted his head, speaking in a trembling whisper. "It's not here, honey. I was hoping, really hoping."

He sniffled, and Shaun turned a little in the bed, so that he faced Evan more. Evan reached out and stroked his smooth cheek with one finger.

"I wanted to fix it all, buddy, take you back and we could try again." A small laugh slipped out. "We could be a family again." A wrenching tightness in his chest squeezed, and then broke. "But that's not going to happen, buddy. I'm so sorry, son, so sorry all this happened."

Evan sobbed into his forearm to stifle the sound. Hot tears streaked down his face, and he remembered the last time he'd cried this much. It was when Elle had slipped away. She hadn't been awake for almost a day when it happened. The morphine in her system was blunting most of the pain, the doctor said, but Evan wondered, he really wondered. He remembered how she'd twitched and then moved her legs and arms, so strong before, now just sticks with drying flesh coating them. It was as though she'd already died and was decaying before his eyes.

He remembered her turning toward him. He supposed it was because of the window; the light had been behind him. She turned and then—

*—opens her eyes. Her beautiful eyes. He stands and clutches the hand she holds out to him, a skeletal thing that grips his palm with no strength. He waits, hovering there beside the god-awful bed, in the god-awful hospital, with the god-awful smell of death. She purses her lips, their surfaces dry and cracked no matter how much water she drinks or how many layers of lip balm they apply.*

*"Be ..." she begins, and her eyes roll back before returning to focus on his face.*

*Something is tearing within him, and he realizes it is her leaving his side after almost a decade of being together. His other half that carried his child. His soul mate.*

*"It's okay, honey, it's okay," he says, knowing full well it isn't. It isn't okay that she is dying. Nothing will be okay ever again.*

*Her eyelids flutter, and she seems to compose herself for the last time on earth.*

*"Be happy," she says, with an effort that looks equivalent to moving mountains.*

*He bites down on the choked moan of grief that wants to spill out, has to spill out, and nods, smoothing the last thin tangles of her hair away from her burning forehead. She rolls further toward him, as if she wants an embrace, and he gives it to her, holds her as he feels the life flow out through a few gasps and tremors. When he finally lets her go, the shoulder of her nightgown is wet with his tears and her eyes are closed.*

Evan awoke to the sound of Shaun moving. He sat up, his arm cocked in a funny angle above him. Pins and needles coursed in jigging lines of fire up and down his leg as he unfolded it from beneath him.

"Wawee."

Shaun's voice made Evan start, and when he glanced at him, he saw that Shaun's eyes were still closed. Dreaming. He waited, the feeling returning to his limbs little by little.

"Wawee."

Shaun spoke the word quieter now, as if falling back into whatever dream that prompted his speech. Evan smiled and touched his hand, holding it for a moment as the tears from his dream dried on his face. Shaun's eyes shot open, along with his mouth, and Evan thought he might scream. But his face twisted into a semblance of a sneeze and his body snapped tight, his small muscles rigid as he bucked off the bed's surface.

Seizure.

"Oh God, no!" Evan said, leaping to his feet. "Shaun, Shaun, can you hear me, son?"

He sat on the bed and slipped a hand beneath Shaun's arched back while leaning over him. His eyes were wide open and staring at the wall, his breath hitching and a strained wheezing sound coming from his mouth.

A million impulses tried to hold sway over Evan as he stood and turned the light on. The floor shifted, and at once he bit down hard on the insides of his cheeks. Blood filled his mouth, and the room came back into focus. He stood over his son, who held the arch of his back like a strange sculpture of pain.

"Oh God, Shaun, no, no, no!" Evan said, picking him up. It was like trying to cradle a mannequin.

*A doll.*

Shaun's normally weak arms lashed out and froze in an unnatural way.

"Okay, okay, okay."

He ran to the couch and wrapped Shaun's convulsing body in the heaviest quilt he could find and picked him up again, making sure he still heard his ragged breathing. When Evan opened the door, the wind pulled the knob from his hand and slammed the door into the inside wall. Squalls of rain spit at them, as the trees rocked in the wind, caught in the throes of the storm. Evan spun and opened the closet, grabbing the rain jacket from its hanger. After slamming the door behind them, he ran into the roaring weather, clutching his son's stiff form through the blanket.

He made a makeshift tent out of the slicker, providing Shaun some cover on the floor of the pontoon. The muscle spasms seemed to be retreating, leaving Shaun to lay flat against the pontoon's carpet, but his eyes still stared and his chest continued to hitch in a way that made Evan sick to his stomach.

Evan fired up the engine, tossed the ropes free, and gunned the throttle. They launched away from the dock, into the embrace of the chopping waves and the rain that fell without remorse.

## 23

"He's perfectly fine," the young doctor repeated.

Evan steadied himself against the wall of the corridor outside Shaun's room, and was able to absorb the words this time, having not understood them when the doctor first came through the door.

"Fine?" Evan asked, not sure he could fully trust his ears.

The doctor nodded. He had jouncy blond hair that moved when he talked, and a stylish set of glasses perched on his thin nose. "Yes, we ran an electroencephalogram, and it showed no signs of a seizure or any signs that a seizure occurred."

Evan let the information sink in, and his eyebrows knitted. "So he's okay?"

The doctor smiled and nodded. "Yes."

"But you can't see that he had a seizure?"

"It didn't show up on the test, no."

The doctor closed his eyes for a moment and crossed his arms over the white coat he wore.

"Are you sure he wasn't having some sort of nightmare or active dream that may have looked like a seizure?"

Evan stared at the man, his eyes feeling like they were bleeding. "Yes, I'm sure."

"Because," the doctor continued, "sometimes people mistake the signs and symptoms for something else. A night terror, perhaps."

Evan held up a hand. "Listen, he was having a seizure. He had one a few months ago, scared the hell out of me, just like it did tonight. I know what a seizure looks like. He had one."

The doctor relinquished his authoritative posture and nodded. "Okay. What we'll do now is keep him for the next few hours for observation, and then send you guys home with a mild seizure medication. Only administer it to him if you're one hundred percent sure he's having one, okay?"

Evan dipped his chin once and rubbed his eyes. His hair was still damp from the ride across the lake, and his clothes were wet but not dripping anymore.

"You look like you could use some coffee," the doctor said. "There's a beverage center down the hall and to the left if you'd like some."

"Thanks. I want to see him first."

"Go right in."

Evan moved past the doctor and pushed the heavy door open to a dimly lit room. Monitors beeped and whirred to the right, and a nurse fiddled with an IV beside Shaun's bed. Shaun lay on the mattress, covered by a blue blanket. His bare chest looked almost white against the surroundings, and a few electrodes stuck like round leeches to his skin. Evan stopped at the foot of the bed. Shaun's eyes were closed, and he slept peacefully.

"You guys had a rough night," the nurse said.

Her voice sounded choked, and when Evan glanced at her, he saw it was Becky Tram dressed in scrubs. Her head was a mangled mess, oblong and crushed on the left side. Raw meat and gray bits of brain hung from shards of bone along her scalp, and her jaw sat like a partially sunken ship off to one side of her face.

Evan sucked in a breath to scream, his hand flying to his mouth. He blinked and saw the nurse coming toward him, concern on her very normal, very whole features.

"Sir, are you okay?"

Her hands reached out to steady him, and he nearly did scream as she touched him, sure that her skin would be cold and hard. Dead flesh.

"I'm fine. It's a shock seeing him like this," Evan said.

The nurse nodded, giving him a sympathetic smile. He realized she looked a little like Becky—dark hair, a little overweight, same chin. Just a trick of the light.

"I'll leave you two be. You can push the call button mounted on the bed if you need anything."

"Thank you."

Evan watched her leave the room before he went to Shaun's bedside. He placed a hand on Shaun's forehead and smoothed back his hair. He could feel a few sticky spots where, he assumed, they'd attached the electrodes for the EEG.

"I'm sorry, buddy, really sorry."

The blood-pressure cuff around Shaun's bicep puffed up on its own accord, and he shifted. Evan glanced over his shoulder at the door, then leaned in close to his son.

"We'll go home soon, okay? There's no reason to stay anymore. I'll write that article for Justin, and if we have to, we'll move in with Uncle Jason for a while until we get back on our feet."

Saying the words somehow made him feel lighter, less burdened, and he realized what it was. He was giving up on the clock, on the crazy idea that had plagued his thoughts ever since seeing Bob's message in the basement.

"We'll go home, son."

Evan brushed Shaun's hair back one more time, and then settled into the chair beside the bed to wait.

~

They pulled up to the dock at five in the morning. The storm that battered them on their journey in was gone. The air was cool and smelled rain-washed, fresh. The somber glow of dawn spread in the east, and Evan had never been so glad to see a sunrise. He carried Shaun up to the house, the feeling of his small arms wrapped around his neck comforting, so right. Evan didn't want to put him down when they came inside. Shaun had woken on the ride back, but his eyes were only half slits when Evan placed him in his bed.

"You can go back to sleep, okay, buddy?" he said, spreading a blanket over him.

Shaun nodded and reached out with one hand toward Evan's face. Evan leaned in, and Shaun's fingers grazed the bit of stubble on his cheek.

"Da."

"I'm right here, honey. Don't worry."

Shaun's eyes fluttered and then closed. Evan waited beside the bed, anticipating the moment when his small body would arch again, wrung with pain and spasms that he couldn't bear to watch again.

*I'd rather die than see him go through that one more time.*

He stood and made his way back out to the living room.

He hadn't flipped on any lights when they entered, and the house held a smoky quality, with shadows beginning to give up their posts. Evan walked to the kitchen and observed the mess he'd created in his frenzy to find the winding key. He sighed. Despite his tiredness, he'd have to clean this up before Shaun rose for the day. He didn't know if the boy would understand or not, but Evan was embarrassed by the scene of chaos. Silverware on the floor, towels strewn out of cupboards, plates and dishes stacked in uneven piles. He placed the heel of his hand against his right eye and wondered when he'd begun to lose his mind.

"You haven't lost it yet, bub. Get your shit together," he said, and strode toward the front door.

The blanket from their trip sat at the edge of the living room, along with the rain slicker. Evan picked them both up, intending to put the blanket on the porch to dry and the jacket back inside the closet. As he gathered up the slicker, he caught a powerful whiff of something. He paused and pulled the jacket to his face, inhaling. It wasn't the jacket, and it didn't smell like mold or mildew—more like something rotten. It smelled like the moment he'd opened the refrigerator their first day in the house.

Scowling, Evan sniffed once more, wondering if a mouse had crawled into the house and died. If so, he couldn't see it in the dark. He snapped on the light near the entry and turned around to put the slicker away.

Two sets of toes poked out from under the closet door.

Evan stopped, his hand reaching out to pull the door open frozen, fingertips shaking. Every inch of his scalp cinched tight to his skull. The toes were discolored, the skin patched with purple and green, like mottled bruises or rot. The smell of decay grew stronger, but Evan couldn't look away from the toes. Some of their nails were missing, and some were broken, sticking up like open car hoods. As he watched, the toes wiggled, a wave of motion from one direction to the other.

Evan wheezed a strangled breath and dropped his hand as he stepped back, his momentary paralysis broken. There was someone—*something*—in the closet, waiting on the other side of the door. His jaw trembled, and the thought of speaking withered away. As if reading his mind, the feet attached to the toes shifted, like whatever waited there was eager to come out, to open the door and rush at him. He didn't want to see what was attached to those feet. Oh God in heaven, he didn't want to see it.

Evan didn't realize he was moving backward until his arm brushed something beside him, and he spun, raising a fist. The table lamp he'd bumped rocked on its edge, and he caught it before it fell to the floor. It was made of a heavy piece of lacquered oak, with a burnished brass base. Its cord draped out and led to a nearby outlet in the wall. With a jerk, Evan pulled the cord free, and yanked the lamp's shade off. He gripped the lamp's smooth torso like a batter waiting for a fastball.

"Come out," he croaked.

He watched the toes for a reaction, but they sat like lumps of decaying clay. Maybe it was a joke. The thought capered through his mind in ribbons of hope. Someone, Jason or Jacob, had come here in the middle of the night and put these fake toes in the closet for a prank.

*Ha, ha! So funny! Now it can be over, and we can go back to a sane reality in which dead things didn't hide in closets and wriggle their toes.*

Evan took another step, his muscles so tight beneath his skin he thought soon he would hear the snapping of his own tendons. The image of Shaun defenseless and asleep in the other room hardened his crumbling resolve. What if it got past him? What if it got to Shaun?

He lunged forward, gripping the lamp with one hand while he reached for the knob with the other, ready to bash whatever came out of the closet. Before his fingers could graze the handle, the closet door flew open with a bang, and Evan leapt back, his bowels loosening almost past the point of no return.

A solid stench hit him, so strong and putrid he gagged.

The closet was empty.

His body shook as he stepped forward, raising the lamp higher over his head. Nothing looked out of place in the closet. The hanger from which he'd snagged the raincoat swayed a little on the bar, and the tackle box he'd dug through sat at the same angle as before. A whispered gasp left his mouth, becoming a moan as he lowered the makeshift weapon and dropped it to the floor. The smell was gone.

*Or maybe it was never there in the first place.*

Evan staggered back until his ass hit the outside door. He slid down it, his legs unhinging at the knees in tandem. His eyes watered, but he didn't attempt to wipe them.

*There's nothing there, there's nothing there, there's nothing there.*

The mocking echo reverberated through him until he couldn't stand it any longer and placed his face in his hands to cry in earnest.

~

Evan couldn't sleep.

The fatigue was a physical thing, a weight of restless hours hanging from his shoulders, his neck, both his eyelids, but he couldn't shut his mind down long enough to drift off. He tried, laying his blankets and pillows beside Shaun's bed again, but the vision of the toes poking from beneath the closet door kept returning to him. He wondered how long it took a person to go crazy, how long someone could cling to the jagged edge of sanity without slipping into the void of gibbering madness. Would he know it when it happened fully? Would the things he'd seen over the last few weeks become solid? Physical enough to touch, or to touch him?

That thought was enough to get him back on his feet. Evan moved through the living room, pausing to throw a look at the closet door before beginning to clean up the kitchen. He whiled away the time in silence, with only a lilting song of insanity playing on an endless loop in his mind. He'd heard once that crazy people didn't wonder if they were crazy; they just went along with it. The idea didn't comfort him as much as he'd hoped. When the last dish was cleaned and put away, he made a pot of coffee, and sat sipping a cup as the sun rose higher and higher in the east.

They would pack and leave tomorrow, he decided, draining the last dregs in his cup. There was no reason to stay now. The promise of the clock, no matter how insane or unbelievable, was gone, leaving an empty cavern, once filled with a mystical hope, inside him. All he had now was Justin's interest in the article, and he could do all the necessary research from the comfort of his own home—or Jason's. Besides, the psychiatrist that he'd seen for grief counseling after Elle died was in Minneapolis. That would be one of his first stops when they got back.

*What about your other shrink? You know, the one you've made dinner for, talked to for hours, and kissed?*

What would he tell her? That he was seeing ghosts and/or losing his mind, so sorry, he had to run away now before he convinced himself that there weren't any ghosts, only the broken shards of his sanity that continued to snag on reality? Yeah, that would go over well.

"She already knows we weren't staying forever," he said to the quiet kitchen.

*But the notion had crossed your mind, hadn't it?*

Of course it had. Just the thought of her pretty face smiling at him in the sunshine the day he'd taken her and Shaun fishing and of the way her lips had felt on his had almost cemented the notion of never leaving. It had been years since he'd experienced anything like the sensation of really being alive.

Evan cast the thoughts away and stood, his feet carrying him to his room. He took out his suitcase and began to fill it with clothes.

Shaun woke a half hour later, and Evan cooked him breakfast in the spotless kitchen. After they'd both eaten, he helped Shaun trace the alphabet and numbers to thirty, saying letters and numerals aloud as the dry-erase marker squeaked on the plastic pages. When the books were packed away, they did Shaun's exercises, though Evan was careful not to push him too hard, for fear of bringing on another seizure. But Shaun looked strong and resilient, with no sign of giving up. Pride washed through Evan, and a smile that would've seemed impossible a few hours ago came to his lips. That was the power of children. Sometimes they were the sail that lifted the adults' minds out of a free fall.

*We're always thinking that we take care of them, and more often than not it's the other way around.*

Bolstered by how well Shaun did, Evan showed him the sunshine glittering off the lake outside.

"Wanna go swimming, buddy?"

The boy looked at him, and then glanced out to the lake, a thoughtful expression on his face.

"Swimming? Do you want to swim?"

"Swum?"

Evan smiled. "Okay, let's go."

The water gripped Evan's ankles like cold hands when he stepped in, and he hissed with the sensation, every inch of his skin tightening. The sun sat behind the island, and the massive trees threw long shadows on the lake, making its surface opaque and fathomless. The dark water pushed a blade of unease into him, and he walked down the beach, with Shaun in his arms, until he found a break in the trees where sunshine sprayed onto the water in a shimmering pool of light.

They eased in together, Shaun making a happy yet comical grimace as the water lapped higher and higher on his body. Evan whooped when it met his crotch, and he dunked them both lower, knowing it was better to get it over with. He walked them out to deeper water and helped Shaun float.

"You remember this?" Evan asked, as Shaun turned his head toward him. "You remember your therapy in the pool back home? Remember swimming?"

Shaun smiled and raised his eyebrows, making his eyes so large Evan burst out laughing.

"You're a ham."

They swam until Shaun's teeth chattered and his own fingertips tingled. Evan waded them to the shore, and then climbed the hill to the house. Once they were both dry and in comfortable clothes, he made Shaun a cup of hot cocoa and coffee for himself. They sat at the kitchen table and drank, the warmth of the beverages sinking into them. He watched Shaun suck happily on his straw, and thought that in this moment things almost seemed normal. The trip to the hospital the night before and the incident with the closet seemed far away, like an island in the distance that is visible but without detail. He could almost imagine them living here indefinitely if every day was like this.

Evan frowned. Had he just been contemplating staying? He shook his head, the disquiet he experienced earlier when looking at the dark water returning.

"More," Shaun said, trying to push his empty mug across the table.

Evan took it and walked to the counter, his movements automatic, his eyes unfocused as the sun climbed higher.

# 24

Evan forgot about Selena coming over for dinner until the moment she knocked on the door.

He and Shaun had spent the rest of the day cleaning and tidying up the house, his decision to leave the next morning as resolute as one of the pines growing outside. When he opened the door—half dreading the conversation he knew they would have to have—his thoughts stumbled over one another at the sight of her standing there in the afternoon sun.

Selena's hair was lustrous and curled, hanging in brown dangles that framed her face. She wore a formfitting long-sleeved blouse that held tight to her flat stomach and a pair of capris that hugged her hips in curves that kept wanting to draw his eyes downward. A waft of cherry blossom crossed the distance between them, and he felt drugged, helpless but to look at her in the doorway.

She smiled, tipping her right shoulder, which held the straps of a reusable grocery bag. "Are you going to let me in or just stare at me?"

"Stare at you."

Selena laughed. "Here."

She handed him the grocery bag, and when he looked inside, he saw the makings of a salad, steaks, a small bag of red potatoes, and two bottles of wine.

"Whoa," he said, carrying the bag to the kitchen.

"Yeah, I got a little carried away, but I thought I'd bring dinner, seeing as you guys have fed me so many times. Hi, Shaun." Selena knelt next to Shaun's chair and rubbed his shoulder, and then tickled his neck until he giggled.

"You didn't have to do this."

"I know, I wanted to. Now pour me a glass of wine and get out of my way, I need space to create a masterpiece."

Evan shrugged playfully and uncorked one of the bottles. Selena worked for the next hour, pausing only to take a small sip from her wineglass from time to time. Smells of cooking steak and boiling potatoes filled the kitchen, and soon Evan heard Shaun's stomach rumble from the other side of the table.

"I think you've got a fan over here," Evan said, motioning to Shaun.

Selena laughed. "You know the old adage about finding a way to a man's heart."

"Through a wineglass?"

"No, quit it."

Selena moved with an easy grace around the kitchen, flipping a steak here, chopping lettuce there. Evan could see her doing the same thing in their kitchen in the cities. Could he somehow make it work if they left tomorrow?

"What's got you down?" Selena asked, taking the potatoes off the stove.

"Nothing. Thinking again."

"Looked like bad thoughts."

"No, just cumbersome, like the song."

"Which song?"

"'Cumbersome,' Seven Mary Three."

"Which is the band and which is the song?"

Evan gave her an incredulous look. "You've never heard of Seven Mary Three?"

"Nope."

"We shall have to remedy that, my dear."

She smiled, and before she turned back to the stove, Evan thought he saw a hint of red on her cheeks.

~

They ate mostly in silence, not because they were uncomfortable but because the food was that good. Evan had never tasted steak like the one he devoured from his plate, its flavor oaky, with a hint of lime mixed in. The salad and potatoes were equally delicious, and before long all their plates were empty.

"Sorry I didn't bring dessert," Selena said, wiping her mouth with a napkin.

"This is dessert enough for me," Evan said, raising his wineglass.

"The way to a man's heart."

"Absolutely."

Evan cleared the dishes away and began cleaning them in the sink while Selena talked about her day. She hadn't seen many clients, but the few she did have were challenging.

"The guy tried to spit on me when I told him his wife might be right."

"You're kidding."

"Nope. He gathered up some spit and hocked it at me, but I was far enough away and it landed on the table between us."

"So what'd you do?"

"I told him, if that was the way he dealt with difference of opinion, then it was no wonder his wife wanted him to have counseling."

Evan smiled. "Are you even supposed to be telling me these things? Aren't they confidential?"

Selena tipped her head from side to side. "As long as I don't mention any details, like names or anything, it's kinda like a case study, and those get printed in magazines and books all the time."

"With the client's permission."

"I'd say once he spit at me, his permission was given."

Evan laughed and glanced at Shaun, whose head was almost touching the table, his eyes closing and opening with long blinks. Selena noticed at almost the same time.

"Oh, poor baby," she said, putting a hand on Shaun's shoulder.

Evan dried his hands off with a dishtowel and came to the table, unfastening Shaun from his seat.

"He's exhausted. I forgot he didn't have his afternoon nap."

"Didn't he sleep good last night?"

"No, we actually had to take a nighttime cruise into town."

"What? You're kidding, what happened?"

Evan related the events of the night before, his throat trying to close up when he described Shaun's seizure. He left out the parts about seeing Becky and the toes in the closet, skimming over the rest of the day's details quickly as he picked Shaun up and carried him to his room.

"Sounds like you guys did a lot of cleaning," Selena said, as he came back into the living room.

She handed him his glass of wine and sat on the sofa. Evan considered the chair  but then rested beside her, a little distance between them. The sun held above the tops of the trees across the lake, a forest fire in the sky.

"Yeah, quite a bit."

"You're leaving soon, aren't you?"

Evan sighed, took a sip of his wine.

"Tomorrow." He chanced a look at Selena and saw a resigned look on her face. "I'm sorry, it's just not working out here."

He regretted the words as soon as they left his mouth.

"I understand."

"No, you don't, you don't. You're great," he said, scooting closer to her, until their knees almost touched. "You've really brightened things up for us. It's me—"

He floundered for a moment, trying to think of how to explain. "I'm afraid."

Selena looked up at him. "Afraid? Of what?"

"Of this, of what's happening between us."

"Evan, I—"

"No, you don't have to say anything. It's me, it's the life I have. I worry, constantly. I'm afraid all the time. I'm terrified that Shaun will have an accident or another seizure and I'll be completely alone, and I couldn't withstand losing him too. I'd break."

Selena moved closer still, as he lowered his head, her thigh touching his.

"But what does that have to do with us? With ..." She shrugged. "Being happy?"

*Be happy.*

"It's everything."

He stood and paced across the living room, watching the sun fall slowly. His heart beat fast, faster, faster still. He could see his pulse in his vision.

*Tell her everything. Tell her about your plans for the clock. Tell her about what you've seen, what you think you've seen. Tell her about—*

"When Elle got sick, I was hopeful. She was young and vibrant and strong, not the kind of person to ever even get a cold," Evan said, facing away from the couch. "I thought, she'll beat this and it will be a courageous story to tell our grandchildren someday. But she got sicker, and sicker, and none of the treatments worked."

He paused. "Like I told you before, I took money from my work, stole it to try some experimental treatments that weren't covered by insurance. The experimental stuff worked better than the traditional medicine did, but barely. It was like she got a toehold while sliding down a steep mountain. Then my confidence started to slip. I caught myself wondering what it would be like raising Shaun alone, and damn me for being selfish, but I was. I suppose we all are on some level, but I kept thinking, I can't do this alone, I won't be able to."

Evan laughed, a choked sound that he drowned with more wine.

"That was when the fear hadn't fully taken over yet, when part of me believed everything would still work out all right. That's sometimes the worst and best quality people possess, you know? To hope in the darkest times. Sometimes it pays off and faith is redeemed, and others—"

Evan swallowed. A lump was forming in his throat, and no matter how many gulps of wine he took, it wouldn't move. He knew what it was, and knew the only way to make it go away would be to keep talking.

"Then one day, I knew. I knew she wasn't going to get better. She'd had another round of chemo two days prior, and it was painful to look at her, to see how much less she'd become. She told me she hurt and she couldn't take much more, and I—here's the selfishness again—I told her she couldn't quit, not on me and not on Shaun."

Evan tipped the last of his wine down his throat.

"She told me to go to her bag, that there was something in there she wanted. She was too weak to get out of bed on her own. When I reached inside, there was a bottle of pain pills one of the doctors had prescribed for her when she was still able to be at home. It was almost full, and I remember how heavy that bottle felt, so heavy. She told me it was too much and she didn't want to suffer anymore. She asked me to help her, to count out a dozen or so into her hand and then get her some water. She told me to pull the bag close to the bed, so it would look like she'd reached down and got them herself after I left."

A vein of tears ran down the right side of his face, and he wiped it absently.

"I told her no. I walked out of the room, and she never brought it up again. I hated her at that moment, for asking me to do it, for getting sick in the first place. But you know what?"

Evan turned halfway toward Selena, who was perched on the edge of the couch, her hands clasped in front of her mouth, her eyes shining.

"I hated myself more than anything, for not being able to save her. And then when I couldn't—for not being man enough to ease my wife's pain, for letting her suffer."

Evan's jaw trembled, and he knew, if he let them, his teeth would chatter, for he was very cold at that moment—*so* cold. He wiped again at his face and glanced at Selena, who had a hand pressed to her mouth, her fingers long and white.

"So I carry that, and I get scared whenever someone else comes close. I want to go back and change things, change everything that's happened, for Shaun and for Elle, for me, and when I realize I can't, it's just too much."

This was as close as he could come to telling her about the clock and his dashed hopes. He turned back to the sunset, only a red smudge on the western horizon now, fading to pink and dark blue where the bruise of night began in the sky.

"I wonder if something in my mind broke a long time ago, if I've been crazy for a while, because sometimes it feels like the moorings are coming loose up here."

Evan tapped his skull. He was as used and empty as a paper cup in a gutter. Any relief he might've had at speaking about Elle's last request was overshadowed by the guilt of saying it out loud. It was like being condemned in front of a judge and jury.

He heard Selena rise from the sofa and begin to move across the living room toward the front door. He grimaced and waited for the sound of the knob being turned, but it didn't come.

Instead her hands gently gripped his sides, guided him around to face her. Her eyes gazed up into his, and she touched his face, traced the line of tears, and then leaned in close.

Their lips met, and heat bloomed within him. First in his stomach, and then lower. Selena moved closer to him, ran a hand down his neck, across his chest, around to his back. Evan wrapped his arms around her, drawing her into the heat between them as her tongue darted into his mouth. She pulled him close, and he let out a small moan as her stomach brushed his growing erection. He tried to draw away then, embarrassed, but she pulled him even closer, ground his bulge against her. Their kiss broke, and she looked at him.

"Take me to your room, Evan."

His heart did a stutter step, but he nodded and took her hand, leading her across the living room and down the hall. He couldn't help but glance into Shaun's room, and saw his sleeping face as they turned to the left. A truckload of shame fell on his shoulders. How could he do this across the hall from his son, whom he'd made with Elle, who was watching now? He could feel her eyes on him as Selena shut the door and came to him, finding his lips with hers in the twilit room.

Evan moved backward until his legs met the bed. He sat on it and momentarily parted from Selena before she straddled him, climbing onto his lap. She guided his shaking hands beneath the bottom of her blouse, onto the warm, smooth skin of her stomach. He wanted to tear her shirt off, to hear the buttons pop free as he exposed her, but he stopped, a sick ball of guilt burning in his stomach. It churned there, with thoughts of Elle in the same position as Selena so many times before. How she'd come to him in the shower sometimes, nude and smiling, washing him off before kneeling before him. The lace she'd worn on their first night together, and how he hadn't lasted more than a few seconds. But he'd recuperated quickly, and she'd cried his name over and over again until they were both breathless.

Selena reached down between them and rubbed him through his jeans, but he was already softening. She kissed him again, but he sat back, withdrawing his hands from beneath her shirt.

"What's wrong?" she asked, her eyes wide in the low light, her pupils huge with arousal.

"I can't," Evan said, not believing he'd spoken the words. "I want to, but I can't, not now."

She tried to read his expression in the falling dark—he assumed to see if he was bluffing, if there was something else there. She slowly slid off him, the sweetness of her heat leaving him, a pang of regret taking its place. He wanted to know her warmth, to slide into it, to bury his face in her cherry-blossom hair and feel himself release inside her.

Evan blinked, feeling himself rise again, desire coming over him in a new wave. He reached out and held her hand.

"I'm sorry, it's not that I don't want you. I do, very, very much. But it's still too soon. Do you understand?"

Selena let a long breath out and nodded. "Yes, of course I do." She smoothed out her blouse and ran a quick hand through her hair. "I suppose I should go, it's getting late."

"Stay with me," he said, holding on to her hand a little tighter. "Stay here tonight."

He waited for her to pull away or shake her head, but she did neither.

"Okay."

Evan guided her around to the other side of the bed, and she lay down on top of the blankets. He did the same, and after a bit of arranging, she scooted close to him, tucking her head against his chest, hugging his stomach with one arm. He put his hand on her waist and pulled her nearer. She sighed, and he could feel her breath, warm through his T-shirt.

The fatigue he'd battled all day collapsed on him at once, a gutted building falling in, piling in with the undeniable promise of rest. He tried to say good night but drifted off before he could form the words.

~

Evan awoke sometime in the night, his eyes coming open like shutters thrown wide. He'd been dreaming of something— darkness so black it was solid. He'd tried to walk through it and felt things touching him, quick, intimate caresses that chilled and made him sick with fear. That's when he'd realized the darkness was alive and nothing but its cold embrace, like a long-dead lover, was there.

He blinked and rolled over, suddenly afraid that Selena would be gone, but she wasn't. She lay on her back beside him, breathing softly. He moved closer to her form, feeling her warmth again, and reached out, searching for her hand in the darkness. He found it resting on her stomach and slid his palm into hers, remembering how he would do the same thing with Elle on nights when sleep eluded him. The comfort of holding her hand, even while she slept, helped send him back into a serene rest. Selena clasped his hand tighter, and he scooted closer to her, the smell of her perfume not as vivid as before but still there, somehow even more enticing as it mellowed. Another scent met his nostrils, and Evan opened his eyes, sleep leaving him fully.

*Decay.*

There was no mistaking the stink. It was the same as the smell from the closet, as heavy and cloying as an open grave. He raised his head a few inches off his pillow and looked at Selena's profile, her lips parted, her eyelashes long against the top of her cheeks. Evan sat up a little more, and Selena shifted, her elbow bumping his shoulder.

His eyes traveled up and saw that both her arms were above her head, hands splayed out on her pillow.

The hand he held squeezed once. Evan tried to rip his arm back, but the fingers gripped him tighter as he opened his mouth to cry out. His eyes shot to the hand holding his, the rotting flesh almost black in the dim starlight that shone through the window, the arm attached to it snaking into the darkness beside the bed.

"Uhh!" he grunted, and managed to break his hand free.

The other hand slid away, and a quiet scuffling sound came from the other side of the bed. A shape rose and stood over them, hunched and broken, its face turned toward him, its outline reminiscent of something ancient, curled in on itself by time. The figure limped across the room, not thin and ephemeral but solid and real. With a turn of its stunted head, it went through the open door toward Shaun's room.

"No! No!"

Evan sprang from the bed, his yells and the commotion waking Selena.

"What?"

He flicked on the light, drawing back a fist, ready to throw it.

The hall was empty.

Shaun's door was in the same position as earlier, or so it looked. Evan rushed into the room, his fist still held high. The light flooded the space enough for Evan to see it was empty except for the boy and his bed. He slept on, not moving but for the rise and fall of his chest.

"Evan, what's going on?"

He turned. Selena was standing in the hallway, her hair sticking out in several places, her eyes bleary.

"I, I thought I saw something, someone."

"You saw someone? In the house?"

"Yeah, it was there in the room. It held my hand." The memory of the thing's grip made him convulse, and he rubbed his palm on his pants leg.

"Held your hand? Evan, you're not making sense."

"It was there, right there," he said, moving past her and into the hall. He pointed toward the bed, looking at the floor, hoping for a telltale sign of the thing's passage. "I went to hold your hand, and it wasn't yours. It was something else. It ..."

His dropped his head as Selena came closer.

"I think you may have been dreaming," she said, touching his shoulder.

"I wasn't dreaming, I was awake. I know I was awake."

"Are you sure? I've had a few clients with night terrors that they swear are as real as waking life."

"This wasn't a night terror," Evan said, shrugging off her hand.

He moved into the hallway again and stood, sniffing the air. A faint hint of rot lingered.

"Do you smell that?"

"Smell what?"

"That smell. It's like something rotten, spoiled meat. Here, come here."

He motioned her into the hall, then pulled her closer to the living room. "Do you smell it?"

Selena raised her face and inhaled a few times. She frowned.

"No, I don't. All I smell is last night's dinner."

Evan closed his eyes, opened them, and walked to the living room. He looked at the dark lake, no light on its surface yet, only a black cloth beyond the trees.

"Let me ask you this," Selena said, moving to the couch. "Was I the first one you told about your wife, what she asked you to do?"

Evan didn't answer for a long time, and then finally said, "Yes."

"Do you know what kind of stress comes with a burden like that? Keeping it all inside, letting it whittle away at you?"

He didn't say anything, just let her talk.

"Releasing something like that can cause stress too, you know. It's like pulling out a knife that's been keeping a wound from bleeding. When you do, there's trauma."

"You know, I'd like to believe that, I really would." His voice sounded strange, far away, not his own. "I want to think stress, the past, is what's doing this, but I'm not sure, and that's the worst part. Not being sure is worse than anything else. You're on a high wire knowing you're going to fall, but not which way."

"I'm sure it's stress."

"Well, that makes one of us."

"What you're experiencing is perfectly normal."

He coughed laughter. "Nothing in the last four years has been normal."

The faint inklings of the treetops across the water became visible. The sun was rising, throwing its radiance out like a candle in another room.

"The how is fine, I can relate to that, understand it," Evan said, after a while. "The how is measurable, calculable, it's numbers and math. It's the why ..." His hand bunched into a fist and shook at his side. "The why is what gets me. It's what makes me dream at night and wonder during the day. It never makes sense, and what really pisses me off is, there is no answer to that one." He spun, seeing and not seeing her. "That's the biggest joke there is, and it doesn't have a punch line."

Evan walked toward the kitchen, meaning to put on some coffee, but instead went to the basement door, pulling it open and descending before Selena could say anything more.

# <u>25</u>

He sat in the basement staring at the clock.

The fucking clock. Its black skin, its quiet contemplation. Serene and uncaring.

"Damn you."

The air was cold, and he shivered, his skin rippling. He could almost see the air he breathed out. Could that be? Evan stood and moved to it, staring up at its height, feeling like he was in front of an avalanche. Power. That's what the air tasted like. An electric coppery tang, almost like simmering blood.

He put out a hand and touched the clock's front. His arm went numb to the elbow, and he opened his mouth to gasp but stopped, letting the thrum travel through him.

*Power.*

Enough to scorch the outline on the wall. Enough to chill the air. He wasn't imagining that. Power to change things, to make them right. He tried to pull his hand back, but it seemed glued there. The clock could explode at any second, he was sure of it, explode and blow him all the way across the room. It could—

The feeling returned to his arm. He let it drop to his side, his eyes staring past the clock, through it.

"It was there the whole time."

His eyes traveled up to the clock's face, and he saw the position of the hands, a startled thrill running through him. A hand on the two, two hands on the zero, one hand on the eight. The year before Shaun's accident—2008. Had he changed that the day before? No. A ripple of fear and wonder went through him as he remembered looking at the clock as soon as he'd come down to the basement. It had been at 1919 less than an hour ago.

Evan backpedaled, pausing to grab a flat-blade screwdriver from the workbench before flying up the stairs, three at a time, and bursting into the kitchen. Selena, sitting at the table, a cup of coffee in her hand, recoiled. Coffee spilled over the rim when she jerked, and she winced, setting the cup down.

"Evan, what—"

"Can you stay here with Shaun for me, just for an hour or so?"

"Sure, I—"

But he was gone, running toward the door, grabbing the key ring from the table near the entry.

"Evan, where are you going?"

"I'll be right back. It's okay now, I know where it is."

He shut the door and ran down the dew-slicked bank toward the dock, a grin pulling hard at his features as he went.

~

It misted the entire way to Kluge House, the van's wipers on intermittent as the day gained more and more gray light, which filled up the land with its cool embrace. The trees that passed on either side were matchsticks, burned in the early day, their crippled branches bent and misshapen against the gunmetal sky.

Evan drove across the small bridge, hearing the tires thunk on the ancient boards, knowing if fate was against him they would break now and leave him stranded. They held, and he emerged in the open yard a minute later.

The door creaked louder than the first time they'd been there, its shriek cutting through him, shaking him from the manic wave he'd rode from the island. The house was a tomb, a crypt of memories stale with history and secrets. Except now he knew one of them, its most precious of all.

The stairs complained under his weight, but he continued up until he stood in the master bedroom, the windows to the east silver squares of light, the floor slanted with dissolving shadows. The clock's outline looked darker today, more pronounced. Evan walked to it, tracing its borders again, and pivoted, facing the opposite wall. He moved in a straight line and stopped in front of the painting, staring at the hole in the canvas.

Without hesitation, he pulled the screwdriver from his back pocket and slipped it into the hole. The driver's tip disappeared, and he listened, knowing what he would hear.

The tool's progress stopped with a little clink of metal.

Smiling, Evan tore at the painting, peeling the dried canvas back from the hole and exposing mildewed wallpaper. The key for the clock was embedded in the wall, its tip driven into the wood from the force that expelled it over ninety years before, splinters in a sharp crown around its black steel. With careful movements, he slipped the tip of the screwdriver into the key's decorative grip and levered it free of the wall. It let out a short squeak, like a mouse being crushed, and popped into his hand.

Its thickness and heft surprised him.

*Heavy with power.*

Without another look around the room, Evan walked out and went down the stairs, leaving the house to mutter its creaks and groans alone.

~

When Evan pulled back into the parking lot of Collins Outfitters, he parked the van and shut it off, considering what would happen to it after he went back to the island, what would happen to it if they were able to go back. Would it sit here in the present and rust until Jacob had it towed away? Would it vanish the moment they did? Would Jacob forget they were ever here? Would Selena?

The implications of what he was about to attempt landed upon him like a giant bird of prey. Any assertions about what might happen fell away. He knew nothing about what would be waiting for them. Instead of a malleable past, it might be different. Alien. Unforgiving and unchangeable. An image of a blank wasteland of time, grim as the morning mist, settled before his mind's eye. An ash-covered stretch that he and Shaun might wander until they died of thirst or starvation. Did the past tolerate visitors?

A rap of knuckles on his driver's window shocked him, and he jumped in the seat. Turning his head, he found Jacob staring at him through the misted glass, a wide-brimmed hat pulled down close to his eyes. Evan tried to smile, then climbed out of the van.

"Mornin', boyo, yer up early."

"Yeah, didn't see you when I came through."

"Yeh, took breakfast with me wife this mornin'. She likes me ta cook least once a week."

Evan nodded and watched as an older golden lab rounded the front of the van and sat beside Jacob's feet. He stared at the dog, feeling his jaw loosen.

"Somethin' the matter?"

"Is that your dog?"

Jacob glanced down at the lab. "Oh yeh, her name's Messy, on accounta how hard she was ta potty train."

He patted the old dog on the head, and she licked her chops once and began to pant. Jacob looked at Evan again.

"Ya sure yer okay?"

"Yeah, I could've sworn I saw a dog almost exactly like her the other day."

"Wasn't a picture out at the Fin, was it?"

"What?"

"Oh, I jest wondered if maybe ya seen one of Dan's pictures. See, we each got a pup from the same litter, both love ta duck hunt and all that. Picked 'em up outside a town almost thirteen years ago from a gal who used ta breed 'em. Ol' Mess here was a right fine retriever up till her hip went bad a year or so ago."

"Dan had a dog like her?" Evan asked. In his mind he saw the golden lab sliding its bloody hind end through the grass, its baleful look before it vanished into the trees.

"Oh yeh, name was Honey B. Beautiful dog, she was, outstandin' hunter."

"Did something happen to her?" Evan asked. The ground was unsteady beneath his feet, and he wondered if it was there at all.

Jacob gave him a funny look, something between puzzlement and distrust.

"What makes ya ask that, boyo?"

"Did something happen to her legs?"

"Aye. I believe it was some sorta accident, if I remember properly. Dan was particular broken up about it. Pup was only a few years old then. Died right there on the island, and Dan buried her down behind the house, 'neath a big pine."

Evan put a hand out to steady himself on the van, the cold, wet steel bringing him back like a slap. Jacob had asked something, and he looked at him as though from the opposite end of a long tunnel.

"What?"

"Are ya okay?"

"Yeah, I'm fine."

"All right. I hate ta run, boyo, but I'm supposed ta be out on the lake soon. Rotten business on a day like today," Jacob said, shooting a look at the sky.

"Why, what's going on?"

"That young girl that killed herself? Well, her father went missin' a few days ago. Someone on the opposite side of the lake found his boat beached up in some weeds, empty, with the anchor rope cut. They're fearin' the worst, I'm afraid."

"Oh God."

"Yeh, terrible business. Poor Tessa's a mess, medicated ta the gills."

Evan thought he might faint. His muscles were jelly, his bones brittle clay.

"Where's Shauny this mornin'? I never see the two of ya apart."

"He's with, uh ..." Evan was sure he would vomit all over Jacob's shoes. "He's with Selena Belgaurd, the psychologist."

Jacob frowned. "Psychologist?"

"Yeah, she's got a practice on the other end of town, near the park."

Jacob shook his head. "Only shrink I know of is old Doc Delly, and he's been shut down a number of years now, mumbles 'n' drools more'n anythin' these days. Kinda ironic."

A cold finger traced its way down Evan's back, something monstrous rising in his mind.

"You're joking, right? I have her card. She said her father and you had a falling-out over some land deal years ago."

Jacob remained silent, watching Evan like an animal on display at the zoo chewing at a weak spot in the fence. Evan dug out his wallet, his hand shaking so badly it took him the better part of a minute to find Selena's card. When he pulled it free, he felt a click, like a cord coming unplugged somewhere in his mind. It echoed to the point that he could hear nothing else as he stared at the soiled piece of paper with Selena's handwriting on it, the other side blank except for a few dark stains.

Jacob gently took it from his fingers, turning it around so he could read it before glancing up at him.

"This a joke, boyo?"

"No, why?"

"This is yer phone number, the number out at the Fin. I've called it a hundred times if I've called it once. Now what're you playin' at?"

Evan snatched the scrap of paper, turning it over a few times, hoping through sheer will that the business print would appear each time he flipped it.

"No ... no, this isn't right. She's a psychologist over by the park, she's—" His mind scrambled as though sliding off a sharp cliff. "She was with us the day you stopped by in the boat. We were fishing, remember?"

Evan waited, watching Jacob straighten up. His lined face became tight, and his eyes narrowed, a glint in them like December sunlight on steel.

"Boyo, there was no one in that boat but you and yer son."

# 26

The mist solidified into fog halfway across the lake and clung to his skin like a spider web.

Evan continued to brush at his arms, knowing full well nothing but moisture was there. There was no wind, and for the first time he wished there was some, to blow away the fog so he would be able to see the Fin. Instead the fog hung in the air, obscuring everything past fifty yards.

A strange sound floated over the water twice, a chilling keening that rose and fell like the wind he wished for. The third time it came, he realized he was making it, deep in his chest. Tears steadily ran down his cheeks, and had been since Jacob caught him before he fell to the ground. He remembered saying something about calling the police and then running, Messy's barks following him into the mist.

A dark shape emerged from the fog, and Evan swerved hard, sure that he'd run up to another boat. Then he saw it was his own dock, as the rest of the island materialized in a looming, grandeur way he would have found majestic any other day. Now, it made him cringe.

Evan didn't bother tying the pontoon to the dock. He ran the boat onto land, rocks and sand playing a horrid symphony on the aluminum pontoons. When he leapt out of the boat, his right ankle turned and he sprawled, a cry of pain coming from him as he braced his hands on rocks and pine needles. His face scraped what he thought was ground, but when he looked up, he saw it was Selena's canoe.

Except it was different.

The canoe had been old before, its hide stained and worn by years and years in the water. Something to be expected from being handed down two generations. The thing that lay before him now would never float. Its sides were broken, with white fungus growing from the cracks. The bottom had a long gouge in it, revealing a smile of darkness. A few dry pine branches, looking like peeled bones, lay on top of it.

"Oh God."

Evan limped up the hill to the house and went inside, the dimmest ember of hope glowing feebly.

"Shaun! Shaun!"

He stumbled across the living room, knocking over a floor lamp on his way through.

"Shaun!"

Sobbing, he opened the door to Shaun's room, the ember inside dying at the sight of the empty bed. Evan staggered to his own room, barely pausing to sweep it with his eyes before continuing to the kitchen.

"Shaun?" A plea now, a prayer.

The kitchen was empty. When he turned toward the basement, any surprise he should have felt bled out of him with the air in his lungs. The door stood partially open, waiting, beckoning.

*Come see, come see, I can't wait to show you.*

Evan could hold it no longer. He bent at the waist and threw up on the kitchen floor. Runners of snot hung from his nose, and he fell to his knees, wetting them in his mess. He gagged again, feeling something tickling the base of his throat. Knowing already, he heaved again, his stomach crumpling like an accordion inside him and—

—forcing the wet lengths of white hair out onto the floor. He let out a shriek and skidded away from the pile of vomit, watching the clumps of hair soak into the bile. He slid to the nearest wall and managed to stand, and forced the basement door open.

Pure darkness held sway, blacker than a mine at midnight. Evan took the first steps and then remembered the light switch. Flipping it on produced nothing like the glow earlier that morning. It looked like the bulbs were less than half power, flickering below him, their light a sickly yellow that barely drove the shadows down.

Evan stumbled on the stairs, hitting the landing and almost falling to his knees. He wiped at the stinging acid on his lips and flipped the next switch, lighting his way with the same urine glow.

"Shaun? Selena?"

Again the hope that she would answer and make this a waking fever dream. He would take insanity now, take it and call it his own with a smile. Anything compared to the anticipation of what reality had in store for him.

A small scuffling sound came from near the worktable, and his heart lost a beat.

"Shaun?"

He moved closer, his shoes rasping on the concrete, his eyes twitching to the clock, to the floor, to the stairs behind him. A silver strip lay on the concrete, and when he tilted his head down, he saw it was tape—the duct tape from the doll's mouth.

The sound again, louder.

Evan slowly walked, rounded the end of the table, and saw the doll standing at the base of the clock. Its head tilted up as its mouth cracked open with a popping sound.

"Go back."

He heaved in a breath to scream, as the doll fell backward, its legs and arms bursting from its plastic sockets. Its head rolled away, its blue eyes flashing, gone, flashing, gone, until it came to rest against the far wall. Evan shuddered, the strength sapped from his legs, his arms cold. His breath plumed out before him.

"Where's my son!"

A small click answered, and the center door of the clock swung open a few inches. The light bulbs began to hiss, and their luminance dipped before flaring. The three bulbs burst, one after another, *snap, snap, snap*. Glass rained down, and Evan sidestepped some of the shards that came his way. Darkness, except for the sallow glow from the stairway, claimed the basement. Silence rushed in.

Evan inched forward, waiting for the dismembered doll to spring into life again. It lay still, and he moved around it, gripping the clock's open door in one hand. Until then he hadn't noticed, but now he saw with utter clarity that the weights were all wound to the highest position, hanging like alien eggs waiting to hatch.

With a last deep breath, he pushed the pendulum aside, ducked his head, and stepped into the clock.

## 27

The first thing he noticed was that it was much larger inside.

Evan knew his left shoulder should be rubbing against the clock's interior wall, but it wasn't. He put out a hand to keep from running into the back panel, but it met only empty air. His footsteps clacked and rang out, reverberating as though he stood not in a three-foot-by-three-foot space but in an empty auditorium. A quiet snick issued from behind him, and though he could see nothing when he turned, he knew the door had closed behind him.

"Shaun?"

His voice bounced back to him, coming from too far away. Impossibly far. The darkness around him was complete, like he'd never known before. He imagined this was what an astronaut felt like staring into the void of space—no end, only pitch black to eat up an eternity in every direction. At least he could still feel the floor.

Something touched his back.

Evan spun, swinging a fist through the darkness before he wondered if it could be Shaun.

"Shaun?"

A slithering sound came from his left, the direction of the door, he thought. It sounded like something long crawling through dead leaves, a snake burrowing into a carcass to feed.

"Who's there?"

Nothing. Another caress from the dark, this time on his right side, toward the back wall of the clock. It felt like a bony hand running down the length of his arm. Evan swung again, this time his knuckles encountering some resistance, but only momentarily. A warm draft of air, then cold.

His dream from the night before came back to him. The darkness alive around him, touching, picking, tasting him. He moved backward, turning in a circle, losing all sense of direction.

"Shaun!"

His yell echoed back to him from a thousand feet, ten thousand. His foot struck something in the dark, and he heard the rustle again, a susurration, and then quiet.

*Evan.*

The voice came from everywhere at once—the walls, if there were any, spoke his name, as well as the floor. Worst of all, he heard it in his head. Not the normal musings of his internal voice but a foreign communication.

"Who's there?" he asked again, hoping for and dreading a reply.

*Evan.*

The voice sounded synthetic, a miasmic blending of tones and depth, not human in the least. The space brightened, lit by a shape behind and above him. Evan turned toward it, squinting at the source until it became clear.

The steel crescent-moon dial had increased in size, along with the rest of the clock. It was now several yards across, and shone with a vague opalescence mixing with the darkness so that the light shifted and moved like a tide through the air. At one moment it would be on his left, and then would flow gradually to the right, all the while the crescent moon grinned its malicious smile down on him as its eye pinned him to the ground.

"What is this?" His voice resounded for a second and then stopped as though crushed in midair.

*Your destiny, Evan.*

He clutched his ears, the voice bubbling through his skull with a paralytic touch of violation.

*You've come through the years to this time and place, and I've been waiting, patiently waiting.*

Evan blinked, his vision hazy with the rolling light of the steel moon. The floor he stood on remained black despite the touch of light, and no defining features were revealed in its glow.

"Where's my son?"

*Here, Evan. Everyone is here, can't you feel them?*

"Who are you?"

*I am one and many. I am the creator. I am the time and the soul.*

His knees unhinged, and he dropped to the ground, feeling something begin to drip from his nose. Hearing the voice was like standing inside a giant speaker, with a smaller speaker in his head. The noise of it was everywhere and nowhere.

"Stop, stop, get out of my head," he said, bracing a hand against the floor.

More blood fell from his nose, splashing to his hand. It looked like tar in the moon's sick light.

*Is this better?*

The voice now came from directly in front of him, and something stood there, just outside the moonbeam's reach. Something rumpled and hunched. Manlike, but so wrong he couldn't find words to describe it.

"Where's Shaun?"

His head felt huge, heavy on his neck, but the nosebleed had stopped, a faucet shut off within his skull. He stood and wiped away the blood drying on his upper lip. The man-shape was gone. He pivoted slowly, trying to distinguish his position within the cavernous space.

"Who are you?"

Evan caught movement off to his right and turned as the figure walked toward him, the moon's light finally illuminating it.

It looked vaguely human, but it wasn't, he was sure of it. It wore a swirling suit of darkness that continued to move even after it stopped walking. Its cloak twisted and crawled with life of its own. Shining eyes inspected Evan from various places on its body and then melded with the rest of the darkness. Its face had no continuity, a wax blur of features without structure. It flowed, melted, a nose erupting and then receding, a mouth blooming, teeth flashing, then gone. Hair grew and shrunk, while eyes, sometimes one, sometimes three, blinked and then sank away. It was then that he realized it did not wear the darkness—its skin *was* the darkness.

Evan took a step back and something crunched beneath his heel. He nearly stumbled but managed to keep his feet as he looked down at the pile of bones he'd tripped over. The skeleton wore a faded pair of women's slacks, their original color no longer discernable. A blouse, thin and flowing, lay around the sunken rib cage like a deflated balloon. Curly strands of gray hair sat in piles above the grinning skull.

*They never found my grandma.* Jason's voice came back to him, the memory nudged either by seeing the bones on the floor or by the thing standing nearby.

He tore his gaze away from the bones as the figure's shape churned and became a kind-looking woman in her seventies who had Jason's chin and cheekbones. She smiled at him, an upside-down grimace.

The swirling moon's light shifted and shone on another rumpled mass a few paces from Maggie's remains. This corpse had some flesh still covering its bones, but death had taken its eyes away, along with its lips, so that it smiled, its teeth bright ivory.

*Bob Garrison. He was the first in many years.*

Evan gazed at the body and recognized Bob, even in death. He looked back to the figure to watch it shift again, taking on the form he'd seen on the Internet while researching the former caretaker's past. Bob sneered at him, his eyes sharpened points.

The light swirled, washing past Bob's rotting corpse. It coursed over the floor, illuminating the unmistakable hind-leg bones of a dog, and then brightened a spot where another full skeleton lay, this one blinding white through tattered suit pants and a limp jacket.

The figure melted again, a long nose and two cold eyes solidifying in a sallow face. The suit pants and jacket came into focus and hung like a loose skin on the man's frame, although they looked brand-new. The man's lips moved when he spoke, but there was a delay as the words crossed the air between them.

*I am Abel Kluge.*

The man-thing walked in a small circle around Evan, its glinting eyes studying him with calculation, a shark's stare.

"You're dead." His mind tilted toward the drop-off of insanity.

*Yes and no. You see, there is a purpose to everything, a reason. You are here because of it. So was your son. Every living thing provides a rung in the ladder that climbs beyond what we know.*

"What are you talking about?"

*Souls, Evan—or I should say time, for that is all a soul is, time. A soul is time for life, energy for living, a drop in the ever-flowing well.*

"Where's my son?" Evan said. Anger rose within him, a fury at whatever this was—hallucination or reality, he didn't know. All he wanted was to find Shaun.

The Abel-shape ignored the question and continued its circle around him. Evan saw the rear of its head shift and warp before coming back into definition. The thing stopped and faced him again. In a split second its face broke, peeling back and reabsorbing its flesh, until long, brown hair sprouted and dropped past its shoulders. Its frame shrunk and took on curves Evan knew well.

Selena stood before him.

As if hearing his thoughts, it spoke in the same ratcheting voice that grated against his eardrums.

*You know her as Selena, but her name used to be Allison. Allison Kaufman.*

Evan stood stock-still, letting its words sink into him. Selena, or what hid beneath her guise, smiled at him, revealing a broken and jagged grin that righted itself instantly. Then the shape became Abel again, the skin flowing like magma until the features solidified once more.

"I don't understand," Evan whispered.

The Abel-thing sprang at him.

It leapt across the distance between them as though teleporting, and had both of its soggy hands around Evan's throat before he could react. Its flesh was like a fish fillet—wet, cold, and pliant—but moved and crawled without releasing him from its hold. He opened his mouth to scream, to cry out in revulsion, and the thing holding him leaned in, touching its now-flowing forehead against his.

A rush of colors and images poured into his mind, a river of life he had only moments to discern before it plunged past. He saw Abel dancing with a woman who could only be his wife in a magnificent ballroom, and they twirl until the scene becomes a workshop in which Abel toils over a bench, gears and sprockets stacked in canted piles, assembling a small timepiece. Kluge House rising from the ground, with dozens of workers lifting, nailing, setting its structure. Selena, her eyes as well as her smile unmistakable, so seductive, before him first on a front stoop, then on a bed, her body bare, writhing beneath him. A young woman bearing a great likeness to Cecil Fenz scrubbing a floor as Abel and Selena walk by, both landing a kick to her ribs, sending her sprawling. Speckles of blood on a mirror, Abel's reflection gazing at the mess, his eyes far away. A dark basement full of tools swaying on their hooks, Abel assembling a large frame—the clock. Abel's hand carving ideograms in the wood, his mouth open and chanting, sweat running in streams down his face. Abel doubling up, hacking out a blob of red and black tissue onto the workbench, his eyes bulging. The master bedroom of Kluge House, Selena lying on a settee, barely breathing, her eyes staring. Abel coughing as he chants again, cutting his wrist on the edge of the clock's swinging pendulum, his eyes alight with fever and madness. Larissa crouching in the corner of the room, her delicate hands covering her head and face from the sight. Abel dropping to his knees before the clock, his arms outstretched in supplication as the darkness within the encasement bleeds into the room. Tendrils reaching, wrapping around Abel's wrists and waist and then yanking him into the clock's dark belly. A shock wave of ichor shooting out in every direction, blazing a shadow against the wall. The key exploding free of its hole, burying itself in the picture across the room as the frame bubbles and welds in place. Selena convulsing and twisting in the clock's oily embrace before spewing blood over her lips, her form slackening. Larissa's open mouth screaming as the wave meets her, engulfs her, drives her body against the wall and then to the floor, where she lies dead, her eyes half open. The clock smoldering, vapors of heat coiling from its top as the pendulum swings, the hands running backward.

Evan broke free of the thing's hold, shoving as hard as he could with his muscles as well as his mind, a coiling, mental tension released. He tumbled and fell onto his back, his mouth open and gasping. He had wet himself, but couldn't summon the energy to care. The thing that used to look like Abel remained where it was, its face no longer bearing any features. Evan sat up and scrambled away from it.

"You caught it from her, didn't you? Tuberculosis." Evan gasped. "The doctors you called weren't only for her, they were for you. And when you knew you were going to die, you built this ... this thing and cursed it somehow." He gestured to the darkness around them.

As if in reply, a ripple flowed through Abel's entire form, a wave of skin rolling and settling.

*My time was cut short unfairly, and unlike other pitiful mortal men, I didn't succumb to my fate, I raged against it. You are correct, I built this, and it welcomed me into its womb, just as the ancient rites handed down through my bloodlines said it would. And yes, my beautiful achievement did need power. The ones that lay around us misunderstood my masterpiece for something it was not. It drew those that had regrets. It gave them hope that they could change their fates, and I waited, luring them closer until I could absorb their energy.*

Evan's mouth opened and then shut.

"You killed them all. Your wife and Allison, all the others—to fuel it."

The list of names and faces scrolled through his mind—Jason's grandmother and grandfather, Bob, Becky, Becky's father.

"They were trying to warn us."

Evan choked and coughed, feeling the strange tickling in his throat again.

"The doll, the body in the lake, everything. They were trying to scare us away before it was too late."

Abel's form writhed as though in ecstasy, the skin opening with sores, bleeding before healing, a scar there and then gone.

Evan slowly stood, waiting to fall back to the ground, but didn't.

*Their weak imprints meddle with my destiny, but they are only husks, hollowed out of the life I took from them. They are nothing but shadows and mist.*

"The hair was from you," Evan said, coughing again. "From Selena, or Allison. You couldn't help leaving a little trace of your own as you guided me, kept me working and hoping I could go back."

*Every soul comes with a price.*

"You give me my son back, right now."

Evan's voice shook, and tears sprang to his eyes. He knew the thing before him was laying out a path, but he didn't want to follow it, he knew where it led to. The creature advanced on him, glided toward him without walking. Its chest opened in a vertical mouth from neck to groin, the blackened ribs beneath splitting, forming teeth, its organs melding into a giant lapping tongue.

Evan retreated, his shoes squeaking on the ebony floor. The crescent moon's shining eye spotlighted him like a star on a stage. The pendulum cut the air now as the chunking of gears and sprockets above him meshed. The clock was beginning its work.

*TICK, TICK, TICK, TICK, TICK.*

Time passing became the loudest sound in the world, and Evan turned to run, to flee from the gliding horror Abel had become, but tripped and fell, his hands barely catching himself before he bashed his face into the floor. He rolled, trying to regain his feet, and saw what he'd stumbled over.

Shaun lay on the floor, his eyes partially open.

Evan's heart stopped dead in his chest; sound peeled away until silence burned in his ears. He saw nothing but Shaun lying there, one arm twisted at his side, his skin pale alabaster. Unmoving.

Evan crawled toward him, touched his skin and felt the coldness of it, the pliancy gone.

"No," he pleaded, his throat tightening against a moan.

He ran his hand up to Shaun's shoulder, pulling himself closer, closer to his son, his boy. He pressed his face against Shaun's cheek, feeling the first tear break free. Reaching around, he got an arm beneath his son's back, curling his small body into his lap. Shaun's head lolled on his neck, and Evan cradled it, the memory of the first time he held him coming back so clean and clear he could have lived in it forever. He heard Elle saying weakly from her hospital bed to support his head, and he was. He would never let anything bad happen to him, not ever. He would die for him; he would protect him and never let him suffer.

Evan rocked as he held Shaun's body, silent sobs racking him as he breathed in the smell of his boy's hair, the shampoo they always used. A sound of pure agony came from deep within him, and it was a breaking, the tearing of something that couldn't be repaired.

The Abel-thing paused in its movement and then continued, stopping only a few feet away from where Evan sat.

*I have enough power to live again, for through their collected energy I will conquer death, and you will be my vessel for life. I will be free of this place and walk again, fully alive within your skin.*

Evan clenched his eyes shut, his jaw spasming so hard he heard several of his teeth crack. He vibrated with loss so deep he thought he would simply rip open and bleed grief onto the black floor until he faded away—away like his wife, and now his son.

Gently, so gently, he laid Shaun back on the floor, putting his palm over his son's cool eyelids to close them. He brushed back his hair one last time.

*My beautiful boy.*

Evan stood, facing the gaping maw of the Abel-thing. The clank and rattle of the gears almost twenty feet above him drew his gaze upward, and he watched their turning progress, interlocking and spinning with perfect timing. The clock's hands ticked backward, and the pendulum slashed the air in swaths, counting off the seconds. Time, delicate and powerful, turning, changing, flowing.

Evan reached into his pocket, drawing out the long, black key, its heavy steel in his hand comforting somehow. He looked down at Shaun's lifeless body and gripped the key so hard he thought it might snap in his fist. Evan exhaled a long breath, and he opened his palm, hefted the key—*everything has a purpose*—and lobbed it upward into the twirling gears.

There was a screeching whine of steel binding, then an explosive bang that echoed through the infinite space of the clock. A haze of brass shavings came down like sharp party streamers, fluttering with golden flashes. The pendulum stuttered and then stopped, cocked to one side, holding its position before another massive boom.

The pendulum began to swing again, the hands running forward now.

The giant mouth in Abel's front bellowed an incomprehensible word—maybe something in the language that brought everything around them to life—and the creature rushed forward, shrieking so loud Evan almost covered his ears.

Another earsplitting roar filled the cavern, and Abel stumbled with the sound, but it recovered at once and was upon him. Its hands grasped his arm, yanking him off his feet. He flew through the air and slid several yards on his back, then sat up to watch it approach.

Abel's face swam to the surface, the eyes maniacal, gleaming with hatred, then it was gone, and he saw a glimpse of Selena before it changed into a conglomeration of countenances. Dozens of eyes and mouths opening and snapping flowed across its face. Ears formed and changed into a mixture of fingers that scraped the air, which then became an empty hole filled with darkness. The darkness seeped like pus from a wound and reached toward him, its edges becoming sharpened into black razors.

Evan watched the blades of shadow lengthen and then shoot toward him, and he welcomed their touch, knowing it would be nothing compared to the agony of touching Shaun's dead skin.

A gear the size of a tractor tire fell from the ceiling and smashed into the Abel thing.

Its head split with the impact, the reaching darkness recoiling and evaporating in a billow of black smoke. The gear traveled into and through it, all the way to the floor, splattering its greasy flesh in every direction. Some matter landed on Evan's bare arm, burning before he wiped it away.

The Abel-shape knitted itself back together, its form becoming whole before several more pieces dropped away, its shed skin hissing like meat in a frying pan.

A sprocket at least two feet in diameter crashed into the floor inches from Evan's left leg, and he stood, backing away from the churning form before him.

The Abel-thing moved forward, two large pincers of bone erupting from its chest, slicing the space before it as it came. A chain fell in a clattering pile somewhere in the dark, and more flesh sloughed off the revenant.

*No!*

The howl in Evan's head was the rending of souls, the tearing of time. Malignant and dark, it was the sound of death itself.

The Abel-thing staggered forward, the pincers dropping from its body and shattering into dust as they hit the floor. It pointed an arm in his direction, the fingers trying to form a fist, but they fell away too, first liquid, then flakes of ash. Eyes bulged in sockets lining its ever-changing face as well as its chest. One by one they exploded outward in pulses of milky fluid, until its body was awash in an acidic pool burning its dark hide into smoke.

Evan's heart thundered as Abel's face came into focus one last time, his features etchings of ancient hatred carved in a melting canvas of flesh.

The horrific amalgam lunged toward him again, its unhinged mouth lined with a hundred teeth. He put his arm up, bracing for impact as the abomination slammed into him. Its teeth flayed through the flesh of his forearm, and it bit down hard, cutting to the bone.

Evan grunted and toppled over, his free arm bracing his fall. He stared into the primal shine of Abel's eyes. An abyss waited there, hatred churning behind the swirling irises.

*You'll not live!*

Evan grimaced with the sound of so many voices intertwined in rage and agony. His fingers brushed something hard on the floor and he grasped it. His eyelids fluttered under the immensity of the pain, but he caught a glimpse of Shaun's supine form on the floor, and leaned in closer to the Abel-thing.

"Neither will you."

Evan heaved himself upright and rammed the winding key he held into its unblinking right eye, which burst under the pressure. The key's tip was mashed into a sharpened point from disrupting the gears, and it slid into Abel's head like a knife. He pushed harder, feeling the slimy tissue give way beneath the unforgiving steel.

The thing screamed, and Evan's eardrums tore. Blood leaked in rivulets down the sides of his face, but he shoved harder, the key sliding in all the way to its grip.

Its teeth released the hold on his arm, and the creature shrunk away. Evan lost his hold on the key, and nearly collapsed, the feeling in his ravaged arm mercifully numb.

The mutating darkness expanded and contracted as it staggered, a writhing tumor. It pawed at the black steel embedded in its face, but the key held fast in its flesh. It cried out one last time and tried to move toward him again, but fell, exploding into a mixture of noxious wax and muddy soot that splashed the floor and ran in every direction. The key tinkled once as it bounced end over end, and then laid still.

Evan shook and waited for the stinking pool to re-form, but other than smoke and bubbles, it didn't move.

The crashes continued in the windings above him, and hot shavings littered his hair, burning for an instant and then gone. The light stuttered and flashed in an epileptic nightmare that made him shield his eyes as he looked up.

The crescent moon's mouth was open in a silent scream of suffering, its eye gouting bursts of light in erratic discharges. Cracks blossomed in its silver skin, and more ill light poured through them.

*Good night moon.*

Evan turned and sat on the floor, hearing more and more gears and sprockets fall, shuddering the ground with their impact. The pendulum let loose and dropped, landing with a hollow gong before tipping forward like a sequoia cut at the base.

He didn't look up when it fell or when the air of its passage brushed his face. The sounds of destruction pounded his ruined eardrums, but he didn't hear even a whisper.

Evan hummed under his breath, a tune from many years past. Something about a baby's bed and soft dreams, a song Elle used to sing when Shaun was young. Shaun's fine hair slid beneath his fingertips, and Evan closed his eyes to the melody in his head, as the clock came rushing down around him.

## 28

The sun was warm on his face, and so bright everything was a red glow before he opened his eyes.

He looked up into a canopy of branches filled with oddly shaped leaves. They looked like long arrowheads with vibrant blue veins running through their structures.

A scent came to him, something warm and wholesome, reminding him of his mother. Baking bread, or the smell of her flower garden in June. The scent made him think his stomach would growl, but he realized he wasn't hungry. He was satisfied, as if he'd recently eaten.

Evan smacked his lips, watching the shimmer of blue sky through the gaps in the leaves, a blue so deep he knew no one could say a name for it.

He sat up, pushing himself away from a bed of sand softer than silk. The little particles glinted at him, miniature diamonds in the sun. He turned a little, looking down a path to where the sun shone, resplendent in the sky, burning in a perfect orb of yellow. He realized he could look at the sun and not squint; it didn't hurt his eyes in the least. It felt right.

Evan stood, brushing off a pair of lightweight pants that he didn't remember owning. His body felt glorious, strong, rested. He wanted to laugh but only smiled, trying to remember how he'd gotten here. There was a memory there, something troubling, horrible even, and it began to form.

*The clock, Abel, Shaun.*

He swallowed, waiting for the grief to plummet into him, an outside force burrowing through his soul. His son was dead, gone forever. But instead of breaking down and falling beneath the pain, a strengthful peace filled him. He heard the rush of water somewhere ahead. The ocean, waves hushing against a shoreline, a breeze still coated with the smell of bread nudging the thin shirt he wore. He had to see the water.

Evan moved, his bare feet sinking into the sand only a little, the walking easy. Trees, their trunks glistening with moisture, lined the path he treaded on, their presence easy, sure, as if he walked down a hallway guiding him.

The ocean was closer now, and he saw it through the trees, a vastness that thrilled and calmed him at the same time. He ran, the trees coasting by on either side, sweet air in his lungs, the sun on his back.

He emerged onto the beach, the forest of beautiful trees falling away to reveal sand finer than and as white as sugar as far as he could see. A turquoise stream flowed into the ocean, and when he looked at the water, two things made him stop and stare.

The first was the utter beauty of the sea, its water as flat and calm as a pond, its color a cousin of the sky. Waves, small and topped with white froth, washed the beach smooth, the sand there even and unbroken but for a short line of little stones running like a stream along the entire beach.

The second was the two people standing at the water's edge.

One was a boy with light hair, wearing the same type of clothes Evan did. He stood with his feet in the waves, his arm cocked back before he slung it out and threw a rock in a straight line. The stone flew a dozen yards and then skipped across the water in bright hops—one, two, three, four, five, six, seven— before it sank out of sight.

Evan turned his gaze to the other figure, a woman with hair that matched the boy's, wearing a flowing white dress that came just below her knees. He studied the curve of her back, the slope of her shoulders, how she shifted from one foot to the other, swaying in time to the waves. She turned then, her face coming into view. His eyes traced her chin, her lips, the nose he'd kiss sometimes, to her declaration that she hated it while laughing. Her eyes, the last time he saw them so full of pain, now clear, glistening in the sun.

Elle smiled at him.

Evan ran down the beach, his legs carrying him before he knew he was moving. The boy turned, hearing his approach, and he saw Shaun's face light up, his eyebrows leaping, his mouth opening in a cry of wonder. Then he was with them, holding them close, feeling their warmth, the realness of them. Elle's hair tickled his face, and he knew that he wasn't dreaming. No dream could be so vivid or so kind.

"Daddy," Shaun said, the words clear, without a slur.

Evan knelt, and Elle came with him, their knees digging into the sand. Shaun looked at him, clear-eyed, studying his face.

"You came, you're here."

The joy at hearing Shaun speak nearly knocked him off balance, and tears slipped down his cheeks. "I'm here, buddy, I'm here."

He pulled Shaun to his chest and felt his son's small arms wrap around his back, strong, holding him tight. Elle leaned close to them, and Evan kissed her, her lips tasting of the apple balm she used to wear. She cupped a hand to his face, holding him, tasting him too.

When they finally broke apart, Elle tipped her forehead against his, their eyes drinking each other in.

"I'm so sorry," he said. "There's so much—"

Elle pressed a finger to his lips. "I know, I know."

She kissed him again, her own tears now flowing. Shaun sat back from them, holding on to Evan's hand. When Evan looked at him again, he saw the scar from the accident was gone, and a memory came back to him, clear and unrefined, poured into his mind by a gentle hand.

"Wawee. You were saying 'Mommy,' weren't you?"

Shaun smiled, nodding. "I saw her in my dreams. She told me we were coming here soon."

Evan turned his gaze to Elle. She smiled, gripping his hand tighter.

"We're together again," she said.

Evan nodded and heard the clack of rocks beneath his hand. He looked down, seeing that they were next to the river of stones, and that each one of them was a perfect skipper.

# 29

The house was quiet except for the wind pushing against the eaves.

Mist beaded on the windows, throwing pinpoint shadows against the floor. The air was still. Dishes sat in the kitchen sink, the food particles drying, milk and juice in the bottoms of glasses hardening. Clothes hung in closets, motionless. The gray light was constant and baleful.

The basement stood silent, a rectangular strip of tape on the floor. A layer of thin glass shards pointed up like leavings of hatched eggs. Pages of diagrams were strewn about, their edges overlapping. A doll's disembodied head lay in the darkness, its sapphire eyes staring at nothing.

A crumbled pile of black wood was against the far wall, jagged splinters in a halo on the floor. A steel disk with a crescent moon protruded from the top of the mound, the moon's open eye burned black, elongated, as though exposed to some great heat. Four timing hands were scattered amongst the debris, the pile no more than kindling, good for firewood but not much else. Bright cogs, their minuscule teeth rounded, poked out like hungry fish rising through a dark sea.

A chime came from inside the rubble, once, onerous. It stretched out, filtering throughout the basement, and then faded into silence.

# Author's Note

First off, I hope you enjoyed the ride.

I hope you were entertained, at times your eyes widened with fear, and possibly tears. All in all, I hope I did my job as a storyteller.

This particular tale came so strong and fast that I barely had a chance to finish my previous novel before it spilled out onto the page. The basis for the story is very close to my heart, maybe too close in some instances, and I pray that shined through in the writing. As I've done many times in my other works, I took musings from my everyday life that scared me silly and sewed them into the fabric of the story. If you've ever held someone's hand in the middle of the night and wondered if it really was theirs, then you know what I mean.

As always I want to say thanks for spending some time with me and I appreciate any feedback you have to offer, whether it be in the form of a review or simply an email to tell me what you thought. I hope you'll come back again and we can set off on another journey together. There's always one more road to walk down and your company makes the trip worth every step.

Joe Hart
November, 2013

# Other Books by Joe Hart

Lineage (novel)
Singularity (novel)
EverFall (novel)
The River Is Dark (novel)
Midnight Paths: A Collection of Dark Horror (collection)
The Line Unseen (short story)
The Edge of Life (short story)
Outpost (short story)